Bloodline
The Awakening
Book 1

R.A. Harris

DEDICATION

For my dad, without whose support, enthusiasm, and
invaluable help, this story might have never been finished.
I love you, pops x.

CONTENTS

ACKNOWLEDGEMENTS

A huge thank you to:
My dad, Mike Harris, my very first editor. Thank you for believing in this book as much as I do. For your tremendous, unwavering support, feedback, and critical eye. You laugh and say it gives you something to do in your retirement days, but I honestly couldn't have finished the book without you. You've crafted and polished it and offered ideas that have really enhanced the story and the characters that I love so much. Thank you for your patience and immeasurable help. I love you.
To Pete Dixon, for designing the book cover. It's exactly what I'd envisioned in my mind. I love it.
To Scott, my love, for letting me sack off the housework, lock myself in a bedroom and write obsessively for months on end. You never complain or make me feel guilty, and you always support my dreams. I love you.
And finally, to my family, for continually encouraging me to do what I love. Again, I love you all.

CHAPTER 1

I've suffered from the same chronic nightmare the whole of my life. Most dreams are spontaneous and triggered by some underlining issue, but this one plagues me. It rattles me so much that I wake in a cold sweat. It plunges me into a fear that's so crippling, that I'm frightened to go back to sleep. It doesn't feel like a dream. It's so vividly real that it's more like a warped memory from a previous life. It isn't easy to explain, but I'll try to do so.

It always begins and ends the same way.

My sight is stolen by the thieving night, and all which surrounds me is unnervingly silent. All I can hear is the voluble throbbing of my pulse, bashing against my temples as I try to catch my breath. The rich fragrance of earth and pine encloses me in the depths of a woodland. Colossal trees constrict the moonlight that's trying to squeeze through the openings of the canopy.

The gasps and whimpers that escape my mouth are alien to me. I don't recognise my voice; it sounds like it's coming from a child. It's like my limbs are too small and delicate for the body I'm familiar with in my waking mind. When I glance down at myself it's then that I realise it's because I *am* a child. I'm barefoot, wearing a threadbare nightgown that barely protects my skin from the harsh temperatures of the night.

I hear the snap of a branch close behind me, and I'm suddenly propelled to my feet, hurtling through the trees and dodging the interlacing tree roots and matted undergrowth beneath me.

'Antonia!'
A child's voice cries out from behind me, but I can't stop running.

'Antonia, wait!'

But I don't wait, not even as jagged twigs that protrude through the wet soil, stab my feet. As I sprint frantically weaving in and out of the trees, I hear the most harrowing, bloodcurdling scream in the far distance, that it forces me to stop.

Panicked, I quickly crouch behind a thick tree trunk and anchor my head, glancing behind me to see if I've lost the potential pursuer on my trail. I don't hear any footsteps. Even the nocturnal beings of the night have been silenced by what sounds like a woman's traumatic screams.

My heart hammers in my chest as I inch cautiously forwards, noticing a flickering glow of light ahead of me through the trees.

It only takes me a few minutes to adjust to the darkness, to see sinister figures moving into an opening, each carrying flaming torches that light their paths. My blood runs cold as I count ten of them all dressed in black hooded cloaks, their faces concealed by the shadows of the night. Another distorted scream strikes terror through my core, but no matter how terrified I am, I must know what's happening.

Every bone in my body seizes in protest. Knotted bushes in front of me, obscuring my vision. I rise to my feet, holding my breath and, I pray that they don't see me.

The low rumbling breaks the silence of ominous chanting. It resonates through the forest, causing the air to thicken with tension. Every hair on my body is now bristling as I feel an impending sense of doom, watching the cloaked figures huddle together, hissing, whispering and chanting in a foreign tongue.

One of the figures moves out from the circle, and I watch its cloak sweep the dirt on the ground and move towards two faint silhouettes in the distance.

'By order of the Elder Blood,' I hear a man suddenly bellow out, 'I sentence you to immediate death.'

My hands clasp over my mouth, horrified. *I can't see who they are. What, in the name of god is going on here?*

The chanting resumes and becomes louder, and the man calls out something incoherent. As I'm about to edge closer, I see something has been set ablaze behind them, and I hear a woman begin to scream deliriously.

The blaze quickly becomes an inferno, and the wild flames illuminate a woman, strapped and bound to a tree with the fire fiercely engulfing her body.

I gasp out in horror and fall to my knees, listening as her guttural cries become shrills of agony.

Why are they doing this to her?
They're burning her alive.

I can't bear to watch or listen any longer and turn away, protecting my back against the cold bark of the trees. I pull my knees to my chest and sob quietly.

My heart pounds as the woman stops her primal screaming, drawing her last breaths. I rock myself back and forwards as hot tears rain down my cheeks, pleading for it to end, willing it to be over, wanting it to be still.

I must have passed out. As I awaken, birdsong bursts through the trees as loud as the sun's morning glare. The morning dew has soaked my body, and my fingers kneed the wet soil beneath me. Frogs croak in the distance as water trickles in a nearby stream and the woodland comes alive at dawn, more than it was at dusk.

I lie motionless for several minutes, absorbing the trees as their branches and leaves sway hypnotically above me. The sunlight seeps through the tiny openings and, for a moment, I feel the most peaceful than I've ever felt before, listening to the whispers of the woods.

The feeling plummets like an act of violence as the stench of burnt flesh hits my nostrils with a vengeance, and then I remember. It's sickeningly sweet, like overcooked pork on a barbecue, now slowly decomposing with age.

It's so rich that it's almost a taste. I heave, rolling on to my knees as it overpowers me. I know I must get out of there, so I force myself to stand.

My bare feet, caked in matted filth, are now showing cuts and bruises. I step over twigs warily and swat away small overhanging branches as I make my way to the opening. My heart accelerates once again, as I follow the stench of death, willing me to turn and run, but the curiosity gnaws at me and drives me towards it.

I hug myself and judge every direction where a possible threat may lurk. The cloaked beings are gone – at least I think they are – *for now.*

The air catches in my throat the minute my eyes align with it. At first, I can't quite make it out as residual smoke is still wafting around it. But the *it* quickly becomes *her*, and *she* is charred to the bone. Her mangled body remains bound to the tree with the remnants of thick smouldering rope. She'd been cooked, like a roasted joint of meat, angled awkwardly with all her teeth still intact. The smell is now so overbearing that it burns my throat. It's hard to breathe. I lift my damp nightgown to my face and bury my nose under it, but something above my head height seizes my attention.

I don't want to look up.

I look up.

My immediate reaction is to scream, and no matter how much I try to strangle it or restrain myself, the sound that bellows from my mouth is the sound of mortal terror. I scramble backwards and plummet down into the mud as I see a man hanging by his neck above me. His body appears unnaturally stiff, and his eyes are on me. I burst into tears, unable to rip my eyes from his. They're bloodshot and unseeing with pools of glazed blue, bulging out of their sockets.

What happened here? Why did this happen to these people? Why have their bodies been left like this out in the open? Will the police come and declare it a crime scene?

I want to run, but I'm rooted to the spot, too traumatised to move. A branch snaps directly behind me, and as I cry out in a dazed state, my ears sharpen too late. Before I can even turn my head, a hand wraps around my nose and mouth and gags me. I get yanked to my feet, and a cloth bag is then forced down over my head. The light is drained away and feeds me into darkness once again.

CHAPTER 2

I woke up gasping for clean air behind the wheel of my car, doused in my own sweat. I'd been driving for an hour and ten minutes in a stuffy tin, nursing a monstrous hangover and struggling with the scrutiny of the unusually hot late June heat.

The south was in a mini heatwave that wouldn't let up, and instead of making everyone happy, it was sapping every ounce of energy one had. It had a bite to it. Even when my sandals hit the tarmac, after swivelling out of my car, I could feel the scorched road eat at the plastic of my soles.

If I hadn't of pulled over to shut my eyes, I'd have killed someone, if not myself. I don't know how long I'd been out for, but it was long enough to plunge me straight back into my nightmare. Even as I came to, for a brief second, I could still smell the bark and pine. I could taste the morning dew on my tongue. I could again hear the skittish movements of the animals within the trees and feel the texture of the earth on my hands.

I grabbed my pack of menthol cigarettes from the glove box and leant back against my Mini Hatchback. I half entertained the idea of finding the bottled water I'd packed, but as my eyes flicked to the entire contents of my life crammed in a chaotic mess in the back of my car, I quickly recoiled.

I'd left my fiancé that morning. I'd hurriedly packed up my car, pushed the keys of our flat through the letterbox, and didn't look back.

Perhaps that's why my nightmare had resurfaced with a vengeance in the weeks building up to the move. My GP, who often had her thumbs twiddling about my mental condition, recognised a pattern when my nightmare would occur the most, and it was always the times in my life when I was highly stressed.

That day was no exception.

I'd been with Jack for five years. We had plans and life goals, not unlike any other couple in a serious relationship. At first, we were both on the same page. I was studying at university; I had ambition, confidence and a real zest for life. Jack always said he loved that about me. But then over the years, he started to change. He got some big, hotshot job in sales, and kept the company of privileged socialites. It was then that he started trying to mould me into someone I was never going to be or wanted to be.

Jack yearned for a dutiful housewife, a stay-at-home mum who baked cakes and kept our show-home in pristine order. He asked me to marry him in front of an audience of strangers in a crowded restaurant one night, and I didn't want to look like the biggest dickhead on the planet by rejecting him so publicly, and thus, through a pained smile, I said yes.

As the room erupted into applause and a celebratory flute of champagne was thrust into my hand, all I could do was swallow compulsively through shallow breaths and try not to choke on my dread. I felt boxed-in and suffocated in a relationship eroding my self-esteem, my identity and independence. I couldn't breathe, trapped and unable to appease his unattainable dreams.

I was twenty-four-years old with my whole life ahead of me. I needed an escape. And then, as if the stars had aligned and the universe was dangling a big, fat, get-out-of-jail-free card in front of my face, I was presented with a teaching job, an offer that I couldn't refuse.

Tucked away in the middle of Surrey, was a little village called Oaks End, where my best friend Zoe lived. She knew the headmaster of the nearby Westfield Secondary School, and all it took was a skype interview, Zoe putting in a good word for me, and I'd pretty much secured my graduate job.

The village had a population of around two-hundred people, which was nanoscopic compared to my area of London, where I'd spent my entire life amongst its hustle and bustle. I craved the tranquillity of a peacefully quiet place, to soothe my loud thoughts, so I welcomed the serenity of a small community, hidden amidst the enclosure of Oaks End's sweeping countryside.

Jack had called my bluff when I told him I'd accepted the job offer. I'd been detaching myself from the relationship for months, knowing fine well he'd have no intention of leaving with me, and when it came down to it, he didn't want to.

I sighed, appreciating the post-card scenery in front of me. According to my satnav, I was a mere ten minutes away from Oaks End village. It almost snatched my breath away how serene and stunning the countryside was. I breathed in the fragrance of the clean, earthy air and looked out to the hills that rolled like green waves and stretched out for miles in every direction against the backdrop of the barren blue sky. Perfect.

I unglued my hair from the nape of my neck, tying it up into a loose bun allowing my skin to breathe, and fanned my face.

As I lapped up the blissful silence, I realised I was exactly where I needed to be at this stage of my life. My theory is that it's usually out of our hands once the wind of fate catches our sails. I've always felt like something bigger was awaiting me; that I'd been born to this earth for something incredibly special. I believe we've already prearranged the itinerary of our life before we're born.

The vivid dreams we have, the chance meetings, being at the right place at the exact right time. The extraordinary instances of recognition we call déjà vu – surely, they aren't a coincidence? The thrill, I guess, is not knowing this and not knowing what or who awaits us - not knowing whether we're going to sail through life on an ocean of luck or power through the obstacle course that attempts to obstruct our paths.

Jack wasn't one to stumble through life. He was methodical in everything he did. He saw spontaneity as reckless, vulnerability as weak, and open minds laughable. I find people with Jack's mentality exasperating.

But then there are people who, like me, are wired differently, and in this way alone, I fit in. I fit in with the small minority of people who stumble upon the most exciting chapter of their lives yet. A life that was not premeditated. A chapter no-one could have written. I was driving towards a fresh new start, but I was sightless to the mind-bending, unfathomable events that awaited me.

I knew that this chapter was not a mere figment of my imagination. I didn't conjure it up as some whimsical story. There are unearthly, preternatural beings who walk veiled amongst us. They aren't a glitch; they aren't a phantom or an illusion. They are real, as real as any human with a throbbing pulse. And I was about to discover them for myself.

CHAPTER 3

'Tell me you're nearly here?' Zoe quipped in her
unapologetically brash tone.

'I'm ten minutes away, I promise,' I stressed,
shouting at my mobile that was sitting in its holster, on
speakerphone.
It was so good to hear her voice. Zoe and I went way
back. We met on holiday as young kids and quickly
became inseparable. She'd always visit me in London
and stay with me and my mum, but as we grew up
over the years our lives simply got busier, and we
spoke more on skype or WhatsApp. I had so much
gratitude that she'd not only found me a job in
teaching, but she was allowing me to stay in her home
until I found a place to rent.

'I'm so excited to see your face!' she squealed.
I wasn't. The sleep deprivation had me looking like a
crystal meth addict rather than the fresh-faced friend

she was used to seeing in heavily filtered pictures and video chat.

'Listen, I have to pop out for an hour to run some errands, so don't go straight to my shop. Grab a drink in the pub, and I'll come to rescue you when I get back. OK?'

I smiled inwardly and frowned. What a request - Zoe didn't have to tell me again. I'd happily sit and soak up the sun in a beer garden with a pint of wine.

'And, Kate,' she added. 'Don't be a cheap drunk. Limit yourself. The day is far too young for me to be carrying you home and putting you to bed on your first day here,' she chuckled. 'Catch you soon … love you.'

My phone fell silent before I could respond. I dropped my cigarette butt and put my foot on it, then eased myself back into the car.

I didn't need my trusted satnav then, nor the resounding echo of Zoe's directions to the village. For some bizarre reason, as I followed the winding country roads, I had an overwhelming wave of déjà vu wash over me. The familiarity of the place was staggering, considering I'd never been to Oaks End in my life – not even for my interview. Zoe had always come to me – in fact – I'd never really questioned why she hadn't invited me to her home until I turned into the village. Maybe the familiarity was because I'd done some research about the area via Google?

It was an utterly charming little treasure. I drove past thatched-roof cottages and cobbled narrow streets that led to the village high street. Since I now had time to mooch around, I clocked the market car park at the top of the road, and reversed straight into a parking space, feeling my body sag in relief that I'd finally made it safely to my destination.

This was it - my new home for the foreseeable future. *Goodbye old life, hello to the new.* I wasted no time in sliding on my sunglasses, grabbed my bag and jumped out of the car to stretch. If only there were a breeze to unglue the clothes from my sticky back. The heat was heavy, and I couldn't wait to shower and change.

I locked my car and started to walk down the street, smiling brightly. *What an adorably quaint place to live.* Everything was so quirky and unique. As I expected, most of the people who passed me were pensioners, living off their retirement funds, strolling up and down the street, window shopping without a care in the world - or a clock to check.

All the shops were emitting overpowering aromas, the freshly baked bread from the bakers, the raw bloodied meat from the butchers, the scones and sugary treats from the clattering tearoom. I peered into the vintage shops and gift shops cluttered with crafts and bric-a-brac. And then, as my eyes searched the street, I saw it; the famous purple fronted shop that Zoe had put in her blood, sweat and tears. I glossed over the name, *'Zoe's Witching Hour'* written above it in a fancy script. It made me smile and was so proud of her. Ever since we were kids, she talked about how one day she'd own her own business and open a shop and there it was, right in front of me.

My sandals slapped against the uneven cobbled pathway as I sped down the street towards her shop. As I slowed nearing her shop, I quickly got side-tracked by a home-made pie deli on the other side of the road. A lady was putting freshly baked pastries in the window, and my growling stomach lured me towards it. As I crossed the street, drooling at the thought of eating slices of carb-heavy dreams, I mentally argued with myself over my lack of willpower to walk away from junk-food. My nose was very much still sniffing at the window while I tried to drag the rest of my body away, but I couldn't avert my eyes away in time to avoid slamming straight into a hard body that almost knocked the wind out of me.

The force of our coming together made me bounce back and a sharp pain shot across my chest.

'Ouch!' I complained, pressing my hands across my boobs. I was about to go full-on London, and passive-aggressively urge him to watch where he was going, but a blur of white, denim and sleeve tattoos had me inching back. Plus, I wasn't in London anymore. *Be friendly to the village folk, Kate.*

It was the solidly built torso and bulging arms filling out the t-shirt that had me gawping open-mouthed. My eyes rolled up the ink that curled around his arms. I craned my neck to reach his face and stopped breathing instantly. The man disarmed me.

Lazily ruffled, ash thick brown hair, hard-jawed good-looks, soft, adulterous lips and the most spellbinding rapturous blue eyes I'd ever seen. I felt the hairs stand up on my arms, and I was immediately awestruck by the notion of instant recognition.

Why did I feel like I knew him? Where could I place his face? Had we crossed paths before? His pupils dilated, and he squinted faintly, as though he recognised me too. *Should I ask?*

'Are you OK?' he asked concerned, gingerly placing a hand on my arm.

My heart pounded in response. All I could do was stare at him with parted lips like I was in some sort of weird trance.

What about TV? Think of all those reality shows you binge-watch, Kate. He has a face for TV. Is he an actor? No? What about Facebook? Maybe he's popped up as a suggested friend? Perhaps he's an internet sensation? Why do you even care? Snap out of it. You've only been single for a hot second! Stop gawping at him. You're making him uncomfortable.

I blinked out of it and swallowed.

'I'm fine,' I finally answered in a breathy matter.

I wasn't fine. Zoe promised me Oaks End was a safe zone, filled with OAPs and no distractions. Yet, there I was, presented with the six-foot-three village hunk who I couldn't stop staring at and had ogled at for longer than I'd intended to.

He squinted down at my chest and scrunched his eyebrows together.

'You don't look OK.'

I traced the shape of his biceps, and the pulsing sinews in his strong arms and felt my ovaries implode. Good, god! Nothing had my pulse pounding quite like a man who looked primordially strong.

It was then I realised my hands were still cupped around my breasts. I dropped them by my sides and fidgeted awkwardly.

'You see,' he smirked, scratching a week-old stubble that coated his jawline. 'Normally I high-five people or give them a little fist bump, but if you want to chest bump, I'm cool with that too. You have to use a little less force next time.'

I liked him immediately. I giggled like a pathetic mess of a human and regretted it instantly. What was wrong with me? I never fell for men's ample charms. I'd just gotten out of a relationship; I couldn't present myself like a starry-eyed melt to the first good-looking bloke I bumped into. My whole demeanour changed as I adjusted myself and shifted my weight forward.

'Well, see you then.' I said casually.

'Well, wait a second,' he quickly stopped me. 'Why don't you come for a drink?'
I paused, rolling my eyes up to meet the pub sign above his head that read, *Moons Tavern.*

I glanced at my watch. 'It's three-thirty in the afternoon,' I protested, even though I had every intention of sitting in the pub all afternoon until Zoe arrived.
He shrugged at me and flashed me a devious grin.

'And? It's also five o'clock somewhere, right?'
My knees buckled.

'Come on, and it's on the house. It's the least I can do for hurting your … erm…,' he hesitated and frowned, '… you know.'
On the house? Does he work there?

'My folks own it. I'm about to start work. The late shift. Come on, before I change my mind.'
He had me. I caved. Willingly.

Two large red wines later, and I was starting to feel loose. I wasn't right when I was loose. I was anybody's.

It didn't help that I'd only eaten half a soggy chicken and mayo sandwich that day, so I hadn't lined my stomach enough to soak up the alcohol. After becoming a little too talkative, I began to realise I may have begun to bore the poor guy to tears. But in between him serving the few customers in the pub, he seemed deeply engrossed by my ramblings.

The place was utterly gorgeous. Inside the dimly lit bar, a smattering of candles and fairy lights added to its charm. Hand-made tables, created using old tree trunks, were scattered around. The décor was a mix of *Olde World* meets contemporary. Clever. It had such a romantic and intimate vibe and I felt immediately relaxed. I was perched on a high-backed stool at the bar, chatting away to him when I realised, I was now boring myself. I stopped talking.

I watched him wipe the bar top with a damp cloth before he registered my silence. He paused, and those pools of sapphire flicked at me and blinked quizzingly.

'And?'

I lost my train of thought. *What the hell had I been rambling about?* 'I've forgotten.'

His lips stretched to a smile, and he burst into laughter.

'You're a cheap drunk - I'll give you that.'

That was the second time that the same day someone called me that.

'I'm not drunk' I cringed, 'I'm just merry.'

'I'll get you some food,' he chuckled.

'Zoe will be here soon, and I think she's made arrangements for dinner, so I'm good thanks. I should probably go meet her —'
I slid off the stool, and the blood rushed to my head.

'Nope!' he laughed and reached over the bar in time to grab me before I could fall. 'Listen, our chef rustles up the best sandwiches in Oaks End. Let me order you one.' I surrendered.

'You sit there; I'll be a sec.'
I followed his long confident strides out of view, and
he disappeared for a moment before returning.

'It won't be long,' he said, pouring me a diet coke.
He slid it across the bar and leaned over on his elbows,
closing the space between us. My eyes found his. He
held me captive in his contact, seizing my attention as
he bore into my soul. Some people have that ability to
arrest your attention completely. Eye-contact was no
issue for this man; he knew how to look at someone
and make them feel completely vulnerable.

'You alright?' he asked.
I nodded and watched his eyes flick down to my hand,
but his smile died quicker than I could blink. His lips
thinned into a straight line, and his forehead crinkled.
He picked up a glass and started to shine it with a
cloth.

'What's the story there then?'
'The story?'
He nodded towards my finger.
'Oh, fuck!'
I immediately tried to yank my gold and sapphire
engagement ring from my finger, cursing myself by
forgetting to take it off.

'You're married?' he asked in an accusatory tone.
'No, I'm not married.'
I managed to pull the ring off and slipped it into my
bag without even hesitating. 'I'm not even engaged
anymore. I left him behind.'
His eyebrows raised, and I could have sworn I saw his
shoulders slouch.

'Where's *behind*?'
'London.'

His mouth curved intrigued. 'You dumped him?'

I shrugged. 'He wasn't good for me.'

'Recently split?'

'Today.'

He straightened and exhaled. 'Grim.'

I smirked at him in response and leant my chin on my hand.

'So, let me get this straight. You had a fiancé, and you left him back in …' He waited for me to respond.

'London.'

'London,' he echoed. 'To move here and stay with your friends Zoe and Danny.'

'Right.'

'And you're working?'

'Teaching.'

'Teaching?' His eyebrows raised.

'English,' I nodded proudly.

'I guessed as much. You have that whole teacher vibe going on.'

'Teacher vibe?'

As much as I wanted to be offended by his blunt assumption, I found myself amused by it. He inclined forward and let his eyes wander up and down my body.

'You're not wearing any make-up, apart from a little mascara. You're not hiding those freckles scattered across your nose and the top of your cheeks. Your hair is in a loose bun.' His eyes flicked down my body, surveying me. 'You have that whole girl-next-door style going on, no visible tattoos, no jewellery, apart from that rock that was on your finger.' He paused and leaned so far over the bar that he was in my personal space reaching for my hands. I didn't have time to hesitate as his large hands lifted my fingers and began examining them.

'No nail polish - nails chewed to the quick - worn bone right here.' His finger stroked the outline of my crooked index finger. The skin to skin contact quickened my heartbeat. His eyes arrested mine again, and the atmosphere between us shifted. I caught a whiff of his man fumes, and he smelt insanely good. His lips twitched and curved upwards meeting his eyes.

'That tells me you're either a writer or teacher.'
 I swallowed hard and bit the edge of my smile.

'OK, so it's hotter than Satan's balls outside, my make-up melted, my hair glued to my back, and I crack my fingers,' I shrugged, throwing him a playful smirk. His eyes wrinkled and a perfectly carved row of teeth flashed at me.

'Is that right?'
'Uh-huh,' I flirted.
 He sighed heavily and kept direct eye-contact with me with a dimpled smile.

'What?' I giggled, blushing under his heated gaze. He pursed his lips grinning. 'Nothing. I've never met a girl with such distinct features before.'

'Distinct features?' I gasped, consciously and immediately turning my head away.

'Yeah, your eyes are two completely different colours. They're insane.'
I twisted my head back to him and fell into his focused gaze.

'The right is electric blue, and the left is bottle green. They're intense.'
I chewed my lip and shrugged at him. 'It's a condition I was born with called *heterochromia iridium*. It results in

the difference of colouration in both eyes and affects the iris.'

A concentrated frown creased his forehead, and he seemed to be curious.

'Well,' his eyelids batted, and he stood up straight, 'It suits you.'

He excused himself and disappeared again for a minute, shortly returning with a huge sandwich.

'Here. Eat something,' he ordered, placing it in front of me.

I was famished, but I didn't care for his bossiness. I picked it up and drooled over the layers of mouth-watering ham and cheese, squeezed in a bed of lettuce wrapped in a soft baguette. I crunched into it, moaning my appreciation to him. His face beamed proudly.

'Good?' he asked.

I gave him the thumbs up and nodded.

'Let me ask you something,' I chomped. I finished what was left in my mouth before I continued. He gave me a nod and waited. 'Have we ever met before? I keep getting this weird feeling like I've met you before, but I can't put my finger on it.'

He blinked at me, straight-faced and then scrunched his mouth up in thought.

'Maybe in another lifetime?' he shrugged.

Somewhere in my memory bank, I thought I'd seen his face before, but I guess I was wrong. Perhaps he just resembled someone I used to know.

As I swallowed the last piece of sandwich, Zoe's name flashed up on my phone. I held my finger up to excuse myself while I answered.

'Hey, I'm back over in the shop, if you want to come to meet me while I close up early?' she said brightly.

'Of course, I'll be over in a minute.' I chimed, sliding off the barstool.

'Danny's just got home, and he's going to help unpack the car and move your bags.'

'Oh, that's great thanks.' I grabbed my diet coke and slurped down the rest of it through the straw and pushed it back on to the bar, smiling at my new friend. 'On my way over now.'

I killed the call and swung my bag over my shoulder. When I glanced up, it seemed as though he was probing me with silent questions. I could see it written all over his face.

'Thank you for the food and for sobering me up, even though technically it was you who got me tipsy in the first place.'

'You're welcome,' he laughed.
I lingered, while he carried on shining the glasses. He had some sort of gravitational pull, magnetising me towards him. Perhaps I was merely mistaking his friendliness for flirting, I don't know, but I liked his company. I could feel it in the depths of my stomach, that giddiness taking hold. The silence between us was soon interrupted with nervous laughter from both ends.

'Well, anyway. See you around, erm, sorry, I didn't catch your name.'

'It's Finn ... Finn Moon.' *Finn. I liked it.*
He extended his hand over the bar.

'Kate ... Kate Littlewood.' I smiled, shaking his hand.

We were still shaking hands in awkward silence, and it started to get weird, so I slipped my hand away. I thought he was about to say something else, so I stood there for several seconds staring at him like an idiot until I realised that was my cue to leave. I waved, but he didn't see it, which made me cringe into myself, and I quickly turned on my heel.

He cleared his throat behind me, and I felt tension fill the air.

'Um, Kate?'

I smiled outwardly before turning. *Thank god.*

He scratched his head and dipped his hand in his jeans pocket, dithering.

I let him suffer a little longer.

'You think you might want to hang out again sometime?'

I had an internal meltdown. I nodded at him and flashed him my comeliest smile before heading out of the pub, into the village High Street. This was a bad idea. Men like Finn were trouble. But like everything in my life that's bad for me, I welcomed it. I loved trouble.

CHAPTER 4

I stepped inside Zoe's shop with wind chimes clanging above my head and immediately heard her voice.

'Is that my Kate?'

'Oh, my god!' I squealed, clocking my best friend standing behind the counter. Zoe had always been into witchcraft and all things spiritual, and it reflected in every inch of the room. The mix of fragrances that oozed around the shop came from scented candles and incense sticks that were almost overpowering. I had no time to dither; she rounded the counter and rushed excitedly towards me.

I flung my arms out and yanked her into a suffocating hug that was so hard that she began to choke and splutter.

'Good grief, Kate,' she gasped, pulling back from me. 'Are you trying to kill me?'

'I'm trying to hug you to death,' I chuckled. 'It's been way too long!'

I pulled back to take in her flawless beauty, raking her from head to toe in complete awe. Zoe was a bohemian goddess, who exuded warmth and always looked exotic by dressing in elaborate patterned flowing dresses. The white maxi dress she wore appeared bold against her tanned, velvet skin and her brown hair hung down in immaculate waves over her back. I was dazzled by all the bangles, beads, and rings she wore.

'You look amazing, Zoe,' I gushed, feeling emotional. I'd missed my best friend like crazy and was so happy to be able to spend quality time with her finally.

'Thank you,' she gasped. 'Two weeks in Tenerife always puts me right. Hey, but look at you, you've lost weight and your hairs gotten blonder.'

'It's all this sun,' I laughed, 'I always go blonder in the summer.'

Her eyes were swimming a glossy espresso, taking me in, but she quickly let go of my hands to roam around the shop, careening around proudly.

'Well?' she asked expectantly, waiting for me to comment.

'The shops great. Fab. I'm well impressed.'

There was so much to explore. I curiously combed the room, admiring the beautifully crafted dream catchers dangling from the ceilings. There were bundles of sage sticks, incense sticks, candles and unique candleholders everywhere. I stepped closer to a shelf full of quirky, colourful crystals, each shaped differently and labelled with unusual names. Amongst them were shiny little pebbles of the prettiest colours; champagne pink rose quartz, lavender amethyst, mint green aventurine and copper brown Tigers Eye, to name a few.

My best friend had always been bubbly and sassy, but spirituality had always played a big part in her character, and she said it kept her humble. She'd always been into otherworldly stuff, but I couldn't make head nor tail of it all. I had her down as a happy hippy, living her best life, and that was enough for me. My hand glided over a brown leather book that had a pentacle engraved into its cover. I lingered on it and opened its blank pages.

'That's a Book of Shadows,' she explained, stepping close to me. 'It's where a witch or a coven write down their secrets and spells and intentions.'

'OK, Regina George,' I mocked, closing it. 'It's like a burn book for witches. I get it; it's pretty cool to look at though.'
My eyes flicked behind the counter to see a shelf that was full of jars.

'What are those?' I asked interestedly.

'Where? Oh!' Her leather sandals clapped against the old quarry stone floor as she wandered off behind the counter. 'These are dried herbs you can use for spells. I grow them in my garden and greenhouse. We've got dill seeds, cloves, blessed thistle, burdock root – you name it. You can also mash them up and put them into creams. Anything that comes out of mother earth is good.'

'I wouldn't be so sure about that,' I scoffed. 'Remember those crazy mushrooms I had that New Year's Eve? Talk about tripping my face off.'
I followed her over to the counter and started to ponder the gorgeous necklaces and pentacles, on view

inside the glass units. Suddenly, the flash of hot pink nails distracted me as she pressed her palm over my hand and squeezed.

'I'm so proud of you, Kate,' she gushed.
I blinked up at her warm gaze as she tilted her head at me maternally.

'For what?' I asked.

'For finally leaving Jack. That was so brave of you. I know it can't be easy starting a new life, but I promise you, you won't regret it.'
Before I could respond, the clinking of the windchimes snapped our heads towards the door and in walked in a pint-sized brunette. She was a pretty little thing, with wispy shoulder-length locks and had that whole book-nerd, preppy style going on.
She stopped abruptly and stared at me in a way which made me shift uncomfortably from foot to foot. The way her bug-like bright green eyes bore into me had me a little nervous. Her lips parted with a gasp.

'Antonia?' she exhaled breathlessly.
My jaw dropped as a pang of recognition hit my chest. *What name did she just call me?*
She swallowed with difficulty and delicately began creeping towards me, with hesitation in every step.

'Jopre Su?' she whispered, 'Jic Latek no obov jo?'
I blinked at her. *What the actual fuck? Is she drunk?*

'Savannah!' barked Zoe instantly. 'This is my friend, *Kate*.' The way she bit on the letter *T* of my name made me glance sideways at her suspiciously.

'Kate, this is my sister-in-law, Savannah. She's Danny's little sister.'

'Oh.' I stepped forward and extended my hand to her. 'Nice to meet you.'

She unfocused with a slight shake of the head, closed her mouth and shook my hand with clammy palms.

'What have I told you about talking in riddles to strangers?' Zoe nagged in a maternal tone before turning to me to sigh. 'Savannah is the languages teacher at the same school. You'll be working with her, so, you'll have plenty of time to get to know each other before you start.'

Languages teacher?
It sounded like gobbledygook to me.

'That's great,' I nodded, dubious about the nervous mute who stood before me.

'Anyway, more dill seeds, Sav?' Zoe asked her, turning to reach the jars of dry herbs on the shelf. I watched her bracelets clatter together and cascade from her wrist to her forearm.

As they chatted, my attention was dragged towards the jewellery under the glass. Rows of mood rings, pendants and stones lit up the glass and absorbed me. One of them bewitched me. It was a stunning pendant attached to a long silver chain, in the shape of a shark's tooth, but the colour – the colour - was like gazing into another galaxy. Spirals of lavender and vivid wild berry, lucent mauve and mottled plum, glimmered like a cosmic rock. It was utterly riveting.

Another flash of hot pink reached towards the pendant, and her perfectly manicured hands slowly pulled out the necklace. She smirked at me with an all-knowing glint.

'So, the amethyst speaks to you, does it, Kate?' She pressed her hand against an almost identical necklace around her neck, although her stone was black.

'Mine's black tourmaline and helps ground my spiritual energy, but this one …,' she ushered it towards me, gesturing for me to take it, '… this one is considered one of the most highly regarded varieties of the mineral quartz.'

I gazed into it, lost in its beauty.

'Its legendary powers are said to soothe, stimulate and help the mind and emotions, and is used for protection.'

'It's gorgeous,' I whispered.

'It's yours,' she replied.

My eyes jumped to Zoe, who smiled a bright, toothy smile at me.

'Really? I can *have* it?'

'Call it a welcome gift. Besides, its name derives from the Greek *amethystos*, which means 'not drunken'. It's thought to ward off drunkenness, so it should help you stop being a plonky.'

I giggled and carefully pulled it over my head and let it drop to its full length. The door opened again, and more customers dawdled inside.

'I thought you were closing up?' I asked.

'I am. You know, Danny's at home if you want to head over there now? I just have to cash up.'

I grimaced uncomfortably. 'I'll wait for you. I've only ever spoken to your husband briefly when he's been in the background of our calls; I don't really want to make small talk and be awkward.'

'Danny loves awkward small talk, but that's OK,' she chuckled.

My eyes jutted towards Savannah, who was still ogling at me like I was an alien.

She smiled shyly and blinked away.

'I think I'll step out for a cigarette,' I sighed, wary of her.

'Disgusting habit,' Zoe tutted. 'You know, I'm going to put a spell on you to quit that shit.'

As I headed towards the door and slid on my sunglasses, I glanced back at the girls as I held the door open for an old lady entering the shop. The way their heads were both turned to me with fixed stares had me a little apprehensive. Zoe's pensive gaze, Savannah's open-mouthed scope, their bodies straight, alert and surveying – had I missed something? Had I said something?

I flashed them a nervous smile before stepping out of the shop and on to the cobbled pathway, but as I leaned against the wall, I couldn't help but question why she called me by the name, Antonia? I hadn't misheard her, she could have picked *any* name in the world to call me, but she chose that one – *Antonia* – the name I hear in my reoccurring nightmare.

There was something off about that girl, but I didn't want to ruffle any feathers too soon. After all, I'd only just arrived, and I would be working with her after the summer break. I shook it off and put it down to the mini heatwave, causing paranoia. Either it was that, or I was going mad.

CHAPTER 5

They lived inside a picture postcard. Zoe's cottage was the last in the village before hitting the country roads. All that separated her home from the fringes of the dark woods was a barren carpet of fields. I shadowed her as we walked across her stony pebbled path that led to a little gate under an archway of vines and honeysuckle. The brown wooden gate was old and rickety. A considerable hedge surrounded the house, and the only thing you could see from a distance was the thatched roof and smoke billowing from the crooked old chimney pot.

It was timelessly unspoiled and beguiling.

I followed her, dragging my suitcase behind me as she struggled with my other bags, and I gaped up at the face of the house covered in aged Ivy. It stretched past all four windows over two stories and resembled a page ripped straight out of an enchanting fairy tale. As she unlocked and opened the white wooden door, I admired the rose bushes brimming with red, peach and white petals. The hanging baskets either side of the door overflowed with petunias and had bee's busily buzzing in and out of them.

'Welcome to Rosewood Cottage, Kate,' she announced. 'My home is now your home.'

We entered, and I could immediately see that the interior design of the home had *Zoe* written all over it. Her personality was painted on every pastel coloured wall, also filled with photographs, mystic and weird hippy art. You could see her stamp on every ornament and her collection of vintage bric-a-brac. Carefully chosen colour-coordinated books were all crammed in an old oak bookshelf.

'We've had to renovate the place,' she panted, dumping my bags in the living room. 'Danny!' she called out.

She placed her hands on to her hips, chest heaving, and trying to catch her breath. I scanned the room admiring the brass wall lights, low ceilings, rustic beams and a central inglenook fireplace that hosted a black log burner. I wondered how cosy it would be in the winter months, curling up in front of the fire on their fabric corner sofa with a good book. The floor flagstones, covered in part with fluffy, grey shaggy rugs looked warming, and there wasn't an inch of the house that didn't accommodate a candle.

I picked up one of her wedding photos which sat on a cluttered mantlepiece and smiled. I never made it to her wedding. I had a bad case of strep throat that saw me quarantined in my own home for a week. She was breath-taking, and both were enough to make anyone envious of their marriage. They were so happy together.

'We had to retain much of its traditional shell as possible,' Zoe explained, ushering me into her kitchen. I found myself in the heart of the home and recognised the open-plan kitchen immediately. It was from where Zoe would always skype or facetime me. All the herbs, spices and seasoning oils neatly lined up on the workbenches, and a fully stocked wine rack nestled in a corner. Low-slung pendants hung over the large oak dining table where a colourful vase of fresh flowers took centre stage. Shiny wine glasses accompanied the three place settings.

'Wow!' I gasped, peering out through the two French doors to the large garden that seemed never ending. It had an alfresco seating area, a garden swing, a pond, a greenhouse and a quaint wooden summer house at the very end of it. 'This is divine!'

I stepped out on to the lawn and breathed in the pure air. I noticed a gate at the very end of the garden that would lead out to the fields. It was so rural and isolated, and I felt lucky to call it home for the foreseeable future.

Zoe came out after me and handed me a glass of red wine. The sun's bite had cooled, and there was a little bit of breeze that fanned my burnt, olive skin.

'There's a beautiful stream that runs a little beyond that gate, too,' she smiled.

A dog's tapping feet and heavy panting snatched our attention, and I spun round to see a black Labrador catapulting towards me. I squealed in excitement and dropped to my knees. Immediately, my face was being washed with a fishy-smelling, rough tongue, as it panted excitedly and was jumping up at me.

'Shadow! Get down!' she snapped, clicking her fingers.

'Who's a good boy?' I cooed, letting him lick my face. 'You didn't tell me you had a dog?'

'Yeah, we adopted him months back from the cat and dog shelter. He's Danny's pride and joy. Speaking of whom …'

I glanced back to inside the house and could see Danny filling the doorframe. He was much taller and beefier in the flesh, and not at all who I'd put with Zoe.

For one, his appearance resembled a homeless person, wearing a sleeveless grey tank that exposed his sleeve tattoos and made him resemble someone that had been attacked with crayons. He scratched at his balls through his baggy black sweatpants that had slashes of white stains all over them. His sandaled feet were hairy and bore unclipped toenails that made me grimace. He didn't look like the cleanest of people. His shaggy, untrimmed beard dominated his entire face and met his brown hair that was greased back under a straw trilby hat.

As we stepped back inside the house, I saw his glossy blue eyes light up when he saw me. He stomped twice towards me, and he scooped me up into a tight squeeze, cutting off my air supply.

'Here she is!' he sang, tightening his arms around me. 'Finally, I get to meet my wife's best friend.'

He released me and dropped me to my feet, and, as the blood rushed to my head, I inched back and nodded at him.

'You too,' I said breathlessly. 'Mind, I also did invite you two to London many times, Danny?'

'I know, but the place stresses me out. Far too many people. Too much pollution. Cars, noise, stabbings. Anyway, it's good to have you here, kiddo,' he smiled genuinely with wrinkles at the corners of his eyes. 'Sorry I didn't help with your bags. I had to run out and catch the last post. I'll take them upstairs for you. Anyway, I'm going to walk the dog and let you two catch up and do your thing. Kate…,' he said. 'There's wine in the rack, and there's food in the fridge. Coffee is on the go, so help yourself. Our home is now your home, and I want you to treat it as such.'

'Aw,' I gushed, pressing a hand to my chest. Now I saw his appeal. What a lovely, hospitable guy. 'Thanks, Danny, I appreciate it.'

'Yeah, yeah,' Zoe clipped, 'Let's go and see your room.'

We moved past Danny and headed up a creaking narrow staircase and on to the landing. There were two bedrooms and a bathroom upstairs, and I crept behind Zoe as she opened the door to a small room that would be my own space for the foreseeable future. It could just about accommodate the double bed, and the peach pastel walls, the baby pink duvet and grey throw over the bed gave it a spacious, cubby-hole feel. Especially with the soft white shaggy rug stretched out on the wooden flooring.

'I've emptied the wardrobe and draws for you,' she explained. 'And there's a dressing table over there, too. Fresh towels live in the airing cupboard on the landing. Oh, we also have Wi-Fi, but it gets painfully slow at times, what with us being out in the sticks. So, don't expect fibre speeds. The Wi-Fi password is on the router downstairs if you want to hook up your laptop or tablet or whatever.'

'I'm taking a breather from social media, but thanks. I need to concentrate on prepping for the school term, and I don't want Jack stalking my Facebook page, which I know he will. So…'

I checked outside through the small window and gasped. I must have had the best view in the entire house, with visual access to the garden, fields and the fringe of the woods. It was so serene and calming, but something was niggling away at the back of my mind.

I flopped outstretched on the bed and flashed my eyes at Zoe.

'What's up?' she asked, scooting on the bed next to me. 'Is it too small?'

'No, no!' I protested. 'The room's great. It's just …' I dithered and began to chew my nails like I always did when I was anxious.

'Spit it out then,' she huffed, staring at me expectantly.

'Why did Savannah call me *Antonia*?' I quizzed. Her eyebrows knotted together, and she blinked at me, confused.

'Earlier today … in the shop?' I pressed, attempting to trigger her memory. 'She spoke in a weird language and called me by the name Antonia.'

Her eyes flicked off me and dipped to the ground, and she stood abruptly, scratching her nails into her scalp.

'I didn't hear her,' she replied dismissively.

She moved across the room towards the dressing table, and I could see her reflection in the table's back mirror. Her shoulders slouched, her body sagged, and her eyes squeezed shut, irritated.

'She did, Zoe, I heard her, and you commented on it,' I insisted.

Her lips pressed in a thin line, and she shook her head, disregarding it.

'Nope. I can't recall any of that- you must have misheard her – Anyway.' She twirled, and her expression was so far away that it surprised me. She wouldn't look me in the eyes. Instead, her eyes danced around the room, searching for a distraction. 'As I said, the towels are in the airing cupboard, the bathrooms to your left and if you need anything at all, shout for me. Feel free to shower or take a bath. I'm going to start cooking, maybe something light tonight. I'll have another glass of wine waiting for you and some dinner when you're finished. About an hour should do it?'

'That's fine,' I replied.

She hurried past me with her white dress skimming the ground behind her. I waited until she'd rounded the corner and audibly followed her steps to the ground floor before hunching over confused. Maybe I had misheard Savannah? Perhaps it was because it had been a long day and the heat was messing with my head? Or maybe she did call me by the name that haunts my nightmare. Was Zoe hiding something from me? Whatever it was, I was going to find out.

CHAPTER 6

Summer always made my soul smile. There was nothing quite like taking that first sip of coffee while sitting in the garden, a cloudless blue above my head with the sun glowing in the sky. I lay on one of the sun loungers with Shadow panting next to my feet. Zoe and Danny had already left for work that Saturday morning and I hadn't intended on moving for the next few hours until I heard a knock on the front door.

Shadow's head cocked to the side, and he ran off in the direction of the door. I was wearing a pair of grey shorts and a white strap top, not exactly attired to receive visitors. I stomped through the house and answered the door. The moment I saw him, I pulled the door back towards me to hide my bare legs. What was *he* doing here at 9.30 a.m.?

He stood tall in a tight white T-shirt, knee-length black shorts, white Nike trainers, and a black baseball cap that accentuated his chisel-jawed good looks.

'Finn?' I stuttered quizzically.

He nodded at me with that winning smile and dropped his eyes, lingering on the one bare leg that was exposed. I looked like crap. I hadn't even cleaned my teeth, and my boobs were hanging free under my strap top.

'So,' he chimed, raising an arm to lean casually against the doorway. 'I heard you were being left to your own devices today. Fancy a coffee and breakfast?' *How did he know that?*

'Erm, well I'm not really. My face, not dressed.' I stammered, trying to find a single English word that would make sense. He cocked his eyebrow at me, working hard to suppress a smirk.

'Won't take any excuses, Kate. The Jazz Café say half-an-hour?'

'The Jazz Café … erm, right, sure. Half an hour,' I agreed, all too quickly. Before I let any other gibberish slip from my mouth, I hurriedly shut the door on him and pressed my back against it feeling like the biggest weirdo on the planet. *Smooth Kate, real fucking smooth. What is wrong with you?*

One hour later, I found myself sitting in the sunshine outside the café located not far from the village market. Of course, I had brought Shadow along with me, and the waitress had kindly given me a bowl of water for him, explaining that it was a dog-friendly village, and you could take your beloved pet almost anywhere with you.

It appeared that Finn was a dog person too. He sat with Shadow between his legs, stroking his fur and leaning in for the occasional smooches. Shadow was all over him and appeared that he preferred his company to mine.

For a while, we were people watching. I envied the seniors sauntering along for their morning paper or stopping to have a gossip in the street, browsing shop windows or doing anything with their retirement days where time was a luxury. I couldn't complain too much. I still had plenty of weeks until the school term started. It was the first day of my fresh new start, and I sat lapping up the sun with my new (unnaturally handsome) friend.

Finn sipped his coffee then whimpered out, wafting his hand in front of his face, which made me chuckle.

'I told you it was hot,' I sniggered.

'Hot!' he squawked in a high-pitched voice. 'There's hot, and there's the fires of Mordor. What have they done? Melted the ring in it?'

I burst out laughing, so loud that Finn's immediate reaction was to laugh with me. That smile would be the end of me. He was funny, hot, and insanely captivating.

'Your laugh's infectious,' he gleamed, focusing his eyes on me. I looked away before I could get trapped in his lustrous gaze again and slipped on my oversized sunglasses.

'So, freckles, what's the story behind you and Zoe, then?' he asked.

I frowned and breathed through parted lips, staring off down the street.

'You already have a nickname for me?'

'I do. As you were.'

I bit my lip and suppressed a smile.

'We've been friends since we were kids. Digital pen pals mostly, but she visits me, usually once a year.' I pushed my sunglasses further up and rubbed my nose.

'This is the first time I've visited her home,' I admitted, turning back to him.

'Really? How come?'

'She's never invited me down here; she always came to visit me. And it's weird because this village is like spookily familiar to me. It feels like I've been here before, but I haven't.'

'How so?' he asked, blowing on his coffee.

'I wouldn't drink that yet, it's still piping,' I warned.

'I'm cooling it,' he grinned, blowing his active lips against the cup.

'I don't know how to explain it. You know when you get déjà vu, and you feel like you've walked in your shoes before, but in a different lifetime? And then that Savannah girl called me by the name, Antonia, when we met in the shop. It's the name that I hear in my recurring nightmare.' I twisted my head to see his eyes burning into me quizzically. 'Never mind,' I sighed, feeling like I was rambling a load of nonsense. 'I haven't been here, but I like the place a lot. So different in every way.'

He exhaled with a sigh and continued to blow on the steaming coffee.

'So, you think you've met me before, and you think you've been to Oaks End, but you haven't. It sounds to me like you have been here. Maybe in another life, in a different dimension or maybe even with me?'
I shrugged laughing. 'I wouldn't rule it out. Everything about you, inside and out, seems familiar. I'm not joking.'

'Well maybe it is just déjà vu,' he grinned. 'You know, in French, it means 'already seen'. Maybe it's love déjà vu? Perhaps we're those people who have immortal love, who fall in love with the same soul repeatedly in different lifetimes?'

I frowned at him. 'Alright, I said I know your face; I didn't say I love you. Easy.'

He laughed and shook his head, smirking from ear to ear.

'I instantly regret saying that. That was probably the cheesiest things I've ever said in my entire life.'

'Like, it nearly knocked me sick,' I joked.

'You and me both,' he laughed, cringing into himself. He paused awhile, and lifted his chin, inhaling the air around him. 'In all honesty, though, I know what you mean.' He exhaled. 'About the recognition thing. I'm kind of drawn to you too, and I can't explain why, so maybe –' he turned his head, blushing and then dismissed the rest of his sentence with a wave of the hand.

'I get it,' I chuckled, feeling a slight embarrassment by his confession. We both felt it.

'So, what's she told you about the witchcraft and the Chambers?' he asked.

Subject change. Thank god.

I pursed my lips and stared at him. 'Chambers?' I asked.

He was focused on the dog, playing with its ears.

'Yeah. It's another word with the same meaning - witches' covens.'

Strange.

'Not a lot,' I shrugged. 'I mean, she makes lotions and has a garden full of herbs which she says she uses in spells, but …,' I scrunched my face, '… I don't believe in all that stuff. It's not like she has *real* magic powers or anything. She just lights a candle and sends

43

things far out into the universe. I think? But whatever, I guess everyone needs an outlet and a belief system.'

'You don't have a belief system?' he asked, cocking his head towards me with furrowed brows.

I felt under scrutiny and was intrigued to know what he believes.

I shrugged. 'I don't have a religion. I think religion just creates wars and controls the masses. Every religion seems to contradict itself too. I mean, take our ten commandments. "Thou shalt not kill". And what do these holier than thou people do, go out and kill, bomb other countries, slay thousands of innocent people. You have these extremists challenging people to repent their sins, but they're the ones standing there mouthing off racial slurs or ostracising people for being gay or different. It's all bullshit. I much prefer to believe in something more spiritual, like the universe, I guess. In fact, one time when I was so skint, I emptied the contents of my penny jar, I asked the universe to do its magic and that I was amenable to receive whatever it sent within the next twenty-four hours. The very next day, I won £40 on a scratch card. I kid you not.'

His face softened, and he grinned broadly at me.

'Anyway, yes, she's mentioned the witches' coven a couple of times. Or, what do you call it?'

'A Chamber,' he smiled.

'Why do they call them Chambers? Why not just call it a coven?' I quizzed perplexed.

He blew on his coffee, not lifting his eyes from me, and shrugged before taking a sip.

'Well, whatever, apparently she's sworn to secrecy, so she can't tell me anything about it.'

'Well, how does that work when she hosts the Chamber meetings at her house?'

'Does she?' I asked.

He nodded with thinned lips.

'Do you think she'll ask me to make myself scarce when she has one?'

His tongue rolled against the back of his teeth, and he tangled his fingers around the hook of the cup.

'If she does, you know where I am.'

My heart flipped. *Yes. Yes, I do Finn Moon.*

I gulped hard and sipped my coffee.

'Can you imagine if I go home and they're all flying around on broomsticks?' I joked.

He leaned his elbow against the table and laughed under his breath.

'Want to know the story behind that?' he grinned.

I rolled my head to face him.

'Go on,' I prompted.

'Well,' he began. 'Rumour has it that practitioners of witchcraft experimented with herbs and potions, one of which was called a mandrake plant.'

I leaned in, giving him my full attention.

'A mandrake plant, it's claimed, has hallucinatory properties, and there's this secret ritual that Chambers perform, completely naked.'

My jaw dropped, gawping at him.

'And it involves rubbing the mandrake ointment in your …,' he hesitated and gestured down to his crotch, '… your bits.'

'What?' I laughed a little surprised.

He shifted forward and rubbed his nose.

'Apparently, it causes a floating sensation likened to that of a floating broomstick between your legs.'

My mouth was agape. 'Wait, they rubbed the oil in their vaginas?'

His chest collapsed with a laugh. 'Apparently. I mean, I've never tried it. So, you don't believe in witchcraft?' he asked.

I shrugged, with a headshake, 'No. Not at all. Why? Do you?'

Curiously, he didn't answer me. He merely smirked and turned his attention to the dog and started stroking its forehead.

My phone began to ring from inside of my bag, and I grimaced at him apologetically. I rustled through the contents to pick it up, but when I saw Jack's name flash up, I rolled my eyes and hunched forward, cutting the call immediately.

Finn side-glanced me and chewed the inside of his cheek.

'Sorry about that … it was the ex.' I sniffed, shoving the phone back into my bag.

'Is he licking his wounds?' he asked, fidgeting with the brim of his cap. I stared down the street.

'Probably.'

'Are you?'

I dropped my head and laughed faintly under my breath.

'I don't know how I'm feeling, to be honest. I've left a five-year-relationship and broken someone's world apart. It doesn't feel good knowing that he's hurting, but I couldn't stay with someone who I no longer saw a future with. We're two different people who want very different things from life.'

I noticed him become unfocused and distracted by a red Volvo that was speeding down the street. RnB music was blasting from the speakers with the windows rolled down, and two women were laughing. The car screeched to a stop and rolled up aside of us, and a twenty-something-year-old redhead turned the music down and leant her arm out of the window.

'Finnius Moon,' she purred, pushing her sunglasses up her nose. 'What have we here?'

Finnius?

He dipped his head and yanked his cap further down to shield his eyes, but I saw the clenched jaw and look of sheer agitation in his movements.

'Beck ... Gia,' he spat.

His pronounced sigh and involuntary knee jerks spoke volumes. I glanced at the driver who's flowing red hair burned like an orange sunset. Her contoured full-face became rigid, her lip fillers pouting with a sultry pucker. She wore designer clothes and had what appeared to be expensive silver and gold rings on her hands, glistening under the sun's rays. I couldn't see her eyes, but I felt them burning into me.

'I've been away for little over a week, and you're already having coffee with another girl?' she snapped accusingly. 'Who is she?'

Wow. Rude.

I'm right here. Hello!

Finn huffed loudly, and shook his head at her, with signs of irritation.

Her passenger, another girl around the same age, had jet black hair and a resting bitch face. She leaned over her friend and pulled her sunglasses halfway down her stub nose. Her face dropped along with her jaw, and an audible gasp hissed from her lips.

'Isn't that?'

Beck, the redhead, rolled her head closer to inspect me, and her mouth opened as if she was in shock.

'It can't be,' her friend gasped. 'That's impossible!' I snapped my head back to Finn, who'd wrapped the dogs' lead three times around his hand and rolled them into a vice-grip. The veins on his arms became enlarged from the strength he was using to dig his fingernails into his palms. He seemed furious.
I stared back at the driver, who flexed her jaw and growled under her breath.

'You're in deep shit, Finn,' she scalded, forcing the hand-break off. 'You and I need to talk. Right now!' She slammed her foot on the accelerator pedal with so much force that her friends head was jolted back against the headrest. I watched as her car screeched away along the road, swerving carelessly into the pub's car park.

'What on earth was that about?' I asked, swivelling my body to face him.
He breathed out of his mouth, exasperated and unwound the lead from his hands that left a red mark. I watched him stand, his expression so far away.

'Was that your girlfriend?' I questioned, already knowing that something must have been going on between them. His icy stare sucked the wind from me.

'Absolutely not,' he scoffed harshly. His razor-sharp tone and cold formality didn't sit right with me. It appeared to me that the woman got under his skin, or they had unfinished business. I wanted no part in that whatsoever - a drama was not going to present itself to me in Oaks End.

'It's complicated,' he said flatly, passing me the dog's lead. 'I should go.'

His coffee lay virtually untouched. I didn't want him to leave, and it was visible in the way I silently pleaded in my movements. I couldn't find the words to ask him to stay, but it was evident from his dipped head and lack of eye-contact that he needed to go.

'We'll do this another time. See you around, Kate.' *What? See you around? Not, 'let's reschedule', or 'I'll see you later'. 'See you around?' Wow.*

I'd barely pushed my jaw back in place when he'd already started down the road taking furious strides. I watched his pace quicken the closer he got to his pub. What was he in trouble for? What was her problem? Why did they react like that with me? I guess there were feet I'd trodden on. I sighed and dropped my gaze to Shadow.

'What am I doing, boy?' I asked him. He panted with a tongue full of bubbling saliva, and his brown eyes rolled up to me. 'Don't look at me like that. I get it. I can't get involved. I know that.' I sighed, staring off after Finn. 'Even if the man is an absolute dream boat.'

CHAPTER 7

I spent the rest of that afternoon sifting through emails which I'd received from my future employers. During the school summer holidays, I had weeks of lesson planning to do, name tags to sort out, seating plans to arrange and everything else that would sharp pile up if I didn't start prepping well in advance. I was both nervous and excited about starting my new job. God knows, I spent years in soul-destroying jobs, losing the will to live. I resented the fact that I was up to my eyeballs in student loan debt, with a First-Class degree not being utilised due to lack of experience. It forced me to spend eleven hours a day listening to arseholes screaming at me down the phone in some shitty call centre, all because I couldn't save them X amount of money on their monthly bills.

When I received a call telling me I'd got the teaching job, I was elated. I knew my entire life was about to change, and I just didn't realise to what extent.

When Zoe and Danny returned home that evening, they were insistent on us going along to the pub where I could meet a mix of their friends. I wondered if Finn would be working that night. Maybe I'd even glam up a little? *Stop it, Kate. You need to swerve that. Pronto.*

'Are you sure I'm dressed OK?' I quizzed Zoe as we approached the pub. Perhaps my denim shorts and grey strap top were a little bit too revealing. However, I'd covered up with a long floral kimono and ankle boots. Zoe's appearance, on the other hand, was fierce. She rocked the shit out of the boho-look. She strutted along with her weave of voluminous chocolate waves under a black floppy sunhat and dressed savvy in a pale pink short floaty dress. Her tanned legs were silken and sculptured as she swaggered along in her suede tassel ankle boots and matching saddlebag. She always made a statement with her fashion, and I envied how effortless she was.

'You look amazing, Kate. Come on. I need a drink. It's been a long day.'

Danny – ever the gent – gestured for us to enter before he did, and I was surprised to see the pub stowed out with people. I guessed that's where everyone assembled on a Saturday night. 'The Moon's Tavern' was villager's go-to place to socialise.

The music bounced off every wall and the pretty fairy lights that draped around the ceiling were twinkling romantically.

With every seat taken, it was a great atmosphere. Immediately, my focus aimed towards the bar, where I could see Finn and a pretty blonde girl, hair in French plaits, serving drinks across the bar.
So, he is working? Keep your cool. Don't stare.

Zoe's warm hand wrapped around mine and pulled me towards a table full of strangers, ripping my attention away from Finn.

'Kate, these are my friends that I want you to meet,' she announced. Their heads arched towards me, and their expressions focused and assessing.

Having that many pair of eyes on me made me feel instantly awkward and uncomfortable. I shifted and fidgeted, aware that my face had turned a shade of strawberry.

'Everyone ... this is my best friend, Kate, who I've already told you all about. Kate, let me introduce you.' Her finger pointed towards a couple who were, quite frankly, exquisitely gorgeous. 'That's Roman, Danny's younger brother and his wife, Ellis.'

Roman's appearance was that of a dangerous animal swollen with muscle and hulking broad shoulders. Like Danny, his arms and hands were covered in tattoos, he had thick dark chaotically gelled hair, and his dark, brooding features smouldered at me. I could see a definite resemblance to Danny. Ellis, his wife, was striking to look at, with feminine features and to-die-for chestnut brown hair that fell in a torrent of immaculate waves down her delicate body. My eyes shifted to Savannah, who I'd already met the previous day, and who stared at me with an unchanging gaze of surprise.

'Sav, who you've already met. Then we have Danny's parents, the lovely Dom and Darcie.' They were the only two who immediately offered me hospitable smiles. It was obvious that Danny and Roman had inherited their fathers' genes, while Savannah's resemblance was almost identical to her mother. Dom was stocky, but Hench for an older bloke, and looked as though he'd once sported the same dark hair in his younger days, only now it was frosted grey and receding. Darcie was a curvaceous, mousy blonde with sage green eyes bright with age and she wore a motherly smile. Finally, I received a scowl from the resting-bitch face of Gia, the passenger from the car.

She sat with her arms folded, in a black jumpsuit. Winged black eyeliner traced her almond-shaped eyes and sliced through me with a sneer.
No smile from that one, then.

'And this is Gia Carmichael. She's Beck's best friend and cousin, who's around here somewhere. Beck is Ellis's sister. They're visiting her for the week.'

I smiled warmly at them, but I was nervous, and I knew that my body language was probably coming across as standoffish and distant. I was never one for big groups of people and crowded places, but I'd deal with it the only way I knew how; by getting pissed as a fart.

'Hi.' I waved shyly, before slinking down into an empty seat in front of the Bloom's.

'Kate, do you want a glass of wine?' asked Zoe, placing her warm hands on my shoulders. 'Danny my love,' she twisted, motioning at Danny to get our round of drinks in. I was thankful when she occupied the seat next to mine. I felt so out of place, with so many strangers' eyes wandering up and down me like I was fresh meat intruding on their space.

'So,' Darcie cheered brightly, picking up her glass. I glanced at the tumbler and assumed she was drinking gin and tonic as a slice of lemon was bobbing about.

The ice in the glass clattered as her thin lips pressed against it. 'I hear you're the new English teacher at Westfield school?'

'Yes. I'm so excited,' I nodded, trying to sound enthusiastic. Her eyes caressed over me.

'Well, Sav and Ellis work there too, so if you need any guidance or advice, I'm sure they will be more than accommodating.'

I searched their faces and met the whitest, comeliest smile oozing from Ellis. She seemed graceful with natural, calm energy around her that I immediately trusted. Savannah was more interested in shredding the beermat in front of her, ignorant to our conversation.

'Of course,' Ellis marvelled, crossing one leg over the other in a relaxed manner. 'You'll love Westfield, plus the kids are great.'

'Pfft,' Dom scoffed nursing his pint. 'Not those little bastards that live next door to us. They need a good hiding, the lot of them. Cheeky little wankers that they are.'

'Dominic!' his wife spat with a disapproving glare.

'What?' he argued. 'Their parents are clueless morons. There's no discipline whatsoever.'

I was grateful when Danny reappeared with a tray full of drinks. Anything to change the subject.

'Good grief!' laughed Darcie peering over the tray, gobsmacked on seeing six shot glasses of tequila, accompanied with a salt cellar and small glass of lime slices. 'Danny, that's a bit excessive, love.'

'Hey, this poor girl needs to loosen up,' he joked, flicking his eyes down on me with a devious smirk. 'The shape of things to come, ha-ha.'

Immediately, I shook my head and dismissed them with a wave of my hand.

'Me and Tequila are terrible together. I puke everywhere, even after a sniff of the stuff.'

'Good,' he laughed. 'Then I'll just keep plying you with wine until they crown you the lightweight of the group, instead of me.'

'Ellis is the worst drunk,' Zoe quipped, adjusting her floppy hat.

'No, I'm not!' she protested indignantly.

'Yes, you are,' Danny nodded. 'You get so sloppy when you're drunk. Remember that night when we had a lock-in here? Roman was asleep in his pint, and you invited Bob the butcher into our space, knowing the man smells like a decaying carcass and then – then - you tried to slow dance with him.'

Ellis shook her head, smirking with guilt written all over her face. 'I can't remember that therefore it didn't happen ... fact!'

'He had his salmonella hands all over your bony arse.' Danny laughed.

'Bony?' Ellis raised an eyebrow and glared at him.

'Mate.' Roman glowered warningly. 'Enough.'

'I do not have a bony arse. Do I have a bony arse?' she gasped towards Zoe, eyes pleading for backup.

'Anyone's got a bony arse compared to Zoe's. Look at the meat on it,' Danny teased.

'Wow!' I gasped, covering my mouth trying to stifle a laugh.

'And proud of it,' she sassed back.

'You do have a lovely arse,' Savannah pitched in, thrusting out her arm to reach for Zoe's behind. 'And you too, Ellis.'

My god.
She speaks.

'I know I have a good arse,' scoffed Zoe, 'It's more meat than you can handle honey. Maybe if you trimmed that mullet on your face, I'd sit on it.'

'Woah!' a chorus from the assembled rumbled out. They all burst into laughter, and Danny flushed red, for once, speechless. They exchanged a private insinuating smirk, and then he winked subtly at her. It reminded me of the way Jack and me would tease and flirt with each other during the first few years of our relationship. I missed that. I missed the sexual tension, the teasing and chemistry that we rapidly lost.

Zoe bit down hard on her lip and blinked up at him with feigned innocence. His smile lifted, and he deliberately cruised her figure.

'Zoe Bloom, you best wash that mouth out with soap in my company,' Darcie cackled in sheer astonishment. Her jaw riveted on the ground, while her husband was keeled over laughing.

I glugged down my wine and felt myself start to loosen up, enjoying the unexpected light-hearted banter that went back and forth. These were my type of people. I did wonder whether to check behind me and see if Finn had even noticed me enter the room, but I was caged in.

'Everyone needs to stop hating on my beardstache, OK?' Danny laughed.
It became apparent that he was the joker of the group and one that kept everyone entertained.

'Beardstache?' Roman jeered, jutting his square chin up to Danny. 'It's a fucking face wig,' he mocked. 'You look like you've just resurfaced from an eighties mosh pit and stole someone's hat on the way out. God knows what's living under that hat or in that beard.'

'Alright, alright,' Darcie quipped loudly, trying to calm the personal jibing.

As they began to talk amongst themselves, I felt a sensation crawl over my back. I had eyes burning into me. I could feel it.

I dared to twist my head over my shoulder and side glanced the bar to see Finn, hunched over, leaning on his elbows, scorching his stare into me. My lips parted, and immediately I dropped my gaze with a flash of embarrassment, but when my lashes swept back up to meet his face, he was now smiling straight at me, probably amused by my blushing. They weren't the only eyes on me. My attention quickly anchored towards the haze of the fiery redhead sitting at the bar in front of him. She'd perched herself on the same stool I'd been sitting on the day before. *Beck? Was that her name? The driver of that car?*

She unglued her eyes from him and dragged her gaze towards me, drilling me with scrutiny. *If looks could kill.* I could sense a viciousness about her, callously assessing me through narrowed slits. I didn't entertain it. Instead, I excused myself and teetered off towards the toilets. I walked with a swagger, knowing fine well her glare travelled with me.

I was only inside the cubicle for two minutes, before I heard the door swing open and the clucking of heels clipping against the hard floor. The door opening brought in the loud background chatter of the punters, and the music booming from the jukebox. And then it faded out, with the click of a door lock. I counted two sets of footsteps and huffed.

I cleaned myself up, flushed the toilet, and took a deep breath, fully prepared for who I'd find loitering outside my cubicle, and low and behold, as I exited, they stood there, waiting for me at the washbasins. *Beck and Gia.*

I moved past them and began to wash my hands, pierced by their silent glares reflected in the mirrors. I slowly raised my eyes from the sink and blinked at Beck, who was death glaring me through piercing blue eyes.

'Do we have a problem, ladies?' I asked while casually washing my hands.

Don't be intimidated, Kate.

Show no fear.

Her entire face was dotted with brown freckles, her eyes popped, and her high cheekbones were full of contour and blush. She screamed extravagance; the overpowering smell of expensive perfume, the lavish jewellery on her fingers and wrists, the immaculate and pristine condition of her black, figure-hugging halter neck mini dress and laced tied heels. The appearance presented her as a posh, privileged princess type. Gia, her sidekick, was the mute that scowled.

'I thought I'd introduce myself, properly', she sneered in an angry, bratty tone. She leaned her curvaceous body against the sink. 'It's Kate, isn't it?'

'It is.'

I turned and stared directly in her eyes, and instantly became cautious.

Her wide eyes stared me contemptuously up and down, deliberately sceptical and insinuating.

'I'm aware you enjoyed a little rendezvous with my boyfriend this morning.'

I rolled my eyes and found myself instantly irritated by her.

'I was given the heads up. I'm no threat,' I replied casually.

She squinted at me and her expression hardened. 'Good. Glad to hear it. Because I don't appreciate strays sniffing around my boyfriend, he belongs with me. He's off-limits, so keep your hands to yourself and stay away from him, do you hear?'

Wow!

I tried to stifle a laugh, but it escaped my clenched mouth. 'Well, you're a ray of sunshine, aren't you?'

Her eyes were hard rimmed glaciers that fixed on me.

'Don't make an enemy out of me. It won't end well. He's mine.'

'Now that doesn't sound psychotic at all, does it?' I deliberately provoked.

'Careful,' hissed Gia, inching far too close in my space for comfort. 'You don't know what we're capable of doing. And I'm pretty sure you don't want to find out.'

I slumped and exhaled sharply, irritated.

'Right. Well, I'm bored with this petty nonsense, and I'm not interested in getting involved in this childlike drama. Keep it in the playground ladies or crawl back into your little bitch caves and bore the fuck off.'

I barged past them, slamming my shoulder against Gia and started towards the door.

'How have you been sleeping recently, Kate?'

I paused, hesitant with my hand on the locked door.

'Or should I say, *Antonia*?'

My heart plunged the second she curled that name

from her vicious tongue. I snapped my head back and met her dilated, menacing pupils of ice. Her lips curved into an antagonising smirk and she arched her chin, folding her arms smugly.

'What did you just call me?'

'Enjoy your night,' she replied haughtily and snidely laughed.

Her eyes flashed to the door handle, and I heard the snap of the lock unhook the latch. My head bounced back to the door to see it was now open. Freaked out, I pushed down on the handle, feeling a disconcerting vibration crawl up my spine. I shuddered and stormed through the pub, bypassing Zoe and the group. I spilled out on to the pavement and my anxiety peaked. Once was enough to stun me, but twice in one day demanded answers. What did they know? Somebody needed to start talking. And how the fuck did she unlock that toilet door without touching it?

CHAPTER 8

Who the hell was this Antonia, and why did people keep calling *me* by that name?

What was going on in this village? Why did it all feel so suspicious?

I dug through my bag angrily with shaking hands and yanked out my packet of cigarettes and a lighter. I didn't want to go back inside just yet. I lit my cigarette and collapsed back against the stone wall, watching the line of grey smog bellow from my mouth and form a cloud against the dark, black street.

The sun had set, and the moon had risen, and the village had become eerily dark. A few dim streetlights lined the road. Shops had long closed, and the street was void of people. The residents must have been in either of two places; their homes or the pub, the only hostelry in Oaks End.

I wanted to leave, but there was no way I was walking home alone; not in a barely lit village that I wasn't yet familiar with.

I sucked the smoke deep into my lungs, exhaled and coughed. I already suffered from anxiety. I guess my smoking habit was my crutch, an excuse to escape awkward or uncomfortable situations. I wanted to enjoy my time in the village, and not to be threatened by some unhinged bunny boiler. That and I didn't want to catch feelings for anyone either. This move was supposed to be a time for self-healing and self-discovery again. I didn't need distractions or drama.

Was this such a great move after all?

I don't need this crap.

A couple bashed through the front doors of the pub and staggered outside. Intoxicated laughter interrupted the still of the night. The chap was middle-aged, tubby and bald. He double glanced over as they hobbled towards me.

'Hey, it's you!' he slurred, stopping to address me. I could smell the rich alcohol fumes on his hot breath. 'You've changed your hair?'

'Excuse me?' I blinked at him, stone-faced.

'You know, in this village, we don't steal from each other. Changing the colour of your hair isn't going disguise that face of yours. I remember it well. Now, are you going to pay for what you stole from us?'

'That's her?' his female companion remarked, hanging off his arm. 'Yes, that's definitely her.'

'What the hell are you talking about?' I snapped, utterly confused and caught off-guard. 'I've never seen you before in my life.'

He squinted at me with eyes like black coal. The woman began tugging him away from me, tutting.

'Leave it, Harold, it was a few pies.'

Pies? What the -

He cursed me under his breath, glaring at me as he swayed on his feet, but succumbed to the direction his companion was pulling him in. I watched as they staggered along the street, fading quickly into the darkness before I jumped to the sound of my phone ringing from my bag.

By this point, my anxiety was through the roof. I angrily rived through my bag and pulled out my phone to see Jack's name flashing up again. My shoulders sagged and, for the first time since I'd left London, I decided to talk to him.

'Jack,' I answered sternly. There was a delay and silence. 'Can you hear me?' I asked.

'I can hear you,' he responded, his voice flat and emotionless.

'Are you OK?'

Everything was off-balance in that village, and, for a just a moment, I missed the norm of my home and the person I'd spent the past five years with. I was distracted by a figure, stepping away from the pub, on to the street next to me. I glanced side-ways to see Finn, his head bowed, and hands slipping into his pockets.

My heart reacted with a skip in its rhythm. He pulled a cigarette from out of a packet, balanced it between his lips and shielded it as he lit it.

'I'm fine,' Jack said tonelessly. He didn't sound like Jack. He didn't sound like the wounded soul leaving angry voicemails on my phone, begging for me to come home. 'I'm at the cottage. I'm here to see you.'

I froze rigid as my stomach hurtled to the ground with dread. *What? Why? How the hell did he get the address? I never told him the address.* I abruptly turned away from

Finn.

'What are you talking about? What do you mean, you're here?'

There was another long pause, and I could feel Finn's eyes on me. I felt him over every inch of my skin, probing with curiosity. I tried to ignore it.

'I miss you. I need to talk to you. Will you come and see me? I'm sat outside in my car.'

'At the cottage?'

'Yes.'

'I'm on my way.'

I killed the call and stared in disbelief at my phone. So many questions were driving through my head. His voice sounded vacant and far removed from the Jack I knew. It was as though he'd given up. He'd probably ridden the waves of hysterics and now was willing to talk, face to face, like adults, almost as if he were accepting of my situation. He just needed to see it in my eyes and hear it directly from me.

'Everything alright?' Finn enquired, blowing a line of smoke from his mouth, watching me through dilated pupils that never left me.

'I have to go. My boyf…' I hesitated, correcting myself, '…*ex-boyfriend* has turned up at the cottage. I need to talk to him. Can you tell Zoe I had to go? Tell her I'll see her back at the cottage?'

His weight shifted on his feet, tensing his jaw as his expression hardened. 'It's not safe for you to walk home alone. Let me walk with you.'

I stepped back, inching away from him and resisted.

'That's not a good idea. I'll be fine, but thanks.'

I didn't allow him to protest and started to run. My boots clinked across the pebbled path with difficulty as it was uneven and jagged. I was never good at running, and my disgusting smoking habit had significantly affected my lung capacity to breathe as deeply as I should. With only a few dull streetlamps guiding me off the main street, I had to run blindly along the road, past the occasional cottage that was mainly, and somewhat disconcertingly, silent at night. A stitch soon caught in my sides, forcing me to stop and walk it off. Like anyone would feel in an almost silent, pitch-black space, my senses became heightened, and my mind paranoid.

Every hair on my body bristled with my hypersensitivity, shuddering with the overwhelming instinct that I wasn't alone. I continually glanced behind me, checking that I wasn't being followed or stalked by some unseen force lurking from behind the corners of the cottages.

I picked up my pace and focused solely on my feet as they thrust me towards the end of the village. With Zoe's house in my line of sight, I powered the rest of the way, skidding across her pebbled path.

I checked around the immediate area. There was no car outside the cottage - no distant rumble of an engine idling or any sign of Jack's presence for that matter. As I fumbled with my house key, my heart pounded, and my hands were shaking.

I felt a presence that I couldn't explain. The feeling that someone was watching me was profound. I thought at any second someone would come and attack me from behind. I fought with the key, jamming it into the hole and heard the patter of Shadow's footsteps run towards the door. Finally, it opened, and I pushed through, slamming the door shut behind me, immediately flicking on the light. The protection I felt behind those doors was instant but was to be short-lived. I dropped down, squatting against the secured door. Shadow was there, wagging his tail and panting, his tongue flopping from his mouth.

Three heavy bangs suddenly rapped on the door. Shadow cocked his head and growled, backing away from me. My heart flipped.

'Hello?' I called out nervously, immediately standing up and backing away from the door.

'Kate?' Jacks voice called out. 'It's Jack, open up.' My entire body sagged in relief. 'Thank god,' I panted, placing a hand over my hammering chest. I opened it and stepped aside, grateful to see his face.

'Where's your car?' I asked, ushering him in. Something was off the minute my eyes met his. Jack had an animated face; he was tall, lean, geek looking with glasses. He was always shifty and aware of his surroundings, awkwardly scanning a room or the people that walked into it and was never good at eye contact. He used to say it freaked him out. But the way he filled out that door frame, upright, rigid, pinning his vacant eyes on me, punched a discomfort in my gut.

His movements were unusually slow as he glided silently into my space, smiling creepily at me without faltering his gaze. He seemed to be different, in every possible way. Shadow whimpered, his tail now between his legs, backing away from Jack.

'How did you find this address … find *me*?' I asked cautiously following him into the room. His head travelled around unflinching, absorbing every detail of the house. 'Jack?'

He turned unnaturally towards me, robotic-like, and

thinned his lips at me. He looked empty, and I couldn't read him like I usually would have. I swallowed and fidgeted with the hem of my top. I'd heard countless horror stories when people break up, and suddenly the dumped goes on a revenge spree, succumbs to a psychotic episode and murders the person who rejected them. Was that going to be me? Was he going to kill or maim me? Jack would cry at Christmas TV adverts or Charity appeals, never mind have the bottle to hurt a fly, so it alarmed me that he was acting so subdued and strange.

'Did you miss me?' he asked, shifting his wandering eyes back to me. His voice sounded different, like strangled and gruff.

'Miss you?' I fumbled with my hands, scanning him confused. 'I've only been gone for two days, Jack. How did you find me?'

He inhaled sharply, holding his breath for several seconds, and collapsed his chest as he prowled towards me. He stared at me like it was the first time he'd seen the detail of my face. He was probing every inch of it with curiosity and intrigue.

'Remarkable,' he whispered.

I jerked my head away from him, and every bone in my body screamed that something was wrong. That I was in danger, and Jack was the intruder, set out to harm me.

'You know, Zoe and her husband will be home any minute, and I don't think you should be here, Jack. You shouldn't have come here.'

He leaned into my personal space, and I recoiled back instantly. His eyes, usually rich hickory, turned almost coal-black and what burst from his mouth was nothing short of a sinister laugh that bounced around the room, promising torment and menace.

I scrambled back and tripped, landing in a violent heap on the floor. His callous chuckle sounded unearthly, like a hollow screech from a possessed soul. As he cackled maliciously, his eyes now spheres of coal, his voice distorted between male and female.

My body cemented into the floor, paralysed in fear. I couldn't breathe, even though I could hear my distress pulsing in my ears, my chest tightened, asphyxiated and fear stricken.

'Did you miss me?' the malignant creature asked, lunging down at me. 'My darling sister?'

Pinned down by stunned terror, my nerves now hacked to shreds, I watched in anguish as my ex-boyfriend's face dissolved and shifted into a face that choked me with recognition; a face I looked at in the mirror every single day – *my* face. I gurgled for air as my body failed to move. She was *me*. All her features, except for her eyes and hair, were identical to mine. She didn't have my eye condition; instead, these eyes were black, harbouring hatred and wrath. Her hair was as black as midnight but styled like mine. She even had the freckles scattered across her nose, just as I did. But she wasn't me. She was a presence of pure evil, rotten to her core.

'Surprised to see me?' she jeered over me, cackling with poison. I couldn't find my tongue to speak and, with no warning, my body was suddenly hoisted into the air, without her even touching me. An invisible force took hold of me, as though someone had wrapped their arms around my stomach and heaved me off the ground. She turned her body and glided towards the bookshelf.

'Of course, you are,' she scoffed, sounding exactly like me. 'They didn't tell you about me. They didn't tell you anything, not even why you're here?'

She was dressed head to toe in black. She picked up a picture of Zoe and tutted at it, before slamming it down. The glass smashed to tiny shards all over the floor, and she turned, snarling at me.

I clenched my quivering fingers together, but my hands went numb. Hot tears burst from my eyes as I floated higher off the floor, feeling the pressure around my body tighten. I couldn't recognise the strangled whimpers spurting from my mouth, but if fear sounded like anything, it sounded like that. *How is she doing this? This isn't real. It's not possible.*

I winced as she stalked towards me. Her body movements didn't mirror mine. Her chin arched up, and she walked like she held high regard for herself, roaming around like she had power spitting through her veins.

'Zoe is a traitorous bitch,' she spat, 'She didn't invite you here for some stupid job. She invited you here because she knew I was coming for you. She led me to you.'

Her voice was penetrating and hostile, and she hissed at me in a harsh, clipped tone. 'Best friend? Ha!'

I followed her as she paced the room with her hands on her hips. 'She knows you have what I want, and she's going to allow me to take it from you.'

Without warning, her arms shot out towards me. Her hands pushed out what I can only describe as electricity or a powerful burst of blue energy. I watched it spiral towards me, but when it contacted me, I felt a severe blow to my gut and my body hurled through the air. The air snatched from my throat, and I cracked with force against the wall opposite. Pain writhed through me, so intense, I wanted to throw up. It winded me so severely that it hurt to draw breath.

'You're pathetic,' she scalded, dropping one hand to her side while the other propped on her hip. She dragged her feet towards me in slow, predatory movements and, as she raised her hands, I felt a force tighten around my neck and pull me high up the wall. I thrashed out my feet as noise ravaged my ears and my eyes blurred.

Was this it?

Was this death?

'You're weak, just like our parents were when they were slaughtered in the Fae Woods.'

My head mangled, and a flash of my nightmare gripped me. *The charred woman's body, and the corpse, swinging from a noose.* I felt sick and disorientated. Was she talking about *those* people?

'You don't deserve your powers, and I'm going to take them from you,' she snarled.

She filled my space and wrenched her eyes up to me, disarming me in a vice grip. Poison escaped from her pores as she seethed violently through flared nostrils and demonic eyes. I couldn't look away, no matter how hard I tried to pry my focus away from her, I could see her black soul festering beneath those discs, corrupt and foul from the inside out. Her lips parted, and her face hardened with deep shadows under her protruding cheekbones. Her eyes bulged and swirled from black to ghost white. There was no iris left, merely a circle of shining, bright white light, like an intense torch beam.

I felt myself slipping in and out of consciousness, as I was a captive, seized by the blinding white lights of her eyes.

I heard the front door rive open and smashed against the wall and became aware of figures running into the room, but she did not release me. She was absorbing my energy, my life. It was only when the white of her eyes blinked back to black, that I felt at liberty to move. I dropped to the floor with a loud thud and winced at the shooting pain spiralling up my spine. I clawed for air and sounded as if I'd just swam to the surface of a deep pool, with a gurgling gasp. It all happened so fast. Danny's arms splayed out, his face like a wild, aggressive lion. His arms yanked a force that grabbed hold of her and threw her across the room.

Zoe moved powerfully, hissing viciously at her and pinning her against the wall, the same as me moments earlier.

But no fear bubbled beneath the surface of my attacker's face. Instead, she cackled bitterly, rife with spite.

'You can't detain me. Jorah sent me,' she said defiantly.

'Then provide me with a fucking warrant,' Zoe spat, inches from her face.

I'd never seen Zoe so possessed with anger before. It startled me. Danny towered behind her, in a stance ready to attack.

'I don't need one. I'm as good as the new Mitral,' she cackled.

'No order or summons, no letter has been addressed to me consenting to this barbarian sacrifice and, until I hear it uttered from his last breath, you will not come near me, my Chamber Vents or Kate.'
I watched her mouth twitch, and her black eyes blink to a cold grey.

'Kate? Ha! Is that what she calls herself?'

'You're no sister of hers, you're nothing to her,' Zoe shouted angrily.

'And neither will you be when she finds out the truth. Good luck with that,' she cackled defiantly.

'Enough!' Danny growled, lunging towards her. 'You send a message back to Jorah. She's not the one - warrant or no warrant.'
Her snarling smirk rose. 'We'll find out soon enough.'

When Danny's hand gripped her arm, she dissolved into thin air, leaving a swirl of black particles. She was gone, in a blink of the eye. I shook, uncontrollably as I lay in the foetal position, barricading my back against the wall. Both their heads snapped towards me, their eyes lowered apologetically, and their shoulders sagged.
I hadn't woken up.
Pinching my skin made not one ounce of a difference.
It was real. That just happened.

CHAPTER 9

'I don't know where to begin,' Zoe whispered, sulking across the table from me with an air of shame.

Her shoulder's slouched forward, her gaze directed downwards, and she kneaded her fingers anxiously. Danny pulled out a chair from underneath the table and slumped down into it, clutching a glass of whiskey. He slid an empty tumbler my way, and I snatched the bottle and poured myself a large one. No amount of alcohol would numb me to the shit show I'd just witnessed, but I was hell-bent on trying.

'Why don't you start by telling me when you two were exposed to high-energy radiation and mutated into fucking X-Men?' I snarled sarcastically. Danny sniggered but was nudged aggressively by a bemused Zoe.

'How did I end up in the *Secret World of Alex Mac*?' I jibed, trying to rationalise what the hell had happened. 'Are you going to start zapping electricity from your fingers or melt into a blob on the floor and start slithering around?'

Zoe eye-rolled me and shook her head, agitated.

'Who is Alex Mac?' asked Danny baffled.

'Danny!' she snapped warningly. 'Look, we didn't intend on you finding out like this, OK? We were handling the situation, but we just needed to get you here so we could make sure you were safe.'

'Safe?' I barked loudly. 'From what? A long-lost demonic sister who tried to kill me. Why did she have my face? Why did her eyes flick from black to white? How did she fly across the room and then evaporate in front of my eyes? I'm sorry, but I'm clearly tripping on acid right now because this is all levels of fucked up.'

'Kate, stop!' Zoe pleaded, winding her thumbs around her temples as if she were nursing a severe headache.

I'd give her a headache, alright. What kind of fresh hell was that?

'Do you have access to holograms? Is this part of Project Bluebeam? Was that what that was? A hologram?'

'What's project Bluebeam?' Danny started, but was quickly cut off by Zoe's death stares and sharp tongue. He mumbled something under his breath. When I cocked my head towards him, his eyes widened at me as though he was an innocent party.

'Don't you dare,' Zoe snarled at him through gritted teeth, 'It'll be the last thing you do.'

'Is this absinth?' I asked, staring down at the whisky. I needed to pace. I got up and began to stomp back and forth around the kitchen. 'I feel like I'm hallucinating again right now.'

'That's it,' Danny uttered matter-of-factly. 'I'm out.' Before I had time to register what he had said, he quite literally vaporised in front of my face.

His image was now a mist, as if he vanished through a portal, out of our dimension, into another.

The shock ripped the breath from my lungs. I felt like I was about to pass out, and my head started to spin. My legs crumpled, and I hit the deck. A pain shot up my spine as I landed awkwardly on my coccyx. I couldn't grasp reality.

Zoe's head dropped at the same time as her shoulder's, and she released her pent-up breath.

'For fuck's sake, Danny!' she called out angrily, before slumping in her chair, appearing defeated. 'I know why he did that,' she admitted. 'Do you believe us now?'

I couldn't speak. All I could do was gaze up at her, horror-struck.

'How do you think I was supposed to tell you? You didn't grow up in our world. You had your own new life and identity. We're different from other humans, Kate. We have inherited incredible abilities that they don't have, and we come from exceptional family bloodlines that go back centuries.'

'I need you to tell me about my real identity, Zoe. Please tell me the truth because I am really freaking out right now.'

Zoe's pupils were dilated, with a rim of chocolate now searching me.

'You're not who you think you are,' she began. 'You're Antonia Wade.' She paused, seeking a reaction before delivering the information that would be life-changing to me.

'That … that was your twin sister, Raven. Both of you once lived right here in Oaks End, until you were five-year-olds.'

My heart swelled. *Raven, my twin sister?* How could Zoe not have told me this?

Who else knew?

Lilian, my mother by adoption, didn't go into specific details about my biological parents. As I grew up, the more curious I became, but she'd always stuck with the same story; that she and her then husband, Joe, had adopted me when I was a baby. He bailed out of the relationship not long afterwards, leaving her to raise me as a single mother. She claimed that they were both killed in a car pile-up. I never pressed it further, nor did I want to, not even when the law was changed to allow me the choice. I had a selfless, loving parent who watched over me, always putting me first. I didn't understand it. Why was Zoe saying that I lived here until I was *five*?

'I know it's going to be a lot to take in,' she continued in a serious tone. 'What I'm about to tell you will probably blow your mind, and it'll be difficult to digest. But if you want answers, you need to come and sit down, listen to me and take it seriously.'

I rose to my feet, holding my lower back and took a seat.

'Difficult to digest? Zoe, I've just seen a grown man disappear right in front of my eyes. Where did he go? How did he do that?'

'As I said, we're witches and have unique abilities. Danny can teleport himself anywhere he wants to, at any time. I have telekinesis powers, which means I can move objects or even people around at will.'

It all sounded so unbelievably farfetched to me; however, I couldn't be so quick to dismiss something I'd witnessed at first-hand.

'So, why did Lilian say that she adopted me as a baby, and don't you think I'd have remembered living here before? None of this makes any sense. I *would* have remembered, Zoe.'

Zoe swallowed and looked at me regrettably.

'I've done some research. The only way I can describe it is that your brain has dissociated with the reality of what happened to you.'

I scrunched my face up at her, dismissively.

'Sometimes when people experience an overwhelming trauma, the brain tries to protect itself. It's like a detachment of the experience, essentially blocking the memory from your conscience. Your nightmare …,' she pressed, '… is reoccurring because it was an early trauma. As kids, we're unable to remember much of our infancy or toddlerhood. Until we get to the ages of around five or six-years-old, then we *do* have *some* memories – especially traumatic events – but not always.'

I took a deep breath and she continued.

'As we get older, those early memories start to fade with time. It's known as childhood amnesia. Lots of kids hear hand-me-down stories from relatives and begin to register those stories as the truth. That's what Lilian did. She told you she adopted you as a baby and you had no reason to doubt that. She was trying to protect you.'

I grimaced. It was my choice not to go searching for more information about my birth parents. The thought had crossed my mind several times throughout my life, tempted to find newspaper clippings of their deaths, or see pictures of them so I could perhaps find my face within theirs, but I knew deep down it might have done me more damage than good. I didn't want to offend or hurt Lilian by doing that. So, I never did.

'Your real parents were Maddock and Allegra Wade. They lived with you at the far end of the village at Rose Bloom Cottage. They were two of the nicest people you could ever meet. They didn't die in a car accident, Kate. They were murdered, right here in Oaks End. Over the back there, in a very remote area of Fae Woods.'

I blinked past her and looked out the French doors towards the woods. Recognition seized me, not because they were murdered, but because it was clear to me now that my horrific reoccurring nightmare was, in fact, a real *memory*.

Pain swelled in my heart, and I had to compose myself. I winced through an immediate flashback. Their scorched faces flickered before my eyes as my head throbbed. That woman's charred body, that man's bulging bloodshot eyes: they were my parents. I'd heard them being sacrificed and saw the aftermath - murdered in cold blood - no wonder I'd blocked it out. Tears dripped from my eyes and rolled on to my lips. I brushed them away with the back of my sleeve and could taste the salt on my tongue.

'Who killed them?' I sniffed.
She reached for my hand and tried to squeeze it reassuringly. I contacted her vibrant, hazel coloured eyes that searched my face and snatched my hand away from her. I felt bitter that she knew all this time and didn't tell me.

'Before I get into that, I need to tell you how all of this works otherwise you won't understand it. The whole structure is based upon the workings of a human heart.'

The human heart?

My head started to pound.

'We evolved centuries ago to ensure that the world stayed a safe place and nothing untoward would happen to humankind here on Earth. Guardians of the planet if you like.'

'Well, you didn't do a very good job of it, did you? The world's fucked.' I snapped flippantly.

'Kate, believe me, it could have been much worse if it hadn't been for our direct interventions. Humans would not have survived, had certain game plans and agendas been followed through to their evil conclusions.'

'By whom?'

'By elites, unseen forces, and the occasional despotic maniac who inadvertently slipped under our radar. Many dangerous agendas are now playing out in the world, and we must be constantly vigilant. We *will* ultimately stop them. There are many of us doing battle for the sake of humanity.'

'OK, so what's any of that got to do with me?'

'Hang on. Let me grab something that will probably explain this a whole better than I am. It's better if I *show* you our structure.'

She rose and went out of the room, returning with what appeared to be a large, old parchment. She unfurled it and laid it on the table in from of me, securing it by placing a salt and a pepper pot on the top and bottom end of it.

'Now, I'll slowly take you through this chart.' She pointed at a detailed drawing of the human heart.

'I'm all ears, go on.'

'OK. This is a human heart. It has four main chambers, two uppers, known as the Atrium, and two lower ones called the Ventricles. Our whole system is based on this concept. There is now a "Heart" presence all around the globe, in almost every country. They're all structured the same as this, the four chambers.' She looked at me, quizzically. 'Are you following me so far?'

'Not really, no!' I replied curtly, which made her huff in exasperation.

'Pay attention!' she bit, frustrated. 'The four individual Chambers of each Heart are known as; The Pericardium, Epicardium, Myocardium and Endocardium ... yes?'

I nodded in acknowledgement.

'Our particular Chamber is called the Endocardium Chamber. We, as individuals of the Chamber, are known as *Vents*. The formal name for the males is *Arterioles*, and we females are the *Venules*.'

'This seems complicated, Zoe ... beyond my comprehension. Is this for real ... seriously?'

'Yes, it's real. Just keep up. It'll become clearer; I promise. Just focus, will you?'

She can't be making this shit up, can she?

'Now, each *Heart* has a controller. It's his or her remit to keep us informed of dangerous events, people, and to advise of what course of action we need to take on that impending threat. The title they inherit is *Mitral*. They also liaise with global Mitrals on any looming International problems. Our Mitral is currently with the Myocardium Chamber, which is based further down south, in Hampshire. Their HQ is at a mansion called Glentree Manor … you'll learn more about that place as we move this along.'

'I think I need another drink. This is way over my head.'

'The Mitral is Jorah De Wyche,' she continued, 'He's our current Mitral. He acts as the heart valve that pumps out his doctrine to the other Chambers. We're answerable to him. There are strict rules and regulations we must follow. He controls almost every aspect of our lives. Even leaking or talking about our Chamber affairs to a non-Chamber member is punishable, by death.'

'Death!' I yelled, frowning and scoffing at the barbarity of it all. 'We're not living in the seventeen-hundreds, Zoe. What gives him the right?'

'His powers, that's what,' she interrupted. I saw the dread behind her eyes and her whole-body shift with discomfort. I squinted at her so she'd elaborate and that I wouldn't have to keep asking questions.

She inhaled through her nostrils and held it for a few seconds before exhaling through pinched lips.

'For many generations, much sought after unique abilities are unused and don't die with the Vent that hosts them.'

'By Vent, you mean a witch, right?' I asked, trying to digest the information.
She growled under her breath and rolled her eyes.

'Yes. We don't call ourselves witches, Kate. We call ourselves *Vents*. Just as I said before.' I nodded and signalled and for her to continue.

She gritted her teeth and carried on.

'These abilities are absorbed and carried on down the bloodlines, through the next generation of Vents, normally via genetics.'

She picked up the bottle of whisky and poured herself a glass, necking it back in one.

'The Mitral generally has a mega mix of powers; one's that he or she needs to pass down the bloodline. Otherwise, they would be lost forever. So, traditionally, when the Mitral comes to the natural end of his or her life, they will choose a beneficiary to inherit their powers.'

'Go on,' I prompted, now engrossed and feeling a little more enlightened.

'It's not all that straight forward. It's morbid, gruesome and not for the faint-hearted.'

I waited, blinking at her as she chewed her lip, deliberating how to word it.

'When the Mitral has chosen a specific Vent to appoint as the next Mitral, the Chambers connecting that Heart, are summoned to an agreed place. In this case, it's Glentree Manor as it's his family home and workplace for his Chamber Vents, who mainly work for the family business. It has a formal room and a former Courtroom, used for blood sacrifices.'

'Sacrifices!' I gasped.

She nodded and grimaced.

'The outgoing Mitral is laid on an altar, which has a semi-circle of pews surrounding it, which the other invited Chambers are seated so that they can participate in the event. The attendees all chant and read the rights of the beneficiary. And then,' she paused and winced, 'and then the beneficiary must take a ceremonial dagger, stab the Mitral through the heart and drink the blood.'

My stomach churned, and I felt violently sick at the very thought of it.

'Years ago, your father was going to inherit the position and be appointed to the post of Mitral.'

I glanced at her with dread. *My father? A father I don't remember, a biological father whom I'd never known.*

'To be appointed, you must be disciplined, respected and demonstrate leadership. The deal was done. He was the chosen one. Except that when the moment he came to do the dastardly deed, he couldn't go through with it.'

I was intrigued. 'So, who did?' I asked.

'His cousin, Jorah De Wyche. He could see that Maddock was wavering and took his opportunity. In a fit of greed, he snatched the blade from Maddock and plunged it through Lourdes De Wyche's heart. Some say he didn't even come up for air when he drank the blood.'

My one hand wrapped around my uneasy stomach and the other clasped my mouth as I became nauseous.

'That's fucking disgusting,' I complained.

'The De Wyche's have always been volatile, unpredictable and corrupt. I guess your father didn't want that kind of blood running through his veins. But Jorah wasn't the rightful beneficiary, and there were severe consequences.'

'Like?'

'Like over the years, he went insane. He was bloodthirsty. He enjoyed the cruelty he could command and got pleasure from death and destruction. Even when it came to the removing of certain people from this world, he did it inhumanely. He became so dark and menacing that everybody winced at the sound of his name. Suddenly, he decided to make an example out of *your* family.'

My eyes pinned on Zoe as she struggled to look at me.

'He saw Maddock as weak. He didn't like weakness. He arranged for the Chambers to meet in the Fae Woods one night for a special ceremony, but it turned into a plan to get them all together under false pretences. He slaughtered your parents in front of everybody and no-one could, or attempted to, do anything about it. You were invited to attend with them, and then you're sixth sense told you that something bad was going to happen. You escaped. You got away, Kate, but your sister didn't follow suit. He had planned on killing you both. For whatever reason in his twisted, evil mind, he decided to keep Raven alive. He wasn't too concerned that you'd ran off, as he still held your parents and Raven. What caused him to spare Raven is still a mystery, but she's been his adopted pet ever since and has taken to his evil ways.' She blinked down to the picture of the heart and sighed heavily. 'They cleared the scene within 24 hours. The Myocardium Chamber was forced to dig your parent's graves and dispose of the bodies. Your parents' remains are buried in those woods.'

'And our home?' I queried, wondering how a family of four could suddenly go missing and nobody report them, ask questions or stop by the house to check if they were OK.

'Your home in Oaks End was emptied, contents disposed of and was soon reoccupied by others. The official cover story was that you had gone to visit family in New Zealand but had decided to settle there. I don't know, from what my mum told me, people in the village speculated for a while, but they quickly got over it and soon gossiped about something else. And then a few years later, that cottage burnt down in an accidental fire. Luckily, no-one was hurt, and it was eventually rebuilt.'

How convenient, I thought.

We sat in silence for a minute while I swallowed her accounts.

All this time, I had a twin sister that I never knew existed. How could I not recall this, or recognise my old home? How could my mind have blocked it out for all this time?

Was it really because of the *Freudian Children's Amnesia* theory?

'And Jorah's dying. The curse of the theft of a Mitral position caught up with him. The man's only in his fifties, but he already looks like a corpse.'

'He's dying?'

'And rightly so. He should never have been considered for the position of Mitral. A premature ageing process is eating through him and has been since he first drank that blood. And now *he* is going to be sacrificed, and he's chosen Raven to do the morbid deed.'

'What does she want with me?' I asked, topping up my glass of whisky. 'What did I do?'

'It's not what you did, Kate, it's what you may hold that she wants.'

'That is?'

'Your powers,' she declared. I blinked at her before laughing.

'Don't be so ridiculous. Powers? I don't even have the energy to get dressed in the morning, and you're telling me she thinks that I have powers?' She stared at me, sternly. 'I don't have powers, Zoe. That's a fucking joke.'

She leaned on her elbows and shrugged slightly.

'Every single Vent of every Chamber has its powers documented in the Mitral Book of Shadows … except you. There are missing powers that need to be absorbed in the sacrifice. They think you have them.'

My mouth opened, and a gasp slipped through my lips. 'She thinks I have those powers?'

She shrugged again and rose from her seat.

'I'm not sure, Kate, but I'm not taking any risks. They were planning a trip to London and seeking you out. I got wind of this and wasn't about to let that happen. She would have found you eventually. She soon found your boyfriend, didn't she? I invited you here to keep you safe, and I will keep you safe: we all will.'

I squinted at her and jerked my head forward as a pixelated human form appeared next to her. Coming into full focus, Danny reappeared.

Zoe cocked her head to the side and glared at him, folding her arms tightly across her chest.

'Well, thank you, for gracing us with your presence, you utter bellend!' she clipped.

Danny tilted his head at me, apologetically and reached for the bottle of whisky. Zoe slapped his hand quickly and snatched the bottle away from him.

'What?' he gasped, acting dumb. 'I thought it was better coming from you. Does she know? *Do you know?*' he asked, leaning towards me.

I curled a strand of hair behind my ear and nodded at him.

'Yeah, Danny. I know.'

He broke into a smile and opened his arms out wide.

'Welcome back, kiddo. Welcome back.'

CHAPTER 10

I could smell the rain approaching. Usually, the all-consuming sun would pierce every window beckoning everyone outside, but not that morning. From the moment I opened my eyes, the world around me drained of colour. The steel grey clouds hung low and clung to the muggy, humid air that surrounded the village. I felt like it was metaphorical for how I was feeling that morning, waking up with no sunshine in my soul, only a thick fog and the feeling of doom.

I stood at the end of the garden virtually chain-smoking, while Zoe's house filled with many of the faces that I'd met at the pub the night before. After the unavoidable exposure to their kind, she'd insisted we meet for a breakfast banquet and discuss everything out in the open.

The table was a full spread of bagels, croissants, fruit, toast, vegan sausages and more. A platter that, quite frankly, miserably failed to reunite me with my appetite.

I was too stressed to eat. I was confused. I had so many questions that needed answering. I could hear them in the kitchen all chatting away to each other; Savannah, Roman, Ellis, Darcie and Dominic – the Vents of the Endocardium Chamber.

Vents! For fuck's sake, they were witches. Why not just call a witch a witch?

When would I be able to digest that notion? It seemed so ridiculous to me. When I thought of witches, I envisioned warts, pointy hats, crooked noses, haggard faces and broomsticks. I couldn't place normal people as a kind that could stand over cauldrons and cast spells. And if witches were now real, who's to say vampires and werewolves weren't? Was I going to start seeing fairies at the end of the garden? Or Pegasus the winged horse flying around the sky? Maybe if I collected my skittles at the end of the rainbow, I'd meet an actual leprechaun?

Christ. Nothing could be ruled out now.

I frowned inwardly and thought of Beck and Gia and the toilet incident. I saw that door unlock by itself. Were they Vents too? Did they have specific abilities? The thought almost made me laugh. I'd existed on this planet for over twenty-four years, and I'd certainly never had the powers to throw someone across a room or make them disappear mentally. God only knows how many times I've wished I had. I guess it explained the curious eyes that had latched onto my every move the night before. They were probably wondering if I *did* have any powers after all.

Thunder rolled in the distance and reverberated across the green landscape in front of me before it dissipated into the surrounding hills.

I craved the rain. I'd welcome it with open arms: anything to puncture the thick air and humidity that anchored me down.

'Kate!' I heard Zoe's feet dash over the grass behind me and stopped by my side. 'Would you come inside? It's going to chuck it down any minute,' she complained.

I ignored her, inhaling deeply. I watched the sky swirl black and exhaled a thick line of grey smoke. A brilliant flash of white split the sky over the immediate landscape, and Zoe squealed. The thunder cracked almost immediately and then rumbled on aggressively.

'Nope!' she said, edging backwards. 'I am *not* about to get zapped by lightning. Come on, Kate, let's get inside.'

'I'm enjoying this,' I shrugged, flicking my cigarette stub into the stream.

'Are you crazy?' Zoe snapped, 'Kate, don't be stupid, it's right overhead now. Are you trying to get yourself killed?'

'Well, I'm sure there's a power or a potion you could rustle up that would protect me,' I muttered. She growled at my sarcasm and stepped further back as another bolt of lightning crackled across the sky. It died within a split second, but the thunderclap sounded violent.

'Stop being a child,' she barked, 'We need to talk to you, all of us.'

I scoffed at her comment. I didn't have the inclination to protest, and I didn't have the energy to stay either, just to have my head obliterated by more information. I needed headspace and time to absorb everything.

I dismissed her, turning abruptly towards the house and stormed off inside.

The gossiping tongues silenced the minute I stepped into the kitchen, but I refused to make eye-contact with any of them. I heard Zoe snapping and demanding I stay to discuss things like an adult, but I wasn't surrendering. I grabbed my phone and car keys and left, slamming the front door shut behind me. As I reversed my car away and turned into the road, the first drops of rain began to fall on my windscreen. I didn't know where I was driving to, but I knew I needed to keep pushing until I had processed everything. I hadn't slept much that previous night, my mind was way too active.

I was born into a supernatural Chamber of horrors. I had unearthly blood curdling through my veins and belonged to a gene pool of witches, or vents, or whatever they called themselves! Someone else had been walking around for twenty-four-years with *my* face. My twin, Raven. A sister I never knew existed. A sister who wanted to take powers from me that I never knew I had. I mean, my entire life had been a lie for Christ's sake.

My mum had lied to me. My best friend had lied to me. Who else had lied to me?
So many questions rived through my head. I wanted to claw my brain out, dump it and start again.

The Sunday silence was evident. For a village that boasted a pre-school and primary, plus a secondary school in the nearby Westfield, I found it weird that I'd neither heard nor seen a single child since I'd arrived. Just to hear or see a family going about their morning would have placed some sense of normality around me, but there wasn't a soul in sight. Perhaps that was because I was the only idiot who dared to venture out with the arrival of a fierce thunderstorm. The thunder continued to rumble overhead, and then a bolt of lightning struck a nearby oak tree, dangerously close to my car. I yelped out, swerving to avoid hitting a lamppost.

'Fuck!' I screeched, realising that I'd made a grave error leaving the house when I did. The sheets of rain had now become a torrential downpour, completely obstructing my view, even with the wipers going at full speed. It became near impossible to continue to drive without crashing, so I made it through the village high street and pulled over into the car park located behind Finn's pub.

I killed the engine and flopped my head back against the headrest. There was something majestic about the sound of listening to the rain thrashing off the bonnet of my car. It soothed me somewhat until my phone rang.

I half expected to see Zoe's name flash up, but I rolled my eyes as I saw that it was my mums' name lighting up the phone screen. I wasn't prepared to have *that* argument with her yet, but I knew my mum too well, and I knew that she wouldn't stop calling me until I answered.

I hadn't informed her that I'd left Jack, or that I'd found solace in Oaks End. I knew that if I told her I was going, she'd have a meltdown, stage an accident or feign illness to find some way to prevent or postpone me leaving.

My nostrils flared as I answered it.

'What, mum?' I snapped viciously.

'Kate?' Her high-pitched tone was full of surprise. 'Why are you answering the phone like that? Where are you, and why is Jack telling me that you've left him?'

I swallowed through a clenched jaw and flicked the windscreen wipers back on. They creaked annoyingly with every repetitive swipe.

'All that money you spent on my therapist,' I began, 'and the entire time you knew who I was, what I was, where I came from and what happened to my biological parents. And I'm not talking about the car crash bullshit story you made up. I'm talking about what really happened to them when they were murdered.'

There was silence on the end of the line, followed by a pronounced sigh.

'Kate, who have you been talking to? Where are you?'

I needed answers.

'Why would you keep something like that from me? You watched me suffer for years with those nightmares, and the whole time you knew. Why couldn't you just fucking tell me?'

'Don't swear at me, young lady. I'm your mother!' Her voice wavered, raw with emotion.

'Except you're not, are you? My *real* mother's name was Allegra Wade, but you already knew that didn't you?'

I heard the audible gulp down the receiver, but I was too angry to continue the conversation and terminated the call. I knew mum would be too stunned to call back. I'd leave her to simmer on that admission, so she could stew on my words and consider an appropriate response. I was furious that the woman who had adopted and raised me, would keep such a vital part of my life buried under a lifetime of lies.

Knuckles rapped against my window, sending an immediate jolt of panic through my core. I could just about make out a blur of navy blue aside of me, before I followed it making its way around the front of my car, to the passenger side. The door-handle unclicked, the door swung open, and Finn's face dropped inside. His face scrunched up; his hair drenched from the rain. Relief almost floored me as my insides fell apart.

'What are you doing?' he shouted over the loud thrashing rain. 'Lock your car and come inside, crazy woman!'

He slammed the door shut and ran off in the direction of the pub. I braced myself, taking deep breaths to slow my pulse down. I exhaled nervously, pulled up the hood of my zipper jacket and made a dash for the pub.

I needed a distraction – an escape from reality, and Finn Moon was just that.

He placed a hot coffee in front of me, and I watched him go about his morning business. He was always busy behind that bar. I perched up on the same stool again, feeling somewhat dampened from venturing out through the rain. I tracked him as he logged figures into a book while sorting out cash in the till. Confidence seeped through his pores with every stride, with every intended stare. That man had a gravitational pull that I couldn't explain.

On paper, he wasn't even my type. Previous boyfriend's, and there have been a few, would be like rotund dweebs or lanky geeks. The only time I'd saw pretty boys were in fashion magazine pages, that I'd rip out and use to protect my carpets when painting and decorating.

It made no sense. I guess I always assumed that if they were that externally beautiful, then something internally had to be amiss.

It was far too early to tell, but usually, I could read characters quite well. Finn had assailable confidence, but I didn't sense anything vain or smug about him. He came across as a humble soul who'd been a friendly face welcoming a stranger in a foreign place. I traced the stubble that coated his jawline and squinted towards the red blotches on his throat where he must have nicked it with a razor.

His face was entirely different in daylight, and I couldn't help but stare.

'So, where were you headed this morning … in this awful weather?' Finn asked, turning his back to me to start restocking the fridges.

I leaned over the bar on my elbows, watching him squat and pull bottled drinks from a crate, stacking them into the fridge.

I swallowed and shook my thoughts. 'I just needed some head-space, I guess.'
He paused, slowing his movements, and I was desperate to see the reaction on his face.

'You and Zoe had a tiff?' he pressed.

'No?' I opposed a little too quickly. 'What makes you think that?'
He shrugged with his back still turned to me and failed to elaborate.

'I guess I'm just a little homesick, that's all.'
Lies.
He craned his neck and frowned at me.

'Already! Would that have something to do with ex-lover boy?'
He turned back to the bottle fridge before I could react.

'Absolutely not. Anyway, what about you? Did you patch things up with your girlfriend because I don't fancy being boxed into a corner by her and her sidekick again, to be threatened and warned off.'
I was met with a scrunched face.

'What?' he half-laughed. 'They did *what*?'
I chewed my top lip with my bottom teeth and drummed my fingers on the bar, nervously.
He stood up, straightening his back.

'Beck's *not* my girlfriend' he insisted. 'She never has been. She's no threat.' There was a significant embarrassing pause before changing the subject. 'You know what we could both do with?'
He smirked at me deviously and rounded the bar, taking off across the room towards a CD jukebox set against a wall. He pulled out some loose change from his pockets and flicked them into the machine. 'Music!'
A nineties club classic instantly blared from small Bose speakers positioned intermittently around the bar area. Within seconds it changed the atmosphere and injected life into the room. It was far too early to be fist-pumping in a closed bar without the aid of alcohol, but Finn smiled at me like he had no fucks to give and encouraged me to do the same.
He raised his hands in the air and reacted to the music, jerking his body in perfect time with the beat. I was impressed that the man could move, without making me recoil away and cringe. He danced towards me and waved me up from the stool, but I flushed with

embarrassment and rejected his invitation. I loved to dance, but not when sober at ten o'clock in the morning.

'Get up,' he laughed, shouting over the music. 'C'mon, dancing's good for the soul.'
So is alcohol, mate.

Admittedly, I was tempted to run behind the bar and empty a bottle of wine into my mouth.
I gave him the thumbs-up, and he flashed his white teeth at me, which dimpled his beautiful smile.
The music stopped abruptly. I glanced across the room to see a seething Zoe, standing beside the jukebox, with its plug in her hand.

A nanosecond later, from out of nowhere, I heard a chorus of synchronised thuds on the stone floor. The atmosphere changed once again, and six bemused entities appeared directly in front of me.

CHAPTER 11

'What are you doing?' Finn panted, slightly out of
breath.

Zoe raked us with fury. She looked as though she was
chewing a wasp, with her arms crossed tightly across
her chest.

'More to the point, what are *you* doing?' she spat.
She was pissed off, but so was I. What were they
thinking by exposing themselves like that? Panic
kicked in, and I turned desperately to Finn, highly
anticipating a reaction, but it seemed delayed. Why
wasn't he bolting for the door? Didn't he see them
appear out of thin air?

'And Sophia, I know you're in there. Quit spying
on us and come out, will you?' Zoe rolled her head to
the jukebox and glared at it, while I scratched my head,
wondering who the hell *Sophia* was.

I peered at the jukebox and frowned. Who was she
talking to?

I concentrated on the machine and had to blink multiple times. Either my lack of sleep was making me delirious, or I really was seeing a large pair of piercing blue eyes flash wide open from inside its glass screen? I blinked several times, trying to convince myself that it was likely to be a trick of the light, that I wasn't seeing a pair of eyes gazing out from the inside of a jukebox. But then it appeared that something was indeed materialising from it. I squinted and felt myself start to shrink with anxiety as I witnessed a body manifest itself and slowly emerge from it.

Once my brain acknowledged that I wasn't hallucinating, the aftershock propelled me to stagger back and trip over a chair. I scrambled backwards on the stone floor, literally terrified. My brain stammered as my thoughts tried to catch up and make any sense of what I was witnessing.

It soon became apparent that the form which had presented itself was the blonde barmaid who had served behind the bar the night before. She stood around five-foot-five, a bleached blonde with dark roots, hair braided on either side of her head. Her protruding cheekbones stood out on her sculpted face, and her thick eyebrows were expressive as she nervously stretched an expression across her face as if to say, *oops!*

Her extreme entrance had rendered me speechless. My mouth hung open, and I felt winded by her arrival. Finn scooped down, and with one effortless motion, pulled me up to my feet.

'Sophia, I thought you were upstairs getting ready for your shift?' he complained, still with his hands gently holding my arm.

I craned my neck slowly towards him as my pulse reacted to his grip. Why wasn't Finn freaking out? Why wasn't he clawing at the doors screaming to be let out? For a moment, I considered that he wasn't seeing what I was seeing and that he was talking to somebody else. Except there was no-one else – just a room full of witches who were doing freakishly weird shit.

He registered my astonishment and double-glanced at me, pulling a face to apologise.

'That's my little sister, Sophia. She's quite a character.'

I felt my knees buckle. Gravity wasn't anchoring me down anymore, and I felt as though I was about to pass out.

'I need to sit down,' I whispered breathlessly, as I staggered towards a chair. I flopped my entire weight on it and tried to calm my unsettled limbs.

He's known all along.

My god, is he one of them?

Zoe clomped her heels across the floor and crouched down before me.

'Kate, look at me,' she insisted in a harsh tone.

I did, and I saw her restless pools of gold melt into me.

'I know that this is a lot to take in. I know you're struggling to process everything, but you can't run away from it. I need you to listen very carefully to what I'm about to tell you.'

I sat with a face stuck in a gormless expression as she braced herself and hesitated.

'He's sent for you.'

My brain sparked a tangled web of questions, and I saw Finn fidget uncomfortably out of the corner of my

eye. He flopped into a chair and rived his hands
through his hair.

'Sent for me? Who has?' I questioned.

'Jorah. The Mitral,' she winced.

'What do you mean?'

Panic began to bubble inside of me.

'After Raven's uninvited visitation, she returned to
Glentree and asked him for a warrant. He gave his
permission, and now they've summoned you, our
Chamber, and the other Heart Chambers to
congregate at Glentree Manor in two days from now.
All Vents must attend.'

Everyone seemed to have dispersed around the
room, keeping a distance from me, as though I was
the *unclean* one. The bizarre unfolding events were
becoming too much. I dropped my head between my
legs and took deep breaths. I was trying to convince
myself that I was having a lucid dream. I must have
been. I began to laugh nervously and lifted my dizzy
head up.

'My god,' I sniggered and smirked at a hard-faced
Zoe. 'I know what's happening here. It all makes so
much sense now. I'm not here. This isn't real.'

The room went silent as they all shared the same
concerned look as they glanced cautiously at one
another.

'A couple of nights ago, I went to some wild house
party, right? I think I'm still there and this is just an
out of body experience I'm having. Who did I drop
acid with? I'm sitting huddled in a corner somewhere,
aren't I? Curled up, gurning my face off, trying to find
my jaw.'

'Kate!' Zoe snapped.

'Wow, how much did I take? This shit is strong.'
Zoe's hand came from nowhere, and I heard the clap
before I felt the sting slice through my left cheek.
She'd slapped me so hard that I felt the welt begin to
burn and sting. My eyes began to instantly water, and
my hand shot up to my face.

'Listen to me!' she shrieked aggressively. 'If you
don't start taking this seriously, you're going to get
killed. Do you understand? We're all witches, get over
it. It *is* real, you *are* here, and you *are* in danger.'
Her words cut through me and hurt more than my
throbbing face.

'If you go to Glentree, you won't come back.
They *will* kill you.'

'Why?' I whimpered unnerved.
I didn't realise how serious this was until she
mentioned *murder* and *death*.

'I already told you. Because they're convinced, you
have at least one of those missing abilities. Raven
needs to absorb it before she becomes the Mitral.'

'I don't have any powers - how many times? I'm
normal. I'm no threat. I can't even get through a
Christmas TV advert without crying, so how the hell
am I supposed to possess superhuman powers?'

'Of course, you have powers, you're a Wade!' she
griped, standing to her feet.

'*Was* a Wade,' I corrected. 'I'm not that person
anymore. Maybe what powers you think I have, have
gone.'

I became distracted by Finn's grumbling, as he
pushed himself up from his seat and strode across the
room. He wandered off behind the bar and began to
pour himself a cold drink. My eyes flicked to

Savannah, sitting on a bar stool with her head bowed and reading a book.

Finn leaned into her space, snagging her attention, and the two of them began muttering to one another. I grazed everyone else and noticed their expressions were all hard-fixed and focused on me.

Danny piped up from behind Zoe, arms folded.

'The only way they'll find out if she has powers is if they put her in the Melladonna.'

'The what?' I asked. My eyes flicked back to Zoe, who mirrored his movements, closing her arms across her chest.

'It's a pool of ancient water in the grounds of Glentree Manor. We must wait until we're sixteen-years-old to visit it. It reveals what abilities we have.'

'It's brutal,' Roman said, rolling his eyes. 'Or rather, *she's* brutal.'

'The Melladonna has to accept you into the water,' Zoe explained. 'When she accepts you, she consumes your naked body and drags you under. Sometimes it can be for only a split second, sometimes it's minutes, and then she releases you. That will enable you to reveal your power. When you emerge from the water,' she continued, 'your body will glow for several minutes. Different colours attach themselves to you, with each representing a different power.'

I could feel my brain swelling. My head ached with taking in so much knowledge and in such a short space of time. I could barely keep up.

'There are only three people allowed to be present at the reveal; the Mitral, a parent or guardian, and Akenna.'

'And who?' I asked with a raised eyebrow.

'Akenna,' she repeated. 'He lives at Glentree; he's always been the council to the Mitrals, and he's the only one who can decipher *all* the powers you possess. Once he's aware, he logs them into the Mitral book of Shadows and places it under lock and key. No Vents have gone unlogged before – except for you.'

'So, theoretically, if I did have powers which you're assuming I have, they will kill me for them? Or what, Raven would absorb them? I'm not fully following?' The room fell silent and everyone avoided my line of eye contact. 'Will someone please tell me?' I snapped, urgently searching their faces.

'It's not good,' I heard Ellis mumble, causing Zoe to tut. 'When Raven absorbs someone's power, she can't isolate it so that it won't cause harm to that individual. She's not allowed to use the power. If she did, not only would she absorb those powers, but she'd drain the life force out of that person too.'

'Besides that,' Danny interrupted, 'if a Vent absorbs the powers of another against their will, there are serious consequences. That person turns dark. They become ravaged by evil forces. Raven would become the cruellest, most inhumane Mitral we'd ever had. What she breeds would have no place on this earth.'

A chill ran throughout me. It didn't sit right with me. That my sister could spread so much hate and fear in the hearts of the Chambers.

'What are these powers? What's so special about them?' I asked, peering over Zoe's shoulder to see Finn and Savannah still having a quiet conversation between themselves.

Darcie made her way over and sat beside me. Her kindly face smiled at me with reassurance, and she placed her warm hand over mine.

'Don't concern yourself with that now, dear,' she said, shooting a look towards Zoe. 'I've known some of the Mitrals who have passed, and I have known some who have ruled. Lourdes De Wyche wasn't exactly a model Mitral, but he had a lot more grace than Jorah. It's a fact that he had possessed forty-four powers that he derived from the bloodline. Six of which were not passed on to Jorah, because he wasn't entitled to them.' She squeezed my hand and sighed. 'It's best you don't dwell on what they are.'

'Bullshit, Darcie!' scoffed Zoe. 'They're aura choking and holograms,' she began, using her fingers to list them, 'pain-infliction, life-draining without absorption, immunity to other Vents powers being used against you, what else?'

'Age-shifting,' Danny added.

'Age-shifting, yes,' she continued. 'The ability to manipulate someone's ageing process.'
I almost laughed at the absurdity of them suggesting that I could have even *one* of those powers. They seemed so extreme.

'If she doesn't have them, they'll dispose of her regardless,' Roman grumbled to himself, before noticing that everyone was scowling at him. 'They're all unhinged!' he complained in defence. 'Kate's not yet part of a Chamber, and she already knows way too much.'

'Not necessarily,' disagreed Savannah, finally swivelling around on the stool to face the group. Finn stood up straight, dipped his hands casually in his pockets and found my eyes. He made me feel vulnerable.

It was as though he was unapologetically dissecting every section of my mind and body.

She jumped off the stool with a simple hop, clutching the black, leather-bound book and quietly stepped towards us.

'I think I know of a way.'

CHAPTER 12

The heavy leather-bound book slammed down on the table directly in front of me, and everybody crowded my space. Sav flicked desperately through the pages, often stopping to lick the tip of her finger to quicken the process.

'Every Chamber has a Book of Shadows, Kate,' she explained, flicking her grass-green eyes at me widely. 'We keep all Chamber business in here; rituals, spells, events, our history and anything that's sacred to our Chamber. However, what we also include,' she landed on a page and slapped her hand on it with purpose, 'is the list of Chamber rules.'

'But that's only *our* Chamber rules?' Zoe muttered, frowning.

'No, no,' Sav corrected her. 'I included the Mitral rules for *all* bloodline Chambers.'

'You aren't just a pretty face, are you?' Zoe mused, leaning further in. Her curiosity seemed to heighten.

'Read this rule,' Sav ordered, pushing the book

towards me. 'Out loud, Kate.'

I hunched forward and furrowed my brows at the unreadable nonsense that blurred the page.

'It's written in gibberish,' I shrugged. 'I don't understand it.'

Finn's hand stretched out and pulled the book carefully towards him. 'She can't read the Ovarkin language, Sav. Let me do it.'

Ovarkin language? Why had I heard that name before? Was it all going to start coming back to me?

'Would this be a good time to ask what that is?' I asked, raising my eyebrows.

He sighed heavily and stared at the page with a focused squint.

'It's Ovar,' he explained. 'It's who we worship. He's everything. He's the earth, the universe, the trees, the animals, the heart – everything. His language is what we call 'Ovarkin'.

I stared at him and thought back to our conversation outside the café about having a belief system. He never did answer the question or comment further on what or who he believed in. Now I knew.

'Rule number twenty,' he began. 'Absorption of powers is only permitted by a Mitral who can absorb or strip a Vent of the bloodline in the circumstance of disease, peril or the process of demise. No absorption of power must result in unnecessary death or inflict ill health on the bloodline Vent.'

'What?' Zoe gasped, crouching to get a closer view.

Finn continued. 'If the Mitral is unable to absorb or strip the power in question, he/she can appoint an able, trusted Vent of the bloodline to carry out the task and gift it to him/her without issue. Should the trusted

Vent abuse power and refuse to gift it to the Mitral, the offence is punishable by death.'

'That's a bit excessive,' I gasped, nudging myself closer to Finn. He paused for a second and seemed distracted by my proximity.

'What's excessive?' A voice bellowed from the doorway, snatching our attention. I couldn't see past Roman and Danny, but I heard the exasperating hiss come from Finn's breath and took a wild guess of who it might be.

'How does everyone keep getting in here?' Sophia complained, inching closer towards me.

'I unlocked it - obviously,' Beck clipped, now coming into my view, followed closely by her sidekick, Gia. Beck's flame hair was swept back into a long ponytail that accentuated her shaved jawline. I saw the wrath harden her face, presumably as a response to seeing me and Finn close together. Once again, she was burning those icy eyes at me. She'd certainly mastered the art of death stares.

'So, you've told her then?' she jeered, snarling at me. 'Isn't that a sacrilege offence?' she asked. 'I'm disappointed.'

'Bore off, Beck,' whined Zoe, ushering her away with a wave of her hand. 'Keep your nose out. I'm trying to have a Chamber meeting here, invited Vents only, so see yourself out.'

'Oh, please,' spat Beck. 'Sophia and Finn aren't a part of your Chamber. They're still officially Pericardium Vents. So, why can't we get involved?'

'Because,' Zoe stood rolling her eyes, 'for your information, Miss Know-It-All, Finn and Sophia currently aren't part of *any* Chamber, they're in transition so they won't go back and tattle-tail to the other Vents, unlike you two loud-mouths.'

Ellis rolled her head and whispered something towards her sister, but Beck was having none of it. She shoved past Ellis and stormed towards us, pushing her way in between Roman and Danny to involve herself in our business.

'What is your problem?' complained Zoe, 'You're such a brat, do you know that?'

It was evident that Beck wasn't interested in what we were doing; she was only interested in what Finn was doing – *with me*.

'Ellis! Roman growled. 'Can you put a collar on it and take it for a walk.'

'Roman!' Ellis snapped, and she tutted disapprovingly, 'Don't be like that with her, she's my family.'

'Who's getting on my last nerve,' he quipped.

'Are you going to let them talk to me like that, Finn?' Beck sulked, desperately searching his face for support. He coughed under his breath and rolled his eyes, refusing to entertain her.

'Goodbye, Beck,' nipped Zoe, in a clipped tone that sounded more like an order.

Beck's chin snapped up as she spun on her heels and stormed across the floor towards the door, while Gia growled at us.

'And take your little barking chihuahua with you,' Danny insisted motioning towards Gia.

Sav lifted her head from the book, becoming impatient and glared at her. 'And yet you're still standing there. Off you fuck.'

'Excuse me? How dare you,' Gia fumed.

'How dare I? You're in Oaks End honey, on the Endocardium soil. Take your snarling attitude back to your own Chamber.'

Gia's nostrils flared as she scowled at Savannah, who'd turned into a complete sass-pot which somewhat shocked me. What happened to the pint-sized mute who'd previously come across as being shy and reserved? I'd got Sav all wrong. As Gia followed Beck out of the door, cursing under her breath, everyone's attention refocussed on Savannah. She was oblivious, folding her attention back to the book. The door slammed shut, and we all laughed.

'This isn't funny,' Sav complained. 'I haven't got time for those two arseholes. We're up against the clock here.'

Her sense of concern warmed me.

'Now, listen up, I have an idea,' she started, demanding everyone's attention, 'I know where the *original* Melladonna is.'

'That's impossible,' Zoe scoffed shunning the idea. 'Nobody knows where the original Melladonna is or was. Besides, legend has it that it's all caved in.'

Savannah's broad expression homed in on Zoe's face, and she smirked cunningly.

'Wait. What? How?' Zoe asked excitedly.

'So,' Savannah started. 'Lourdes De Wyche recreated the Melladonna in the grounds of his estate, long before we were even born. It was a power thing. Glentree Manor reigned, therefore, why not have *everything* there? All Vents would eventually have to go to Glentree. The water in his pool came from the original Melladonna, and it is pure, but it's also stolen. The records of the original Melladonna were erased from our history so that future generations would easily accept the story that it's always been at Glentree - but it's not.' she paused, 'It's right here, in Oaks End.'

'Here? As in here in the Fae Woods?' Finn questioned eagerly.

Sav nodded and smiled. 'I have the directions up here,' she said, tapping the side of her head. 'But roughly, I'd say it's an hour's trek into the forest.'
Just how big is that forest?

'Can Danny teleport us there?' asked Zoe.

Danny quickly shook his head and furrowed his brows.

'Zoe, you know I can't teleport us to a specific place if I've never visited there before. And, for the record, you of all people should know that it's not teleportation when there's more than one in transit, it's *apportation*. I can certainly use apportation to bring us back, but we're going to have to do the trek there.'

'Sorry,' Sophia stepped in, 'I'm confused. You want us to go to the original Melladonna to discover what powers Kate holds?'

'Yes,' Savanna quipped.

'Aren't you forgetting that we need Akenna?'
Sav spread an all-knowing smile and tapped her head again.

'No way,' Danny laughed. 'You know how to decipher the auras?'

'Yup,' she gushed.

'Since when?'

'Since I met Akenna and read the entire contents of his brain – aged sixteen.'

'Sav,' questioned Zoe. 'You sat on this information

for years, and you haven't thought to share this with any of us?'

She shrugged with an air of nonchalance and exhaled. 'Well, I didn't need to share the information with you until the time was right, and that time is now. I know everything about everyone – except the full extent of their powers.' She flicked her eyes toward me. 'I have a literary manipulation ability,' she explained. 'I can quickly memorise the contents of a book, word for word, and store that information in my head. I understand every single language around the world. It's called *omnilingualism* if you want its formal name. Also, I can scan someone's brain and clone their knowledge for my own gain.'

I gawped at her, astounded.

'Not that I'm boasting or anything. It lays dormant in there, locked in my brain and then suddenly, I'll just come out with these facts and figures, that I don't understand, but I kind of do. You'd think I'd have some deformity with the shape and size of my skull which holds all that information.'

'Sav,' Roman huffed, 'you're making *my* brain hurt. Can you stop?'

'OK, but,' Danny slouched, rounding Zoe and rested his hands on her shoulders. She reached up and pressed her hands against his and leant back into his body. 'If you can scan the knowledge in someone's brain, wouldn't that mean you'd have scanned Akenna's, who knows who has what powers?'

Sav shook her head quickly. 'That's what I thought, but no. I just contracted how to decipher the auras.'

Danny blinked down at Zoe and pursed his lips.

'What happens after that?'

'Well, I'll document what I find and someone, not me, will go and present the Chamber rules information to Jorah and remind him that it's forbidden to allow someone to absorb powers if it leads to needless death. He can't deny the hard-written facts passed down by our ancestors. The Gods to whom he answers won't let him near the Elder world.'

There was much I didn't understand. So much alien talk – and my mind and body were now beyond exhausted. My eyelids were getting heavier by the second. All I wanted to do was lay down and have a nap, but it appeared that I was running out of time. I yawned loudly and slumped on my elbows, propping up my face.

'OK, then,' Zoe nodded, shifting her attention to me. She watched over me as a worried mother would, but there was a strength that she exuded that gave me hope. 'I guess the question is, who's going with her?'

CHAPTER 13

'You do not need to worry about getting naked in front of me, Kate. I've seen you strip off a bunch of times,' Zoe laughed, following me into my room. 'Remember the night we got drunk at that holiday park, and you bared all in our chalet when we got in, asking me if I thought you were *shaggable*?'

I cringed, lifting my jumper over my head and dropped it to the floor. She leaned down and swept it up immediately.

'I'd rather forget that night,' I grimaced, 'Besides, I'd had a belly full of vodka. That was different from getting into a cold pool of water, stood butt naked in front of a bunch of strangers who I barely know. Why do I need to be naked? Why can't I just go in with my underwear on?'

I climbed out of my jeans and discarded them to the floor, to watch Zoe swoop them up too and immediately shove them in the washing basket.

'Because it won't work. It has been attempted.'

'This is crazy,' I complained, digging out another pair of jeans and a black hooded jumper from my wardrobe. 'To think, yesterday I was Kate Littlewood, an ordinary human being. Today, I'm Antonia Wade, a friend of the *Avengers*, a marked woman who's about to go trek through a forest and swim in cave water, naked. My head is mangled.'

'You're welcome,' Zoe chuckled.

'And I'm sorry, but why is Finn coming?' I groaned out in a hushed tone, trying to keep my voice low enough so that he wouldn't hear me from downstairs. 'Why did you choose him of all people to come along?'

'He actually *asked* to come along,' she argued. 'I told him, no, but he insisted. To be honest, I think he wants to cop an eyeful of your bits, the pervert.'

'God, this is so awkward,' I huffed, climbing into my fresh clothes.

I grabbed a backpack and shoved a large fluffy towel inside, as well as a spare pair of trainers and some pro-plus.

'It'll only take an hour or so, and then we will know, OK?'

'And then I can sleep?'

'Then you can sleep.'

It took us over forty minutes to travel from the end of Zoe's garden, through the fields to an opening in the forest. When I saw the clearing, it hit me like a ton of bricks. I wanted to be sick.

It was almost identical to the area that had savaged my dreams for so many years, and the instant recognition weighed down on me. I couldn't help but envision my parents' brutal murders and had to take a few deep breaths before entering. I tried to imagine those thoughts wrapped up in a soaking wet towel and mentally rinsed them out.

I exhaled nervously and followed Sav, Danny, Zoe and Finn, into its enclosure.

'You alright?' asked Finn, slowing down to walk beside me.

His hands latched around the straps of his backpack, and he looked fit wearing in his khaki shorts, black hoody, hiking boots and a black cap that accentuated his hard jaw.

'Ish,' I shrugged, craning my neck to admire his stature. 'Honestly, I feel as though at any moment I'm going to wake up next to Jack back in London and tell him all about this crazy dream I had.'

'But then you wouldn't have met me,' he smirked mischievously. I bowed my head, trying not to give anything away.

The group had decided to take a detour, thus avoiding the exact spot where my parents were killed. I knew it was deliberate, for the sake of my feelings, and I was grateful for it. It just meant it would take a little longer to get there, but I didn't mind walking with Finn. It would give me a chance to get to know him a little better.

It was colder in the wooded areas. Mud squelched under our feet, but it smelled the same as it did in my dreams, rich with an earthy fragrance.

'Beck mentioned that you don't currently belong to a specific Chamber. Why's that?' I probed, deliberately making conversation.

His eyes shifted around the woods, cautiously checking no-one was following. 'It's a long story,' he sighed.

'It's a long walk,' I grinned.

He chewed his lip and inhaled so hard that his chest puffed out.

'When we lived in Berryness - that's a few hours from here - we were part of the Pericardium Chamber. Things didn't work out so well for us there, so we all moved to Oaks End. My folks bought the pub, renamed and refurbished it, and the rest is history. Because we're not part of Zoe's Chamber, we don't practice our craft anymore. But if needed and called upon, then we would.'

I was desperate to know more and wondered what dormant abilities he possessed.

'You don't practice, but your sister walked out of a jukebox?'

'When I say *we don't practice*, I mean, we don't do rituals anymore. There's a lot that goes into being an active Chamber Vent. It can be all-consuming, and we don't have the time.'

'But you can tell me what powers you have though, right?' I asked, grinning playfully.

He swept his eyes down with a smile and blinked.

'Whatever powers we have, we can only use them for doing good.'

He kept tight-lipped, but I still wanted to pry further.

'Isn't that the rule for everybody, though?' I enquired.

'Ours is different. Our great-grandfather, Apollo Moon ...'

'Apollo Moon?' I gushed, 'What an epic name.'

He chuckled.

'Sorry, go on,' I urged.

'He lived with the same generation as Lourdes De Wyche, who was the Mitral at that time. The De

Wyche's, unfortunately, are from my mum's side of the family.'

'Your mum is a De Wyche?'

'Was,' he corrected.

'Wait, so Apollo Moon and Lourdes De Wyche are both your great-grandfathers?'

'Yes,' he nodded, tightening the grip on his backpack straps. 'The Moons are my dad's side, and the De Wyche's are my mums. It's complicated, but basically, the two bloodlines didn't see eye to eye. I think there was a clash of ethics and a lot of tension between the two of them. I mean, the De Wyche's are rotten to the core, they always have been. They're feared for their greed, power and money. That's the complete opposite to how my dad was raised in the Pericardium Chamber.'

I tried to keep up and follow his story.

'My mum met my dad and left the Myocardium Chamber to be with him, and this didn't sit right with his family. They didn't trust her. I mean, how can she be the exception, when her families are poison and her grandfathers the Mitral?'

'Well, that's not fair,' I jibed.

'Exactly, but they weren't taking any chances. So, when Apollo Moon was on his deathbed, he placed a curse on our family, banning us from using our powers to inflict harm, kill, or disarm anyone. He died with that curse, and we've never been able to reverse it since.'

'What's the curse? I mean, what happens if you *did* use your powers in that way?'

'We can use our powers for good. I can heal you if you have an injury or if you're unwell. Sophia can

119

disguise herself or invisibly cloak herself. We're not hurting anybody by doing that, but if we used our gifts to harm other Chamber Vents, then there are severe consequences.'

I nodded at him encouraging him to tell me more.

'He put an age manipulation curse on us so that if we hurt someone, we age by five years each time we do it. We'd literally be signing our own death sentences.'

I flashed him a look of surprise.

'Wait, what's the difference between the age manipulation curse and this age-shifting power that the others were talking about?'

'The age-shifting is a slower process, and it's also reversible. But the age manipulation isn't. It's a curse, and the curse only becomes active when the person who placed the curse is dying.'

'My god,' I gasped. 'There are so many rules. It's so confusing.'

'Tell me about it … but it's a good thing, otherwise think how many curses would be thrown around left, right, and centre. They also have to be approved by the Mitral.'

'So, say I was in trouble, and my life was in danger, you couldn't protect me?'

He shook his head and bit down on his lip. 'I don't need powers to right-hook someone and break their face, Kate,' he chuckled. 'Whoever tries to attack you, I hope they like hospital food.'

My stomach flipped the minute he said it. I'd never had anyone talk protectively like that before. My old boyfriends couldn't have swatted a fly never mind play fisty-cuffs with someone. I remember one night I went to a nightclub with Jack and had some drunken twat try to chat me up. He kept groping my arse in front of Jack and wouldn't take no for an answer, as if he were deliberately trying to antagonise him and goad him into a fight.

Jack was never a fighter, and he pretended like it wasn't happening to save himself from confrontation. In the end, it was me who made the threats to the drunk. Then Jack dared to *apologise* on *my* behalf and escorted me out of the building! Our relationship started to go south soon after that night.

'Perhaps, I won't need protecting. Perhaps, I'll come out of the pool with some serious bad-ass martial arts moves I never knew I had.'

'What … like, Kate Littlewood, the teeth-shatterer and bone-breaker?'

'Ha-ha! It has a ring to it.'

Finn flicked out a hand in front of me, as a warning not to trip over a snagged tree branch. I noticed that every few minutes, Zoe would turn around to keep a protective eye on me. Finn had seen it too.

'She's like an overly strict parent, isn't she?' he said, nodding in her direction.

'Who? Zoe?'

'Honestly, I'm not scared of many people, but that woman *terrifies* me sometimes.'

'She's harmless,' I cackled. 'She just takes no prisoners, that's all.'

'Takes no prisoners. Have you seen her when she gets angry? She's like a whistling teakettle. She goes from nought to one hundred in a nanosecond.'

'She's the boss of the Endocardium Chamber, isn't she?'

'Ha!' he burst out, 'The boss? Yeah. Her official title is the High Priestess, and Danny is the High Priest. Dom and Darcie used to be, but when they hit a certain age, they have to hand the title down to someone else, so they chose Zoe and Danny.'

'And she cracks the whip?' I grinned.

'What are you like in a relationship?' he asked, abruptly changing the subject.

His question caught me off-guard. Why was he interested in knowing that?

I found myself blushing a little, and shrugged, pursing my lips.

'When you're not dumping a fiancé, that is,' he mocked.

'What an odd subject change.' I giggled, thinking aloud. 'That was a long time coming. I don't know, what you are like?'

'I'm a nightmare. I know I am. I'm all bickering, fights and make-up sex.'

'So not difficult at all then,' I grumbled sarcastically. I was surprised he'd admit something like that.

'Not at all,' he chuckled, 'I'm just picky, and I get bored easily.'

'Wow. Do you type that in the *'about me'* section on your online dating profile? How can anyone resist?'

'Honesty is the best policy,' he sniggered, defending himself.

'Well, honestly, you sound like a *dick*.'

'Ouch,' he laughed, before furrowing his eyebrows together slightly offended.

'I'd be exhausted by you. Life's too short to be entertaining someone constantly, so *they* don't get bored.'

'Says the person who's just left a relationship because she was bored,' he pointed out. 'Pot…kettle!'

'After five years,' I snorted. 'How long does it take you to get bored?'

'Oh, a couple of days,' he shrugged.
I couldn't tell if he was joking or not. I pulled a face at him as to say, *'get over yourself.'*

'Don't look at me in that tone of voice,' he smirked, pushing on my shoulder playfully. 'I'm winding you up. Of course, I'm not like that, ha-ha. The horror on your face … look at it.'

'Oh, that was you being funny?' I said dryly. 'Sorry, I missed the memo reminding me to laugh. Cue, laugh!' I waited a few seconds. 'Ha.'
He broke into laughter and playfully pushed me again.

'Will you two stop the joking around back there?' Zoe snapped haughtily, stopping to wait for us with her hands on her hips.

'Well, if you don't laugh, you die, right?' I mumbled under my breath. No one was else was laughing. She glared at me, stone-faced and serious.

'I'm glad you find this so hilarious, Kate. It's not like we're risking our lives right now for you.'
She silenced me with the harsh truth, and I didn't want to piss her off any more than I already had.

'Awkward,' Finn muttered. 'That's you on the naughty step when you get home.'

CHAPTER 14

Soon, we were so deep into the forest that my legs were buckling from the relentless trudging. My socks were soggy inside my filthy matted trainers, and I was cold, damp and physically sapped. When Savannah shrieked and pointed towards a huge ivy-covered rock, my entire body sagged in relief.
We'd arrived.

'Someone give me a hand,' she ordered racing towards the rock. 'We need to push it away. The cave entrance is behind it.'
I watched everyone flock to the boulder and struggle to push on it with all their strength. It wouldn't budge.

'Don't just stand there,' Zoe barked at me, red-faced. 'Help us.'
I was about to help them when Finn swooped in and waved them aside.

It took one effortless push, and the boulder rolled aside, exposing a black hole. We all gawped in utter disbelief. Was that one of his abilities? Superhuman strength? That boulder must have weighed more than a ton. He didn't even break a sweat. He brushed his hands together, slapping off the dirt and gestured for us to enter it. It wasn't the most significant hole for us to squeeze through, but it was doable.

Sav went first, turning on her torch. Her voice echoed and called Zoe in next. One by one, we all followed her into the black space and had to crawl and squeeze our bodies through a tight tunnel, until we were able to climb out into the main cavern.
I couldn't believe what I was seeing.

We stepped into an enormous dome-shaped grotto. Limestone wrapped the entire space, with the occasional spotting of marble and dolomite. The stone had moulded into jagged stalactites above us, pointing threateningly downwards. If one of them was to fall, it could easily slice through us. Huge boulders lay scattered around, reminding me of a Moonscape, rocks that had not moved for millennia. It was echoey, and it smelled like a mix of algae, mould and fungi. A stream trickled delicately past us. I knew we'd have to follow the flow of the water that would ultimately lead us to the Melladonna.

As the high-powered torch beams flicked around, we marvelled with our jaws hanging open in awe. There was so much beauty inside the cave; so much to take in.

The further we got past the algae-covered rocks, the wider the stream spread. The air changed as we rounded a corner and became fresher. Strangely it became brighter in there too.

'Oh, Ovar!' Zoe gasped in amazement, sidestepping into the open space. A loud gasp also wisped past my lips. It was hypnotically beautiful.

The stream veneered over a rock and into a vast oval-shaped pool of clear water. The pool was quite transparent and reflected our forms.

I watched Finn trace his fingers along the uneven walls and then he turned around to face me. 'Why is it light in here?' he called out, looking aloft for the source. There was none.

Suddenly, I became overwhelmed with nervousness. Finn must have seen it written all over my face because he rushed up and placed his hands on my shoulders to offer some comfort. My heart palpitated uncomfortably, and my breaths were shallow and quick. It had all been some sort of a blur, until the moment I was presented with the reality of having to go into that water and uncover my truths.

'Hey! Look at me, Kate. You've got this,' he said reassuringly. 'There's nothing to fear. We've all done it at Glentree. Nothing bad is going to happen to you.'

'Has anyone died from doing this?' I panted anxiously.

He sniggered at me. 'No. Never.'

I swallowed hard, lingering on his face for longer than I should have. Zoe approached me and gave Finn the nod. When her eyes found mine, she smiled faintly.

'Finn is going to keep watch over there,' she said, pointing back towards the entrance. 'Danny will be stationed opposite, obviously with his back turned. I will be right here with Savannah, watching over you, OK?'

I nodded frantically and began to shake. To me, it appeared to be an undisturbed pool, serene and unspoiled. I was unnerved by the unknown, with the knowledge that I now had to take my clothes off. I waited for Danny to wander away, and he hunched his shoulders forward, folding his arms across his chest. I glanced back to Finn to see him shifting from foot to foot, doing the same. Both Savannah and Zoe urged me on with nods of encouragement.

I took a deep breath and slipped out of my trainers. My heart was flapping quickly, getting faster with each item of clothing I removed.

Something shifted in the air again, and the fear began to subside slowly. The warm ambience of the cave rushed over my sensitive skin, and as I discarded my underwear, a surge of excitement gripped me. I felt unadulterated liberation.

The air gliding off my naked flesh felt incredible. I felt sensual, womanly, alive and exposed. I suddenly didn't care who saw my body, and I wanted to celebrate it. I felt primal and animalistic in a way that I'd never felt before.

Was this the doing of the Melladonna?
Is this how she makes us feel?

'Go on,' Zoe encouraged, 'She won't bite. Promise.'

My heart steadied. I felt amazing before my feet had even touched the water, but as my toes dipped into what felt like a lukewarm bath, I sighed heavily and plunged into the water, with my head exposed.

'Swim to the middle,' she instructed. My nerves dissimilated as I stroked the soothing water and swam into the centre. 'OK, that's good, Kate. Now turn around and face me.'

I stopped and bobbed up and down while treading water. I attempted to touch the bottom of the pool, but it was too deep.

'Now, what do I do?' I shouted.

'Just wait. Melladonna will take you when she's ready.'

I remained calm and focused my attention on the outline of Finn's back which was still turned, his head angled to the floor. He was keeping to his word and being a gentleman, but I wanted him to see me and watch his reaction.

It wasn't about his good looks or the way he smiled at me. It was the familiarity of our souls and the pleasure of being around him – even when he was incredibly annoying.

Suddenly, as I lost myself in thoughts of him, I felt a pressure start to build under my feet. It wasn't strong at first, but in a short while, it seemed that there was an undercurrent beginning to spiral, like a whirlpool.

'Stay calm, Kate,' Zoe shouted, 'Take a deep breath.'

The undercurrent caught my feet, and without warning, it took hold of me, yanked me down and submerged me entirely under the water. I hadn't taken a big enough gulp of air.

It came too soon, and I wasn't ready.

My immediate reaction was to panic, kick my feet out and wriggle my way free, but the pressure fastened tightly around my legs and restrained me.

God, this isn't good. I need to take a breath.

I tried to kick out, but the force cemented my feet together so that I couldn't separate them. I was anchored down in a dangerous vortex and couldn't escape. Dread invaded me as the seconds passed.

How long can I hold my breath? What happens if I can't? Will they pull me out?

The seconds underwater began to feel like minutes.

128

Let me go, please.

The Melladonna ignored my pleas. The force felt menacing and starved me of oxygen.

My eyes sprang open. I could see everything so clearly. I dared to glance down at my feet but

I saw nothing but the water spiralling violently around my ankles. My uncooperative body solidified, and I couldn't flay my arms around or pedal my way to the surface.

It was then I really started to panic.

I can't hold my breath much longer. I'm going to drown. Please let go of me.

Thirty seconds must have gone by, and I could see faces at the water's edge.

Thank god. I'm not going to die, after all, they're going to pull me out. Right?

I was at the mercy of the Melladonna, who seemed to enjoy crushing me with the unremitting pressure. My instinct not to breathe underwater was so strong that it suppressed the distress of running out of oxygen. If I opened my mouth to draw breath, asphyxiation was the only outcome. *Pull me out. Why is no-one pulling me out?*

Panic rived through me. I could see them all. They had crouched down at the edge of the pool. All they had to do was jump in and rescue me. They couldn't let me drown there. They wouldn't watch my life end in a brutal struggle, *right?*

What's taking them so long. Help me!

My mind pleaded, over and over as more precious seconds ticked on. No matter how desperate, I was determined to resist the urge to inhale until I was on the verge of losing consciousness.

You promised me nothing terrible would happen. I can't hold on any longer. I have no breath. Pull me out.

It was at the same moment I heard their muffled voices begin to shout, as my mouth opened. I tried to buy myself some time and let small bubbles of air escape, but my brain prompted an involuntary breath and dragged the water into my mouth and windpipe.

Oh, fuck! No! Please, not like this.

My nose filled instantly with strangling water, my vision blurred, and my mind clouded over. It burned so bad, scorching my nose, my throat, my lungs and stomach. They were on fire, as the rapid decline of oxygen ravaged me. Slowly, I was starting to lose consciousness.

They weren't going to save me. They were watching me drown. I anticipated the inevitable that I was about to die.

This is it. This is how I die. Surrender to it.

CHAPTER 15

Tinnitus whistled unbearably loud in both ears, and the shrill of it travelled around my skull. Amidst the piercing ring, I thought I could hear whispers calling out my old name.

Antonia, Antonia.

The voice came in with a swooshing echo, and I recognised it. I'd heard it before – not in my dreams – but during my lifetime. It was like a silky, motherly murmur.

Antonia, you must find us. He has us. Please, release us.

How? Who was she? Who had her?

Jorah.

Her voice trailed off and was replaced by the distorted shouting of my frantic friends.

'It didn't work. She's drowning. Get her out of there!'

My body floated, ever so lightly, like I was gliding above the water. Was this my soul leaving its shell? Had I died? I couldn't feel any pain because I couldn't feel my body. I felt inner peace. Perhaps death wasn't so terrifying after all?

'Kate?'

Someone slapped me repeatedly across my cheek in quick, numbing bursts and I felt a hot mouth over mine.

'Kate, can you hear me?'

I heard the panic in his deep rattle.

Finn.

My eyes snapped open, and my body jerked forward. I violently convulsed while trying to clear my airways - the whole time I was clawing at my scorched throat. I choked and coughed up so much water that it made me puke, and then came the loudest, death-rattling gasp for air.

My muscles were now shot, and my body concrete. I rolled on to my back, gasping the air back into my aching lungs. I began to shake uncontrollably, feeling cold. Through chattering teeth, I requested a towel to cover my modesty, but instead of being handed one, there was silence.

They'd all inched away from me, mouths hanging open in shock. It was when I mustered enough energy to roll on to my knees, that I realized what had stolen their attention. I was glowing.

My entire naked body radiated the most exquisite colours. Auras of colour swirled ghost-like over different areas of my body. My arms were a shocking pink, mottled with glittering cherry-rose. My hands and palms were grape purple, with the tips of my fingers a liquorice black. Crimson red swelled over my abdomen and swirled into a watermelon red, down to peach-sorbet orange, coral orange and blizzard white. All I could do was look down in disbelief. This was real. I *was* a witch, and I had powers.

Oh, my god!

It hurt to swallow, it hurt to think, and it hurt to move. Finn had his head tilted at an angle, smiling at me like a proud parent. He must have registered the pain on my face, and his smile died. He quickly crouched down beside me and placed a hand gently on my lower back.

'Let me help you,' he insisted, not lifting his gaze from my face.

I felt a low vibration from under his hand that heated and tingled my skin for a slight second before the pain dissolved almost immediately from my body.

'Easy, try and sit up.'

Danny held a towel and my backpack and went to hand it to Finn, but Zoe quickly snatched the towel away and clicked her fingers at Savannah.

'Get the book, Sav. You need to note this down while she's still glowing,' she ordered, still scanning my body in awe.

Savanna stood before me with the leather-bound book and began furiously scribbling down words on the page, without taking her focus off my body.

'You did well,' Finn exhaled, beginning to rub my back. His comment infuriated me.

'I did well?' I bawled, 'I was drowning! Why didn't you get me out of there sooner? Could you not see I was struggling? You said you wouldn't let anything bad happen, so what the fuck was that?'

He appeared stunned by my outburst and stood up abruptly.

Zoe rolled her eyes at Finn.

'You were under a long time; we hadn't seen that before,' she declared.

'You think?' I yelled.

'Look, we can't intervene, Kate. She's much stronger here than she is at Glentree Manor.'
I glanced back at the water that had since calmed and slowly got to my feet.
I anchored my head back to Savannah, trying to read her expressions as she dissected my auras.

'I want to know what you've written down,' I demanded.

Finn cloaked the towel tightly around me. I welcomed the warmth while awaiting Sav to acknowledge me. She slammed the book closed and stared at me with a poker face.

'And you will when we get home. We don't disclose the powers in front of the Melladonna. She doesn't like it.'

'Oh, dear, let's not upset *her*?' I scoffed, 'The bitch nearly drowned me.'
The still waters started to bubble, and I took that as our cue to leave.

*****

I nursed a hot coffee back at Zoe's and nuzzled up to a pillow on the corner sofa. We'd been teleported back to Oak's End, a weird experience to say the least. It involved us linking hands in a huddle, heads bowed, and eyes closed tightly.
Danny mumbled something I didn't understand, and I immediately felt a sting of the cold brush through me.
I opened my eyes to discover we were still in a huddle, but now standing in Zoe's cottage. It was trippy enough without letting myself spiral into an overthinking frenzy once again, so I just let things be.

I'd changed into a jumper, jogging bottoms and thick fluffy socks. Zoe placed a comfy throw over my lap. The rest of the Chamber came to sit either side of me, with Finn nudging up close to my side, to make room for everyone else.

Sav, however, sat on her chair in the middle of the room, facing us all. She had the book opened on her knees, and she sat idly waiting for us all to settle. Finn's body wedged against mine. He was in my personal space, and I liked it. His body was a radiator, and for some reason, the closeness between us had my heart racing again.

'Well,' she started. 'There's good news, and there's bad news.'
I watched his hand reach for mine, and he gave it a reassuring squeeze without looking at me.
My eyes flicked around the room and stopped at Ellis. Her brown eyes homed in on our hands, and she squinted with suspicion. I wondered if she'd report back to Beck and make a big deal about it, or if she was quietly judging. He didn't let go of my hand, and I didn't pull mine away.

'You don't have any of the missing powers that Raven needs,' she announced.

Our bodies sagged in a synchronised wave around the room. 'But,' she quickly added, 'you do have sought-after abilities. I can't promise you won't be a threat to the De Wyche's.'

'Abilities … like what?' Zoe piped up very impatiently.

'I'll get to that,' she bit, glaring at her.

'OK. So, based on what I saw today, I was able to identify *eight* different abilities.'

'Eight,' shrieked Zoe, snapping her head to me in shock. 'I only have *one*.'
I felt my cheeks burn with everyone staring at me in astonishment.

'She's coming after your HP title, Zoe,' Roman teased, nudging her a little too hard. Zoe spat out her dummy and growled towards the ground.

'High Priestess? Shut up, Roman,' she barked. 'She's still clueless about our craft and how to use it. She's unassigned to a Chamber, and even if she were, it takes six months of initiation before she can become a fully-fledged Chamber Vent and she would need to have an initiation ceremony.'

'Oooh!' Roman jeered, sniggering. 'Jealous, are we?' Even I was surprised at how heated Zoe was getting because I had more powers than her. I'd never witnessed that side to her before, and I didn't like it.

'She's right.' said Darcie. She sat forward pursing her lips and threw me an apologetic smile. 'You haven't a title sweetheart. You don't know the Ovarkin language, and you haven't channelled a Goddess yet. That takes months and months of work and offerings.'

'Nobody said anything about becoming a High Priestess,' Sav snapped, frowning at Darcie. 'It was a joke. Get a sense of humour or leave the room. Now, can I please continue, or does anyone else want to interrupt me?'
Bossy.
The room fell quiet again.

'As I was saying,' Savannah huffed, picking up her mug of tea. 'You have eight abilities. Most of us have only two or three, that's if we're lucky.'
Eight abilities? How?

'First, you have enhanced danger warning. You can sense danger a mile off. You also have healing powers, like Finn.' She lifted her eyes from the page and winked at him before returning to the page again.

Healing?

Could I heal people?

'The coral orange represents something we call audible inundation, which means that you can actively overwhelm someone's mind with voices.'

I cocked my head to the side, confused.

'We'll get to that in a while. You also have psychokinesis, which means you can move objects that aren't in your line of sight. There was a hint of calling in there too.'

She registered that I didn't understand and tutted.

'It means you can summon an object into your hand. There was only a hint of green, so I don't think it's that strong. Moving on, this is where it gets good.' She took a deep breath and exhaled excitedly.

'Not only do you have power extraction, *but* you can gift powers to people too.'

Everyone's heads riveted to me, impressed.

'Oooh,' Roman chuckled rubbing his hands together. 'Happy Christmas to us!'

'You can temporarily strip powers from other Vents without absorbing the power,' Sav continued. 'However, that also contradicts something else you have.'

I waited.

'Power mimicry,' she added.

'Power mimicry?' Darcie enthused, pulling a face at Dom. He nodded back at her, impressed. Finn leaned in closer to me to mumble in my ear.

'That's a cool one to have, that means you can permanently copy another Vents power if they use them on you.'

I pulled away from him and blinked into his hypnotic eyes. He lingered a smile and then dropped his gaze, almost shyly.

'Yeah, so be careful people. She could potentially mimic your abilities if you use them on her,' Sav laughed. 'Oh, and the last one. You're clairaudient.'

'Clairaudient?' Zoe frowned.

'Yes, it was all over her.'

'Wait,' I gasped, lunging forward. I remembered the voice speaking to me when I was half-conscious underwater. 'I heard someone when I was under the water.'

Hard squints pierced me.

'It was a woman's voice. She called me, Antonia. She said I had to find them.' I racked my brain, staggering through the foggy memory, and then it hit me. 'Jorah. She said Jorah had them.'

Dom let out an exasperated sigh and rubbed the space in between his eyes, while Darcie squeezed her eyes shut, grimacing.

'What? What is it?' I asked, edging off the sofa. Dom ran a hand through his grey hair and chewed his lips.

'Well,' he exhaled. 'We knew your parents well. We were there when it happened.'

Darcie tutted, arching her head to the ceiling and grimaced through her memories. 'Before they passed over, Jorah extracted their souls and used soul projection with them.'

'You're making no sense,' I quipped.

'It means that he's trapped their souls in an instrument or object,' Dom bit. 'They haven't been able to pass over to the Elder World. He has their souls contained somewhere.'

'Not even our medium friends can contact them,' Darcie sulked.

'Do you think that was my mother speaking?' I asked, raising an eyebrow at them.

Darcie nodded slowly.

'I don't understand. Why now? If I have all these so-called powers, why haven't I been able to use them before today? I get the danger, but everything else?' My voice trailed off as I shrugged.

'Oh, my god,' Sav gasped, lunging from her seat. She passed back and forth, throwing her hands over her head. She clasped her fingers together and forced out a laugh. 'How did I not see this?'

'See what?' Zoe clipped, tracking her movements. Sav turned suddenly and flopped back down on her seat. 'It all makes so much sense now.'

We all waited with bated breath.

'The Melladonna!' she nipped. 'Why did the De Wyche's replicate her at Glentree? Why did she drag Kate under for so long?'

Everyone shrugged at each other.

'Because she doesn't just reveal your powers, she *gives* you them.'

Dom and Darcie's head turned towards each other in bewilderment.

'How long has it been at Glentree Manor? Before you were born? You hear of all our ancestors, the likes of Lourdes and Apollo and how many powers they had. Why do we all have so little? Because we didn't get fully revealed in the *original* Melladonna, right here in Oaks End. The one at Glentree is not strong enough.'

'Wait!' Danny stood up and folded his arms across his chest. 'You really think Kate *didn't* have those powers until today?'

'She'd have had some of them, but the Melladonna has given her more *and* enhanced the ones she already does have,' Sav explained matter-of-factly. 'I don't even think Jorah is aware of this?'

'And it should stay that way,' Darcie warned. 'If he knew if Raven found out …'

'What would happen if we all went back to our Melladonna? She might give us more abilities?' asked Roman, searching the faces in the room for a response.

'No. I'm not messing with that,' Ellis piped up. 'There might well be consequences. We've all done this before. We've had our reveal. What if she strips our powers?'

'Ellis is right,' Dom agreed. 'I say we don't meddle with the unknown.'

'But I feel robbed!' Roman complained. 'We've all been robbed. We could have had more powers if we'd gone to the original Melladonna. How is that fair?'

'Son,' Dom huffed. 'Leave it.'

'Regardless of any of that,' Darcie interrupted, seemingly stressed. 'The point is that Allegra is communicating with Kate. She desperately wants our help. We have to free them.'

'This is the start. *Fibrillation* is upon us,' declared Zoe.

'Fibrillation?' I pressed.

'It's like a human heart,' Zoe explained. 'If one or more of the chambers of the heart stops working properly, it causes the heart to fibrillate. It becomes irregular and abnormal, and it can't pump blood to the rest of the body efficiently. That's *exactly* the same for us. If one of *our* chamber's falters, it affects every one of us. We can't function properly. Our powers aren't as strong.'

'This is going to end up in violence, isn't it?' Sav huffed.

Roman chuckled obnoxiously under his breath and rubbed his hands together as if he willed it to be that way.

'Then, violence is the way. It's going to have to be,' he declared.

I flinched away and suddenly felt my entire body seize up with fear. The situation was about to escalate beyond my control, but was I prepared for it? The idea of real violence unnerved my soul, but I knew it was inevitable, and I could feel the dread begin to course through my veins. The outcome equalled bloodshed, and there was nothing I could do about it.

CHAPTER 16

I collapsed on top of my bed in an exhausted heap and felt the cushion of clouds beneath me. *Sleep,* that's all I craved.

Downstairs, everybody was starting to leave, but I couldn't muster the energy to go and say goodnight. I lay there, like a starfish, staring up at the ceiling with heavy eyelids, waiting for the onslaught of overthinking to begin.

That's when I felt a presence lingering outside my room and knuckles tapping lightly against my door. I flicked my eyes to see Finn filling the doorway, smirking at me.

'What's this, crawling into your bed at nine o'clock at night?' he chuckled.

I yawned and fluffed up my pillows, sinking my head back into the air-dried quilt that smelt like fabric softener and clean linen.

'I'm done in, Finn,' I admitted defeatedly.

'Well, I just came to say that I'm heading off now.'

'OK, then.'

I didn't know what else to say to him, so I stared at him in awkward silence as he lingered expectantly. The silence lasted longer than it should have, which made him shift on his feet and laugh gawkily. He patted the doorframe and nodded as if he got the hint that he should leave.

'Well, sleep well,' he chuckled.

'Wait!' I blurted out, way too quickly. I didn't want him to leave as I needed a distraction to intervene with my over-analytical mind.

He slowly turned and pressed his back against the frame.

'Do you want to hang out for a bit longer?' I asked, hopefully.

His blue eyes flicked along the bed and reached my face. He didn't give anything away; just a hint of a grin and then it was gone again.

'You want tucking in and a bedtime story?' he teased.

I pulled an unimpressed face at him, which caused his smile to light up.

'Alright,' he sniggered. He pushed himself away from the door and ambled over to me.

'Scoot over,' he said, tapping my leg.

I budged over the bed, making room for him, and he plonked himself down next to my feet.

'Long day, kiddo?' he asked, anchoring his head towards me.

I yawned and nodded, rubbing my eyes.

'The longest.'

Even with the dim light from my bedside lamp, his eyes still dazzled. They were by far my favourite feature of him. Those forget-me-not pools of lagoon blue would forever captivate me. Surely, he knew the affect he had on women.

'Well,' he said, stretching. I followed the shapes of his arms bulging, and his muscles tightened. He then sagged and leaned back to rest on his elbow. 'What do you want to talk about, freckles?'
I had no idea. I guess I just wanted to be near him a little longer. I liked his company even if he did have an irritating nickname for me.

'Anything,' I shrugged, pulling the quilt further over me.

'Narrow it down, what's on your mind? Do you want to talk about the meaning of life? Aliens? Conspiracy theories? What?'
I giggled at him and rolled my eyes, tutting.

'OK, smartarse, how about you? Let's talk about *you*,' I suggested.

'Me?' He rolled his shoulders back and relaxed. 'I'm not interesting enough.' He began picking at the quilt fabric and batted his eyes back to mine. 'You always were a smart-mouth, even as a five-year-old. Always giving me sass.'
I was confused.

'What do you mean? You've only just met me?' I questioned. He burned into me with a sudden intensity.

'Wait. What?' I sat up and shuffled, so I had my back against the headboard and brought my knees up to my chest.

'I have a long, long memory, Kate. This isn't the first time we've met. We were pretty close as kids.'
I had to take a moment to digest his words. I *knew* I had met him before. I knew that his soul was familiar, though I could never place it. I still couldn't place it. My fragmented memories were impossible to piece

together. No matter how much I strained to recall it, I couldn't.

'I don't expect you to remember. You were only five. I was eight. That's the last time I saw you.'

'That night?' I asked, lifting my eyes to meet his troubled face.

He huffed and rearranged himself so that he was sat with his feet on the ground, hunched forward. He cleared his throat and started slowly fumbling with his hands.

'Yeah, I remember everything about that night, Kate.'

I waited.

'Every weekend, for the longest time, we would all come here to Oaks End and have family time. The Moons, The Bloom's, The Wade's and The Carmichael's, we were all close. Your parents were like the glue that held everyone together. They were so much fun,' he smiled remembering. 'They used to host parties all the time … barbeques, birthday's, Chamber events and more. They were so welcoming and kind.' His head lowered with a shake. 'And then it all changed.'

I watched him become uncomfortable as he tuned into his memories, but I remained quiet, allowing him to continue.

'You probably don't remember Zoe's dad, Henry?' he asked, batting his eyes towards me. I shook my head. I only knew her mum, Bessie. They were a duo, just like my mum and me, that's why we bonded so well. Bessie had a scar that travelled from her forehead, down her cheek, and then to her chest. When I asked how she got the injury, she told me she had survived a car accident. Zoe later told me her dad had died in that same crash.

'He was the one who got you out of the Fae Woods that night. He was your rescuer.'
I frowned at him, and my jaw swung open. He nodded silently and dropped his head again.

'He had a premonition about your parents' impending death a couple of months before it happened. He warned them what was going to happen. He told them that no matter how much they tried to run, or however long they tried to defer it, the outcome would always be the same.'

'How?' I quizzed, feeling the dread stab at me. 'How could it be the same? Why didn't they run?'
He dragged his hands through his thick hair and sighed.

'One of the De Wyche's could see where everyone was at any given time. Jorah would have hunted them down one way or another and killed them.'

'They knew they were going to die that night?' I gulped, unable to fathom it.
He twisted his face and nodded apologetically at me.

'They knew. They sensed it the minute he requested a meet, a congregation in the Fae Woods. All the Chambers received an invitation but under false pretences. The De Wyche's would never visit Oaks End, so everybody was suspicious of what was going to happen that night, but your parents knew, so did Zoe's and so did mine.'

'Why didn't they tell the rest of the Chambers and ask for their help? Three Chambers against the De Wyche's? They could have fought! They could have at least tried to intervene and prevent it.'

He shook his head and stood abruptly.

'No, Kate, they couldn't have. You have no idea how fucked up the De Wyche's are. They're too powerful. They'd kill anyone who got in the way. Your mother didn't want blood on her hands. Her main concern was making sure you and Raven were safe and got out alive. Jorah was going to kill you two as well.'

'He'd kill children?' I gasped horrified.

'To make an example, yes, he would. And he would have if your parents hadn't of devised a plan to get you out. In your nightmare,' he replied, turning slowly, 'that kid you hear call-out your name. The kid who's chasing after you …'

His voice trailed off, lingering until he waited for me to put two and two together.

I stared at him in disbelief. 'That was you?' I whispered breathlessly.

His head dropped, and his jaw flexed. 'I had one job,' he scoffed, 'Henry told me to stay close to you and Raven. To keep you as far back as possible as we walked through the woods. He told me to hold your hand and not let go, and when my mum gave me the nod, I was to get you and Raven to Henry. He had a car waiting on a dirt track nearby to deliver you both to Lilian. She was a close friend of your mums. However, she was completely unknown to the De Wyche's'. Although you were only a five-year-old, you instinctively knew something was off the minute we stepped into those woods.'

I swallowed hard and inhaled deeply. I was slowly finding the story ever more incredible.

'You sensed immediate danger and became hysterical. You made such a scene, screaming that

something bad was going to happen and you wanted
to go home.'
I turned my head and squeezed my eyes shut. It was all
a blur, and I couldn't recall that part of the night. I
couldn't remember anything before my nightmare start
point.

'Raven ran to your parents, and they heard you
crying in the distance. They kicked up a fuss, insisting
that they wait for you to catch up with them. It was
then that their hands were bound by the De Wyche's
and dragged off. I tried to calm you down, Kate. I
tried to tell you everything was going to be alright, but
you struggled away from me and sprinted off in the
complete opposite direction to where Henry was
waiting. I shouted that I'd go after you, and I did, but
you were just too fast for me, and I lost you.'

I knew how the rest of that night played out.
I scrunched my face up, blocking the images before
they could invade my mind. The pain was all over his
face, as he stood disturbed and taunted by the memory
of it.

'You think you have nightmares, Kate?' he scoffed,
'I had to go back to the opening. They forced us all to
watch it unfold. You can only imagine what that does
to a kid. No amount of therapy has numbed the pain
and scraped those images from my head.'
I puffed, exhaling loudly. 'He didn't kill Raven … why
not?'
He flexed his cheeks and shrugged. 'I guess he saw
something in her that he could salvage. He raised her
and installed his sick ideologies into her, so now she's
a carbon copy of him. She had no hope once she was
under his control. Kids are a product of their

surroundings and upbringing, and she doesn't know any different than what she's been taught.'

I struggled not to feel a little sympathy towards my twin. If you train a dog to bite, it will bite! My thoughts flicked back to Henry.

'Zoe's dad saved my life?' I swallowed, feeling a wave of guilt wash over me. Was that survivors' guilt I was feeling? His eyes blinked up at me, and his face hardened.

'Yes. He combed the forest all night for you and didn't give up. He got you out. And they eventually killed him for it.'

I winced, feeling a pain stab at my chest.

'Why do you think Zoe is the way she is with you. She doesn't want her father's death to be in vain. None of us do. She could have lost her mum as well, but she didn't. Someone ran them off the road. They tried to stage it as an accident, but Bessie survived and now she lives with the scars. She stays well away now; she won't have anything to do with the Chambers.'

I understood why.

He shifted around the room slowly, gliding his hand along the wardrobes, reaching the dressing table, from where he pulled out the stool to sit on.

'And where does Lilian come into all of this? Is she one of us too?' I asked.

'No,' he frowned. 'She was Allegra's best friend growing up. Allegra was careful to keep their friendship shielded and not tell her anything that would pose a risk to Lilian's life, but Lilian's a smart woman. She knew snippets here and there, but she never talked. She was happy to take you in, but she wanted you to have nothing to do with the Chambers.

She wanted you to have a normal life. It was only by sheer coincidence that you ended up bumping into Zoe and Bessie at the same holiday resort when you were kids. Lilian was terrified you'd recognise them, but you never did.'

It was difficult to process his version of events, but it helped cement together the missing pieces of a broken jigsaw. Now everything started to make so much sense.
He scrubbed his face with his hand and wrinkled his nose, bowing his head.

'I was told not to speak of you again, and I never did. But I always knew you were out there somewhere, clueless to your true identity. And then one night I saw you.'
I froze as his eyes pinned on me. His expression changed as he altered his memory.

'I'd always try to imagine your appearance now. I wondered if you were a dead ringer for Raven, if you'd cut or coloured your hair. If you still had the same eyes, the same mannerisms and the same laugh. And you were everything I imagined you to be and more.'
I smiled at him instantly, and tilted my head, listening intently.

'I was in London city for a friend's birthday night out. We went around all the popular bars and ended up in a nightclub. It was my turn to get the round in, and that's when I first saw you, at the bar, ordering drinks with your friends.'

I tried to track my mind to the many times I'd been to nightclubs in London. It could have been any night because I was always out partying when visiting the bright lights of the capital.

'You wore a black dress and shiny silver heels.'
My eyes nearly popped out of my head. I remembered.
The only silver heels I ever owned were a gift to me on
my 21st birthday, and I only got to wear them for one
night before the heel snapped, and I had to hobble to
the taxi with one shoe on and the other off.
So, that was the night he saw me.

'I can't even describe the feeling, Kate,' he
chuckled, awkwardly.
I was absorbed by him.

'Try,' I said.
He chewed his lip and flashed me a weak smile for the
first time. 'I guess I just remember being floored. My
world stopped. Everything became dark, and you were
the only light. You appeared so happy, so alive,
dancing and laughing with your friends. It was an out
of body feeling like seeing an apparition. Like I was
seeing someone who I'd mourned and grieved for,
resurrected from the dead.'

He was impassioned recounting the story, in a
trance-like state, as though he could see it all
happening again in front of him.

'And then you glanced over to me, and my heart
stopped. You ripped the air from my lungs. I was sure
I saw a flicker of recognition on your face, only for a
few seconds, and then it was gone. You smiled at me
and blinked away, and that was that. You got your
drinks and walked off, and I knew at that moment that
I had to have you back in my life. I just had to wait.'
My heart throbbed. I had no idea.

'That was three years ago.' His cheeks flushed red,
and he began to chew down on his lip. *Did he like me in
that way?* He was blushing.

I couldn't take my eyes off him. I half dithered whether to jump from the bed and go to him, but a loud knock at the door interrupted us, and I found Savannah slinking into the bedroom.

We both sat up and straightened as her green eyes bounced between us. She was holding the Book of Shadows and looked at Finn with a raised eyebrow.

'Zoe wants to lock up,' she stated, hinting for him to make himself scarce. Finn nodded and slowly pushed himself to his feet, but dawdled in the middle of the room, waiting to hear what Sav had to say to me.

She opened the book and began flicking through the pages until she landed on one.

'Chamber rules,' she quipped. She placed it on my bedside table and tapped on the open page. 'It's important you familiarise yourself with them.'

'I'll check it out in the morning,' I yawned, dismissing it and glanced back to Finn. Sav followed my gaze and huffed.

'You're still here,' she said with an air of irritation. Finn smirked and rolled his eyes.

'I'll see you tomorrow, Kate. Night.'

He moved past Savannah and left the room, and I listened to his footsteps going down the stairs. When I glanced back at her, she lifted her eyebrows and gave me an all-knowing smile.

'What?' I laughed innocently.

'Uh, huh. Read the book!'

'I can't read that, Sav. It's written in gibberish.'

She tutted and huffed, staring at me without saying a word. It made me uncomfortable, so I laughed awkwardly and turned my head.

'Ah-ah!' she snapped, clicking her fingers at me to snatch my attention. 'Look at me.'

My body sagged, and I rolled my head to look at her. Her bug-like eyes locked onto me, unblinking. For a fraction of a second, they suddenly glowed a blizzard white, and it startled me. I felt something shift inside me, like a sharp sting inside my head. Then, as if nothing had happened, her eyes blinked back to green, and she grinned broadly at me.

'Now see it with your new eyes,' she suggested in a smug tone.

Slowly, I motioned my head back to the book and was stunned to see the words now written in plain English, and I could understand everything.

'You were taught how to read, write and speak Ovarkin at a young age. You've just forgotten how to.'

'How did you do that?' I gasped, stunned.

'I used my power on you,' she shrugged in a blasé way. 'And now you've got the same gift as I. Have fun.'

The same gift as her? What?

I watched her as she sauntered out of the room. She stopped abruptly and turned her head.

'Omnilingualism,' she winked. 'Add it to your abilities. You'll never have another language barrier ever again. It's great.'

She skipped out of the room, leaving me awestruck.

Omnil- what?

CHAPTER 17

Somewhere, between Savannah leaving me and flicking through the seemingly endless pages of the *Book of Shadows,* I'd conked out and succumbed to my severe need to sleep.

There was an overload of information inside the book, and most of it consisted of spells and ingredients, Chamber rules, its Vents and their abilities.

I was intrigued by every aspect of it, but I couldn't keep my eyes open long enough to focus. When I awoke in the middle of the night feeling parched and needing a glass of water, I tossed and turned and eventually gave up trying to fall back to sleep. I rolled on to my knees and pulled open the bedroom curtains. Immediately, I was awed by the stars that littered the sky and the undisturbed silence that surrounded the land. No harsh streetlights were stealing the beauty from the sky, no traffic, no sirens or cars, or drunks jeering in the distance. Night-time in Oaks End was a far cry from night-time in London.

I sighed, half-tempted to get up and go into the garden and be a sponge to the night, absorbing the paradise and harmonic ambience of the nature that encompassed me, but I knew I'd probably wake everyone up. Instead, I settled back in my bed, propped myself up and opened the *Book of Shadows*. I skimmed the pages until I landed on the Chambers' powers while thinking of my own.

How did I even use my powers? When was someone going to explain that to me? I didn't exactly have a magic wand; I couldn't yell out *abracadabra* and will the objects to appear in my hands. How did everyone else use their craft? I was desperate to find out. I glided my finger down the page and began to read.

The Endocardium Chamber

Zoe Lockhart Bloom – *High Priestess – Sister of the Setting Sun.*
 Abilities: Herbalism, telekinesis – (the ability to move large objects and create a powerful burst of telekinetic energy)
Danny Bloom – *High Priest – Brother of the Fading Moon*
 Abilities: Apportation/teleportation – (the ability to teleport oneself, objects or people through space).
Savannah Bloom – *Sister of the Divine Teachings.*
 Abilities: Knowledge absorption, Literary Manipulation (the ability to absorb all the information a book can contain) and Omniligualism (the craft to understand and speak any language without training.)
I smiled inwardly, smug that I now had that last power.

Roman Bloom – *The One who Protects, Brother of Protection*

 Abilities: Sleep Induction (by physical touch or wave of the hand).

I paused my finger on his name. He could make people fall asleep at the wave of a hand. I'd bet there wasn't an insomniac between them – except for me.

Ellis Carmichael Bloom – *Sister of the Morphing World.*

 Abilities: Illusionary (the ability to create illusions which alter an individual's senses and perception of their surroundings.)

Darcie Bloom – *Denounced High Priestess – Keeper of the Black Mirror*

 Abilities: Empathy, enhanced senses, catoptromancy (the ability to see people or places through mirrors).

Dominic Bloom – *Denounced High Priest – Friend of The Fae*

 Abilities: Fire Manipulation (ability to generate fire).

I had to hand it to them; they were cool powers to possess. I couldn't wait to see them in action.

My name was pencilled in at the bottom of the page. As much as I tried to lift the words from the page, I still couldn't believe it was real.

I became distracted by the sound of Zoe's bedroom door creaking open and heard Shadow's feet walking across the landing. I waited to listen to his body slump down and then ignored it, returning to the book.

Something suddenly shifted inside of me, and I couldn't pin-point why, but I became unsettled. Something felt off.

Shadow began to pant loudly, and he groaned as he rose to his feet again. Usually, he slept soundly at the bottom of Zoe and Danny's bed, but I'd always been in a comatose sleep and didn't know if his walking around in the middle of the night was typical of him. He seemed restless, so I patted my bed and whispered out his name to try and entice him into my bedroom. He didn't come and began to growl instead.

Good god, dog, you're going to wake them up. Does he need to go outside? Is he thirsty? What is it, boy?

I waited and closed the book.

I could hear him shuffling, and then I followed the sound of his feet pitter-pattering down the stairs. Within seconds, I heard what sounded like a pot or pan clatter against the kitchen floor, and a yelp came from Shadow.

I immediately threw back my covers, swung my legs out of bed, put on my slippers and crept towards the door. I peeped out to the landing with apprehension. I felt along the wall for the light switch and flicked it on. Zoe's bedroom door was wide open, and I could see an outline of them sleeping soundly. I moved along, then tiptoed down the stairs to see what the hell had gone on. I must have only been four-steps down when the light flicked off and immersed me into darkness. *What the?*

I froze, and my stomach plummeted. *I'd just turned that light on.* Neither Danny nor Zoe were behind me. My spine tingled, and I legged it down the rest of the stairs. I paused at the bottom to switch on the living room lights. My heart hammered as I glanced around the room. Everything was as it should have been. Nothing was out of place or had been disturbed.

Shadow's growling beckoned me to the kitchen. I stomped through, switched on the kitchen light and searched around. However, nothing had fallen to the laminate flooring. *Strange, I was sure I had heard something fall?*

Shadow's head snapped back, and he drooled from his mouth.

'What is it, boy?' I whispered, crouching down next to him. His head suddenly tilted, his panting stopped, and his eyes shifted behind me. In that second, I felt an eerie presence surround me, and I could see that the living room light had gone off.

My heart dropped again. I spun around, and as I tried to focus into the darkness, I heard the most sinister child-like laugh ripple from inside the room.

My stomach caved as my heart thrashed in terror. Fear pinned me rigid.

I couldn't move.

I couldn't speak.

I became immobilised with profound terror.

Adrenaline was pumping around my body, and I began to tremble. I wanted to scream out to alert Zoe and Danny, but I was voiceless. An uneasy breeze bristled against the back of my neck and Shadow whimpered behind me. I turned, as my heart accelerated to dangerous speeds, and watched him begin scratching frantically at the French doors.

He wanted to escape. And in that second, so did I.

The noise that burst from the living room again was nothing short of a demonic, child's giggle. It reverberated around the house and was followed with quickening footsteps, thudding towards the kitchen. They trod boisterously, and the child's menacing cackle boomed. My entire body was now shaking uncontrollably, and the kitchen lights began to flicker on and off above me. I stepped backwards, and Shadow's growling became so aggressive that he bared his teeth in a defensive stance. He was now snarling towards the living room.

I glanced in every direction, searching for the danger when suddenly, the lights flicked back on in the living room. I dared to walk in, trembling with my foot about to leave the kitchen and cross the threshold into the living room, but I dithered as the threatening entity hadn't gone. I took slow, cautious steps through the room, and dared to turn my head in the direction of the staircase. What I saw next will forever fill my heart with immortal terror.

It was the silhouette of a cloaked woman, masked by the darkness on the stairway, her outline now hovering above the stairs. Her head was angled to one side, eerily watching me. It sounded like she was whispering something. I strained to listen as my heart raced uncontrollably, but the hissing whispers were inaudible.

Her head cocked to the other side, and a warped, gurgling cackle poured out of her.
I recoiled to the wall, pressing my back tightly against it, closed my eyes tightly and held my breath. Then I heard a clattering. Something was happening back in the kitchen. I opened my eyes, and she was gone. *Was she now in there?*
I took a deep breath and legged it into the kitchen to witness a cupboard silently opening, and its contents of utensils begin to rise from its draws. They drifted up to the ceiling and then became suspended there. My

voice seized, and all that escaped my lips was a rasping fear that again had me immobilised.

I pinned myself to the wall, rigid. I heard a grinding sound coming from the French doors and flicked my eyes to see the key, turning in the lock. I let out a whimper, as hot tears began to rain down my cheeks. Shadow panted as the doors quickly slid open. As the night air brushed against my face, he leapt out into the garden and began barking aggressively, as though he was warning something away.

What occurred next was too fast to comprehend. Everything dropped from the kitchen ceiling, crashing down on to the floor with a crescendo of ear-splitting noise. I watched in horror as the knives hurtled downwards, one by one, sticking into the wooden flooring and getting closer and closer to me. Was I going to be the final target?

Before my brain could fully register what was unfolding before me, I heard the windows in the living room explode inwards, and the glass smashed into thousands of fragments, scattering dangerous shards across the floor. I screamed out and hit the deck, shielding my body with my hands. I heard feet pounding down the stairs, then Zoe gasp.

'What the hell is going on?' she screeched, dropping to her knees as I cringed.

'Why did you let the dog out?' Danny huffed, storming towards the open doors.

I lifted my head, wiping away my tears with the back of my hand and turned my head abruptly both ways. Danny whistled and patted his leg while calling out for Shadow. The kitchen appeared completely normal. There were no knives, pans and utensils scattering the floor - no shards of broken glass. I snapped my head to the intact window and sat up.

'I don't understand,' I cried, still shaking. Zoe stroked my head and got to her feet.

'Did you sleepwalk … have another nightmare?' she asked, turning towards Danny with a fretful gaze. My head pounded with confusion. *What just happened? That wasn't a nightmare. I was awake – more awake than I'd ever been before.*

'You're trembling,' she stressed, pressing her hands over me. 'Come on, come with me. Get some air.'

I rolled on to on my wavering knees, and she helped me up. Danny pulled a cigarette out of a packet and handed it to me, taking one for himself. We all walked out into the chilly night. The sense of danger had diminished, now that they were with me, but that didn't mean it didn't happen. *Who was that woman? Why was she messing with my head?*

We lit up our cigarettes – much to Zoe's disgust - the lighter flame flared in front of me, and my eyes soon readjusted to the darkness, but were beckoned to something in the distance.

A perfect silhouette of the same figure now stood at the bottom of the garden. The cigarette dropped from my mouth, and I whimpered out.

'She's still here,' I cried, pointing towards her with a quivering finger. Both Danny and Zoe frowned while straining to find something in the distance. I must have only blinked away for a split-second, and when I looked back, she'd completely vanished again. Zoe rubbed my back, silently helpless to my ordeal.

'I know what I saw, Zoe. I'm not going crazy. You have to believe me.'

'OK, honey. Shush! Nothing's going to happen to you. Just calm down. We're here.'
As she stroked my back, I saw the looks they exchanged with each other. It wasn't a disbelieving glance, but more like a dubious glimmer. It told me everything that I needed to know. I wasn't losing it. I wasn't going crazy, and they knew something.

CHAPTER 18

'You really did scare us last night,' Zoe said softly, sipping her coffee.

We were seated at the garden table and I was hiding from the sun under the umbrella. Zoe ended up having to give me some herbal concoction that sedated me and knocked me out cold, and I was grateful for it. I wouldn't have slept otherwise.

'I don't want to re-hash it again,' I moaned. They couldn't enlighten me on what or who I'd seen. Nobody could, and I didn't want to think about it anymore. It made my spine tingle just thinking about it.

'I just want this over with so I can have my life back.'

They glanced at each other and their forehead's creased.

'Well, you won't be getting anything done by going off with Finn this morning, will you?' Zoe swiped.

My body sagged.

'He texted to invite me for breakfast, what's the big deal?'
I felt like Zoe was turning into an interfering mother, criticising my life choices. She began to drum her nails across the table and threw me a glare.

'The big deal is, he's distracting you. You can't get that man out of your head now. I don't trust him. He was with Beck, and suddenly since you arrived on the scene, he's dropped her like a hot snot, and now you're the flavour of the week.'

'He says he wasn't ever with her, and I believe him,' I snapped. She was now rubbing me up the wrong way, and I felt the tension grow between us. I was over-tired, mentally broken, and the only person who brought me joy was now a target of judgement. I threw up my hands and rose to my feet, turning my back on her.

'Please just be careful, Kate, that's all we're saying,' Danny chimed. 'He's a man-whore, admittedly a good-looking man-whore, but still a man-whore.'
I snapped my head back and glared towards them both. Zoe slid on her oversized sunglasses and sipped slowly on her coffee in a bid to conceal her thoughts. My phone bleeped, and Finn's name flashed up.

'Well whore or not, he's here,' I huffed. 'I'll be back later.'

'You'll be back by noon and no later,' Zoe dictated. 'You haven't got time to mince around, Kate.'
I growled under my breath and stormed off. I couldn't stand her dictating to me, but I knew I shouldn't piss her off either. I was against the clock, and they were putting their lives at risk for me. I just needed some headspace, even if it was merely an hour or two.

Finn drove me out of the village to a town that was less than five miles away. This town was Westfield, home of my new school. The music was blasting, windows down, Finn singing along as loudly as he could. He created so much energy and fun that I couldn't stop laughing at him. He wanted to get away from the prying eyes of the village and spend some alone time with me, and I went willingly.

He offered to show me where I'd be working, and we briefly pulled up alongside Westfield School. The green gates that surrounded the large building were locked, but as I peered through past the open playground, I could see more detail. The buildings stood tall and were made from solid red brick, although they did look decades old. A small carpark was situated right next to a large school field that smelt like freshly cut glass.

'That'll be you soon, Miss Littlewood,' Finn smiled, ducking forward to glance up at the school. 'Soon you'll be the inconspicuous fresh meat, walking down the bustling corridors and crowded halls, probably being wolf-whistled at by all those horny teenagers.' I rolled my eyes at him and bit my smile.

'Well, let me concentrate on *not* dying first, and then I can start to get excited about this place.' I mused, to which Finn eyeballed me and tutted.

We drove on for a while longer and then pulled into a small car park that served a picturesque lake setting. It featured a little café-come-shack close-by. Finn insisted that they made the best breakfast in the whole of Surrey.

The view was outstanding. We settled ourselves at a table near the Café's window which overlooked the sleepy lake and ordered coffees and a full English each, which arrived promptly.

'God, it's so nice to have some *real* food, Finn,' I gasped, cutting into my sausages. 'Zoe's vegan food…I just can't. It's foul.'

'Danny tells me that, too' he laughed. 'He's a sneaky eater though. He occasionally comes to the pub on his lunch break for some food, and then I'll see him five minutes later walking by stuffing a pie in his mouth.'

I chuckled. 'Well, that's because she's a total control freak, demanding and dictatorial.'

'Do I sense some hostility building between you two?' he quizzed, looking suspiciously at me.
My shoulder rolled forward, and I leaned on my elbow, huffing.

'Just a difference of opinions that's all.'
His tongue rolled inside his cheeks as he side-glanced at me.

'Let me guess?' he dropped his head slightly laughing through his nose. 'They've told you I'm a man whore.'
My eyebrows creased as I stared at him, bewildered how he'd know that. His face softened the minute he saw my reaction.

'It's nothing I haven't heard before.'

'So, you *are* then?'

'No!' he spluttered.
He picked up a napkin and covered his mouth while he cleared his throat and swallowed, flicking his eyes to the lake.

'There's been a lot of family gatherings since we were kids. The Chambers meet up once, maybe twice a year for special ceremonies, and the girls, well …,' he exhaled irritably. 'We can only mate with other bloodlines.'

'I read it in the Chamber rules. What was it again?' I tracked my memory. 'Rule number –'

'Five,' he interrupted. 'Mating with Vents from other bloodlines is essential to keep the bloodlines pure.'

'Right,' I nodded. 'So, fucked up.'

'Yup. Tell me about it. We're not allowed to have kids before the age of twenty-five, but we can get married earlier than that.'

'Why do you have to be twenty-five?' I asked, thinking the whole thing was ridiculous.

'I don't know. It's always been that way. Maybe it's to stop overproduction. But we must keep the abilities in our genes. We can't mix with normal humans; we'd eventually die out.'

He cleared his throat again, 'We have to try and build a connection with someone in the Chambers from an early age. I mean, you haven't met the De Wyche's yet. They are not the *prettiest* bunch in the world.'

'Really? How bad are we talking?'

He hiccupped and swigged his coffee. 'Nova has a face like a crime scene, Jett's teeth could stop traffic, and even Walt Disney would have a job at drawing Isaac.'

I burst out laughing and shook my head. 'Wow.'

'What?' he shrugged defensively, 'I'm not shallow, Kate. They're slim pickings. Trust me. I have very little to choose from.'

'So, you tested the waters with more than one, is what you're saying?'

'God, no!' he shivered at the thought. 'There's the De Wyche breed; Cora, Nova, Jett, Raven or The Carmichael cousins; Gia or Beck. Those were my options, but none for me. The De Wyche sisters make Wednesday Adams appear more appealing. They dress morbidly and are genuinely horrible people. I'm merely scraping the barrel with Beck - who I can just about tolerate.'

I was about to frown inwardly, but he stretched his arms out defensively. 'I know, I know, she's having some issues taking no for an answer, but ultimately she has to accept that it's never going to happen between us.'

'Have you ever dated someone outside of the Chamber? Or dated a normal, regular girl?'

His lips thinned, and he stared away from me.

'Once.'

I sensed that he didn't want to talk about it, so I didn't dwell on the subject or pry any further.

'So Roman and Ellis and Danny and Zoe got lucky, huh?'

'Absolutely.'

He blew on his coffee and sighed, raised his gaze to me and smiled contently.

'You have no idea how happy I was to hear that you were coming to Oaks End, Kate. You have no idea.'

I curved my lips and cocked an eyebrow at him.

'That's very assuming of you. Who's to say I'm interested?'

He tilted his head, and my question caught him off-guard. He didn't know what to say. Instead, he smiled inwardly and cringed away.

'I mean, that just backfired in my face,' he laughed.

'It did. What if I friend-zoned you?'

'Then I'd be very disappointed.'

Oh, Lord. He does like me.

He doesn't want to be friend-zoned? Does that mean he wants us to be a thing?

Am I getting ahead of myself?

Stop smiling.

You're so transparent.

He didn't faulter his stare and smiled into my eyes with intensity. There was something building between us - undeniable chemistry.

CHAPTER 19

After our morning breakfast, we started to head back into Oaks End. I didn't want to go back. I could have sat in that café with Finn all day talking, flirting and soaking up that sense of excitement injected back into me.

As we approached the village, he passed the turnoff that a driver would usually take, and continued up a narrow road instead, and into the hills.

It was beautiful. On the right-hand side of me looked like a stitched patch-work quilt of green and yellow field. To my left, was the infinite ensemble of the ancient Fae Woods.

I wondered why he was driving around the opposite side of the forest, but he kept tight-lipped, driving along with his window down, leaning an arm out casually.

Finally, he turned left into an off-road track. We endured a bumpy, few minutes longer until he slowly rolled up next to a rutted pathway that had partially dried by days of sunshine. He yanked on the hand-break and killed the engine.

I cocked my head to him and frowned. He smirked, hooked his finger around the door handle and climbed out of the car.

I mirrored him, slid my sunglasses on to the top of my head and probed around the area. It was a lot lighter on this side of the forest, with a less cluster of trees.

The car beeped and was locked.

'Is this where you take the axe and disposal bags from the boot?' I joked.

'An axe?' he scoffed, dipping his hands into his pocket. 'Why an axe?'

'Well, what's your choice of a murder weapon?' He dawdled beside me as we began to trudge along the dry dirt path.

'Chloroform and my bare hands,' he teased. 'Less messy and much more effective.'

He waited for my reaction, but I was already intrigued by the direction we were walking in. I felt like I'd walked the same steps before, instinctively turning off the footpath and stopped to stare down a steep bank, covered with tangled weeds and overgrown ferns.

I could hear the distant sound of running water and felt drawn to it. Although the bank was steep, the soil was thick enough to dig my boots into and keep my footing. Finn shadowed me down to the bottom until we stopped at a small wooden fence with a broken gate. I felt lightheaded for a few seconds as a wave of recognition washed over me.

Finn was silently observing me, never giving anything away. It was as if he was waiting and watching to see if something triggered my memory.

The gate immediately did that. For a split second, I heard children's hearty giggles echoing, in a vision of when I was a child, running care-free through the gate. I swallowed, dithering with my hand on the splintered worn wood. The instant my hands touched it, I squeezed my eyes shut, and I could see and hear kids running towards a stream, and then loud splashes and squeals of happiness. I anchored my head towards Finn.

'Did we play here as kids?' I asked.
His eyes never left mine as he prised open the gate, smiling. He gestured for me to go first and stayed close behind me.

As I stepped through the gateway, I walked on to a paved path, cracked and uneven through age and overgrown with weeds. My eyes took a moment to recalibrate the most spellbinding vision in front of me. Stretching down a long path, was the most enchanting carpet of purple flower petals.
I gasped, awestruck, and glanced above me, stunned by the arch of interwoven branches, forming a semi-sheltered tunnel. Speechless, all I could do was gawp in amazement.

'They call them purple rhododendron's,' Finn explained, stepping to my side. 'It's beautiful, huh?'

'Beautiful? It's the most mesmerising thing I've ever seen in my life.'

'It should be,' he smiled. 'Your mum created it.'
My head cocked towards him, and he began to walk ahead of me.

'My mum?' I echoed.
The trail was like a light mauve blanket of light. So scenic and extraordinary.

'She was an enchantress of nature,' he clarified. 'She could augment, grow or revive dying plants and flowers.'

My eyes danced around the tube of radiant violet, and I shook my head beyond impressed.

'Allegra was all about being good to the earth. She loved this forest. She said it supplied the oxygen we needed to survive, so the least we could do was be kind to it and keep it alive.'

'And she did all this?'

He nodded, beaming from ear to ear.

We walked a little further and Finn placed a hand on my arm to stop me. When I glanced at him, he nodded to the side of me. I followed his line of sight and found an opening in the tunnel which lead to what appeared like a small wooden bridge over a brook. Sound of water dragged me away from the tunnel, and down to the bridge, where the fragrance of moss and earth expanded my lungs as I inhaled it. The fresh, cooler air was a relief on my skin as my cupped hands reached down to scoop up some of the slow-flowing water.

'It looks clean and clear enough to drink.'

'It flows from a natural spring further up the hill. I think this stream flows down to the Melladonna,' he guessed.

The small bridge led towards an abandoned cabin. I frowned, and a feeling of unquestionable recognition engorged my stomach.

From the outside, it appeared like a crooked wooden shed, eroding and rotting with time. The roof, low and slanted, was covered in leaves and green moss and the rustic brown rotted wood. Glass was missing from the window frames too. I knew instinctively that it once been humming with life.

It triggered a flashback of hanging baskets buzzing with insects, and flowers proudly flowing out. My head glanced back towards the stream, where the clear water trickled against uneven rocks and stones, exposing bankside roots of weeping willow trees.

'Wait,' I insisted, turning on my heel in the direction of the trees.

I distinctively recalled a rope swing. I wandered off towards one of the overhanging willow trees and low and behold; there was a rope swing.

'Oh, my god,' I laughed, rushing up to it. The wooden seat was splintered and broken, and the rope frayed, but the nostalgia that it brought me was immense.

I *did* remember.

I spent a lot of time there.

That *was* my childhood summer retreat.

Finn took my hand in his and guided me towards the cabin.

'Understandably, it's become an eyesore inside and out,' he admitted. 'In fact, I wouldn't risk going inside. It's far too dangerous.'

I didn't care. I had to have a peek.

I moved ahead of him, gingerly stepping towards the broken door. Once white, the paint was faded, and the wood was falling apart. I carefully pushed open the door and stepped on a slab of rubble and debris-covered concrete.

The interior was much smaller than from what I could see from the outside, with two rooms divided by a thin wooden partitioning wall. It was foul-smelling and stagnant, and void of any furniture. There were no signs of electric wiring or plumbing, no cooking stove or fireplace. How did my mother prepare the meals or wash us? Where was the loo?

Finn folded his arms behind me and cleared his throat.

'Believe it or not, but this place spruced up nicely when your mum had it. It was basic but always kept clean and tidy.'

I side-glanced him, noticing dust coating the remnants of old shelving and cobwebs all over the place. He watched my every move, quietly observing me.

'After your mum was gone, the place went to shit. The whole place was cleared, and it's been falling into dereliction ever since.'

I turned back to Finn and chewed the inside of my cheek. 'Why did you bring me here?' I asked, tilting my head to one side.

He stared down at his feet with a smile creeping up the corners of his mouth.

'Well, aside from the fact that I wanted to see if you would recognise this place, I also wanted to show you my future project.'

'Future project?

'Yeah,' he lifted his head and smiled.

'You're going to restore this place?'

'Yeah, I think I am. I've spoken to the farmer who owns this land, and he's up for it. As your mum did, he only requested a peppercorn rent from me. It needs a lot of work done, but with some furniture and a lick of paint, it'll be a good little getaway when you want to escape from the real world.'

We stared at each other, smiling in silence. He wasn't saying anything, and I wasn't saying anything. We stood awkwardly, and the air shifted between us. His hand dipped back into his pocket, and he shyly half-laughed.

'Maybe there was another reason I wanted to bring you here.'

I swallowed as my mouth pooled with saliva.

He rolled his tongue over his front teeth and bit down on his bottom lip, suppressing a spreading grin.

He flicked those dark lashes up towards me, dragging my attention to his heated gaze as he stepped towards me. My immediate reaction wanted to back away, but I didn't. The ground had roots that strangled around my feet, locking me in place.

My heart started to pound for him as he towered over my frame, glancing down at me in a way that he never had before. This time, I gulped audibly, as his expression transfixed with desire. I blinked up at him as he closed the space between us and reached his hands towards me. Slowly, he glided his fingers through the strands of my hair, then cupped the back of my head. My heart began to stutter, as his restless eyes dilated and glossed over. The tension was so substantial you could slice through it.

Suddenly, his other hand stroked around my back, and I felt his hands splay out as he pulled me against his hard chest. Our breaths shook as our faces were almost touching. My eyes dropped to his parted-wet lips, swollen and sensually arousing me.

I swallowed compulsively, anticipating his mouth on mine, and as I watched him slowly lean in, I closed my eyes and felt his soft lips press against mine.

He pulled away for a second, beckoning me to exchange a look at him. I was practically seeing stars as I blinked them open to see him reading my face for a few seconds.

His other hand cupped my chin, and the pad of his thumb began to stroke my cheek, as he flashed me another heart-accelerating smile.

I wanted him.

I wanted to taste him.

Lose myself in him.

Be with him.

He knew the effect he had on me, and this time, lugged me into him and took control. My limp body melted into his arms as his mouth hungrily and passionately kissed me.

Every thought in my head exploded like fireworks. Nothing mattered at that moment, and nothing needed to make sense. It was as if the rest of the world just slipped away, and we were the only two souls alive, living in a moment of unadulterated passion.

Warmth smeared my bones like a comfort blanket, and it was so intense that I had to rip my mouth away to gasp oxygen back into my lungs. Finn didn't stop, his lips moved from my mouth to my throat, and he began nuzzling my neck as he teased me with delicate kisses that tingled my skin.

I grinned appreciatively, but as my eyes rolled up to the open doorway, and focused on the stream, a bolt of indescribable terror made my blood run cold.

My knee-jerk reaction pushed Finn away, and I staggered backwards, uncomprehending of what I was seeing.

We were no longer alone.

A band of hooded, black-cloaked beings lined the bank before us, their faces obscured and their silence, menacing.

I couldn't speak, frozen in immediate fear as I began to process that their feet weren't touching the ground. They were hovering above the stream, some above the bridge, and others on the bankside.
My heart jerked into fifth gear, furiously pounding as I was rendered speechless.

'Kate?' Finn pulled away from me, noticing the distress crawl over my face. All I could do was pant like a dog, voiceless to my fear. My trembling finger pointed towards the stream and slid along the faceless cloaked beings. But when Finn turned around, he peered out of the door, cocked his head both ways and turned back to me in complete bafflement.

'What is it? What's the matter?'
I skimmed his befuddled expression, unable to respond with words, and choked on the horror the dark, faceless entities brought. They didn't move. They were static, hovering above the ground, like foreboding, intimidating presences of pure evil.
I compulsively swallowed through a dry sand throat and wheezed with anguish.

'Kate, you're starting to freak me out,' he complained, moving in front of me to block my view. 'What's the matter with you?'

I became disorientated with panic, and when I heard the slaps of bare feet pad on to the bridge, I fell to my knees, sure my heart was about to burst from my chest at any given second.

Finn crouched before me and took the back of his hand to press against my head to feel my temperature.

His head glanced backwards, and he stood abruptly. But he huffed and stomped towards the door and out to the path.

I stared – trance-like – towards the bridge. That familiar demonic sound of a child's distorted giggle resounded around the cabin.

I flinched. Was it the same bloodcurdling entity from the night before? The one who crept in the shadows in the dead of night? Was there now more of them? What did they want with me?

Why were they prowling me?

My stomach lurched as an over-familiar smell of death wafted into the cabin. The fragrance was unnaturally sweet, like unrefrigerated meat left to rot, like singed hair and burnt decaying skin. The smell forced me to my knees, and my hands covered my nose and mouth. I heaved.

The sight that then filled the bridge submitted me into a frenzied hysteria, and a guttural, delirious cry screamed from my core. I knew the instant I saw it *what* and *who* it was.

A mangled body, with bones, twisted unnaturally, dragged its damaged legs over the hump of the bridge. Its dislocated jaw visible and dark red and black calcinated flesh peeled away from its bones and organs. The skin hung like tattered charred rags. Its eyes were now hollow black sockets.

It was my mother.

I'd seen the same heinous sight dominate my nightmares, bound to a tree.

Her scorched body was beyond the point of recognition, with only her teeth intact. The horrific atrocity began to stagger over the bridge towards me.

Tears began to burn down my cheeks like a rain of fire. My anguish forewarned Finn, but he could only glance around with a look of disdain, utterly perplexed by what was supposedly happening beyond the naked eye.

The undead screeched in the most distorted, inhuman, piercingly loud shriek that it shook me to my core, and I recoiled back, scuttering across the debris-strewn floor.

It growled at me, revving itself up, and then without warning, lunged over the bridge at an aberrant speed, erratically and violently pouncing towards me. I screamed out again and cowered behind Finn, grabbing him by the scruff of his neck to shield me. I anticipated bloodshed. I expected a violent death, awaiting the swipe of claws across my throat.
I winced, holding my breath.
But it never came.
My arms were in vice grips, being forcibly shaken.
'Kate!'
Finn's voice came in like a screeching echo as my ears tried to retune. I was cowering in the foetal position on the filthy ground, my limbs trembling uncontrollably. Even as he placed a hand around my arm, my body jerked aggressively.

'Kate, what's happening to you?' he shouted in a panicked tone. 'You're freaking me out. What did you see?'

My eyes sprang open, and I lay there waiting for my heart to compose itself. I inhaled and exhaled slowly, now drenched in sweat. I felt sick, and I sat up, quickly dodging my attention back to the bridge. There was no-one there. No carcass and no hooded beings.

Nothing. I pulled my knees into my chest and concentrated on my breathing. Finn was still crouched before me, looking genuinely concerned. Finally, I swallowed hard and snapped my head to face him.

'Get me back to Zoe,' I demanded. 'I need to unlock my powers, Finn. And I need to unlock them now.'

CHAPTER 20

Finn grumbled as we pulled into the pub's car park. There was a white Citroen parked up, and a blonde, middle-aged woman struggled to lift shopping bags from its boot. She stopped to track us as we rolled up alongside her, and her curious squinting suddenly turned to wide-eyed joy, as she recognised Finn and began to wave to him.

'Who's that?' I asked, unbuckling my seatbelt.
I watched his chest deflate while he puffed tetchily.

'My mum,' he sighed, opening the door and swung out his legs. 'They've been away on a short break.'
His who? Holy crap.

Nerves began to pierce my stomach as I hated meeting men's parents for the first time. It was so nerve-wracking and uncomfortable. I already felt her eyes on me before I'd even climbed out of the car.

Her blonde, thick, shoulder-length hair fell over her oval face, and her hazel eyes – sunk deep within their sockets - pinned on me with the same intensity that I recognised in Finn.

Her mouth was agape, and suddenly, the shopping bags she held dropped. She covered her mouth with her hands. I raked her petit, slender frame, feeling confused by her reaction. She had pain written into her face, with her eyebrows slanted, and eyes teary. Was she crying? She pulled her hands from her face, sniffled, and tilted her head ardently.

'Antonia,' she whimpered, her voice filled with emotion. 'I can't believe it's you.'
Before I could react, she stepped towards me and yanked me into a motherly embrace, squeezing the air from my lungs. I felt her tears land on my shoulders. The air was already sticky enough without a stranger's eye juice splashing off my raw skin. She pulled back, taking a minute to study my face and body, and then chuckled.

'You're a Wade alright,' she said. 'The image of Allegra.'

'Mum,' Finn groaned. He tutted and turned to pick up the bags. 'This is Kate Littlewood. She's changed her name. Can you stop that snivelling?'

'But I haven't seen her in so long. You were only this high when I last saw you,' she declared, raising her hand up to her waist. 'And now look at you.'

Of course, Finn had told me she was once friends with my parents. She tried to help us escape. Suddenly, she reached for my hand and placed hers over mine.

'Come inside. I want you to meet Quinn. He'll die when he sees you. I'm Athena, by the way, I knew your parents well.'

'Mum!' Finn complained, huffing loudly.
She linked arms with me and practically marched me around to the rear entrance of the pub.

All I wanted to do was get back to Zoe and tell her what I'd witnessed earlier. I needed help to unlock my powers. Time was running out.

Once inside the pub, I found myself in a small corridor. An array of garments was overloading a wooden coat and hat stand, and a corded phone was attached to a corridor wall. A staircase lay ahead, one that I presumed led to the upstairs accommodation. She dragged me through a second door that brought us into the main bar, where I noticed that the pub hadn't yet opened its doors.

Sophia raised her head from behind the bar. She smiled and waved at me, while an older man – who was Hench for his age – stood across from her, flicking through paperwork on a clipboard.

'Quinn,' Athena sang, pushing me ahead of her as to show me off like a prize.

The minute his eyes rolled up to me, his jaw dropped, and he leaned in further to get a better inspection of me.

'Well, I'll be damned,' he gasped, slapping down the clipboard on to the bar, 'Antonia Wade, back from the dead.'

He stomped towards me with heavy feet and extended his hand for a handshake. I felt surprised at the sight of Finn's doppelgänger. The only difference was that Quinn was shorter, stockier and his hair was greying.
His handshake was strong and firm.

'It's like meeting Allegra again,' he said in amazement. 'You're the image of her.'

'Can I get you a drink?' asked Sophia from behind the bar.

'Oh, not for me, thanks,' I politely refused. 'We're heading back out now.'

'Already?' complained Athena, rounding me. 'At least stay for dinner. I have so many stories and photographs to share with you.'

Finn's feet shuffled behind me, and he dropped the last of the bags near the door.

'We've got plans, mum,' he said, clearing his throat.

'Like?' she quizzed, raising an eyebrow at him.

'Like, I'm twenty-eight-years-old, and I don't have to run everything by you. We're going out. That's all you need to know.'

I flinched and bowed my head while thinking how unnecessary his comment was. Quinn immediately narrowed his eyes in at Finn.

'Finn, please don't speak to your mother like that, she's trying to be hospitable. What's the attitude for, huh?'

I felt awkward and wanted to leave.

'Because the last thing Kate wants to do right now is to be looking through old photographs and shown pictures of her dead parents that she can't rightly remember.'

'Finn!' Athena protested, shocked.

I crawled inside my skin and grimaced. Why did he say that? He was making this whole meeting more awkward than it had to be. I shot him a disapproving glare and shook my head at him, which made him huff loudly and turn his back on everyone.

'Whatever,' he shrugged, 'Are you coming, or what?'

Athena's eyes flashed from me to her son, and she squinted, suspecting something was up.

'What's going on?' she asked, 'You're hiding something from me.'

The guilt was written all over my face, and I could no longer make eye contact with her. I stared down at my feet and fumbled with my hands, wanting nothing more than to leave.

'Finn,' she repeated with a curt, warning tone.
Finn turned around slowly, grabbed a chair and sagged into it.
He dragged his hands through his thick hair and drew a deep breath.

'Jorah's sent a warrant for Kate,' he admitted, finally rolling his eyes up to his mother.
I flicked between their faces, watching the discomfort wrinkle over them.

'What do you mean, a warrant? What are you talking about? Why?'
I stepped forward, attempting to break the growing tension in the room.

'They think I have the missing powers, which I don't. We've been to the Melladonna and checked.'
Finn's head and shoulders slumped in a synchronised manner, and the defeat on his face made me realise I probably shouldn't have disclosed that information. Her stony expression burnt a crimson red, as both Quinn's and Sophia's heads snapped in my direction.

'You did what?' Quinn bit, with fury brewing behind his voice.
Finn stared at the ceiling and groaned.

'Before you blow up,' he huffed, 'Nobody knew Kate's capabilities. If she'd gone to Glentree Manor, and she had even one of the missing abilities, Raven would have killed her for it. We had to know.'

'You idiot,' Athena cried. 'How could you be so stupid? Do you not realise what you've done?'
I flashed my eyes to Sophia, who winced at me regretfully.

'Don't you know the Chamber rules?' Quinn yelled, his face burning the same shade as Athena's. 'Rule number nineteen. All abilities must be witnessed by the Mitral, a parent or guardian and identified by Akenna, the trusted council of the Myocardium Chamber when absorbed by the Melladonna.'

'Trusted council,' Finn scoffed. 'He certainly made exceptions for you.'
Quinn's fist suddenly slammed down on the counter. He was almost spitting with fury.

'How dare you!' he shouted, his booming voice reverberated around the entire room and shook me. Finn stood up and puffed his chest powerfully, clenching his fists.

'Rule number twenty: no absorption of powers should result in death unless it is the sacrificial ceremony of the Mitral and his beneficiary.'
I didn't know where to put myself. My heart was beating hard with all the animosity in the room - what a way to meet the parents.

'I can't believe you're doing this to us again,' cried Athena, dabbing her eyes with her knuckle. 'Every time you involve yourself with a girl, you nearly get your family killed.'
Woah!
My mouth dropped open, offended. Was this my fault? Was I putting him and others in danger? I didn't even ask for his help. I decided to intervene and speak for myself.

'With all due respect, Athena, I never asked anyone to help me. This is all very overwhelming and happening at lightning speed. The information is like a tornado that's sweeping me up and spitting me out. All I want to do is get this over with and to live like a normal person again. I don't want anybody to get hurt.'

She narrowed her eyes at me and exhaled.

'We're dealing with the De Wyche's here. Somebody *always* gets hurt.'

'You never listen,' Quinn complained to Finn, 'Has it escaped your memory that this family has a curse over our heads? That we can't fight back. We can't protect ourselves, and we certainly can't protect you if they find out what you did. They'll hang you for what you did, all of you. I thought you had more sense than that.'

'What do you want me to do?' Finn snapped, clenching his teeth. 'Throw her to the wolves? What happened to having the courage to do what's right for another person? I'm not going to send her to what could be a slaughterhouse. And neither is anyone else.'

Athena stared down at her nails and bowed her head, with a face of fury.

'We lost our powers because of you and your actions,' she hissed. *Wait. What? I thought the curse was because of her. What did she mean?*

Finn cocked his head at me, trying to decipher my reaction, but when I looked back at him, his head quickly turned away.

'We've kept out of trouble. We've kept ourselves to ourselves and never got involved in anyone else's business. And I'll be damned if I let you.' She spat.

'I'm not asking him to,' I complained, defending him. 'I'm not asking anyone. All I want is to unlock my powers so I can go and get this over and done with. I need to be able to protect myself. There are forces after me, that nobody else can see. It's happening more frequently now and need those powers.'

Athena blinked at me and sighed. 'What do you mean, forces?'

'It's now happened two days in a row. Last night I saw someone or something in my home. No-one else could see it but me. And then again today at the cabin in Fae Woods.'

'You went to Fae Woods?' Athena jibed.

'Yes,' I answered matter-of-factly, 'And that's when I saw it again, except this time, there were at least a dozen of them, and my mother's corpse was running around like in a zombie movie. Finn didn't see anything, so either I'm going insane, or someone's screwing with me.'
Quinn and Athena shared a worried glance and remained silent, but I sensed that they knew what was happening to me. I raised my eyebrow at her, waiting, and she exhaled defeatedly.

'It sounds like someone's using fear amplification on you. One of the De Wyche girls has that power, which means their probably close by, watching your every move.'

'Fear amplification?' Sophia gibed, pulling her eyebrows together with confusion while wiping drinks glasses, oblivious to our heads craning towards her. 'No, fear amplification is your *worst* fear. Like spiders, heights, confined spaces, or clowns. That sounds more like an illusionary power to me.'

Everyone shrugged to each other, but something registered in my memory. I recalled scouring the list of Zoe's Chamber Vents and their abilities and distinctively remembered one person who had the power of illusions: *Ellis*.

I decided to remain quiet, even ridiculing myself at such a thought. The girl had been nothing but welcoming to me. Why would she want to mess with me? I wouldn't point the finger and accuse her of doing something she probably hadn't done; instead, I focused on making my excuse to leave.

As I was about to speak up, the corridor phone began to ring, and Athena excused herself and left to answer it. We were all stewing in silence and my stomach began to summersault with dread. It came in strong waves, and the creeping feeling of anxiety had me recoiling to the back wall.

Something felt off again.

A few minutes later, as I eyeballed Finn for us to leave, Athena returned to the room and the colour had drained from her face. She was ghost white and looked like she'd just received news that someone had died.

Please let it be Jorah.

Please let it be Jorah.

She held her stomach and swallowed, shaking.

Quinn was in front of her in a second, cupping her face, forcing her eyes to meet his.

'What is it?' he demanded, 'What's wrong?'

She moved past him and had to hold on to a chair to keep her balance. Sweat glistened on her forehead, and I instinctively knew that something was *very* wrong.

'That was Tabitha De Wyche,' she gulped, trying to keep her decorum. 'Jorah's in his final stages of life.

They've decided to bring the sacrifice forward. We have the summons to bear witness tomorrow evening. All Chambers must attend.'

She was trembling, and I couldn't understand why. Why was she so terrified to go to Glentree? It appeared that the news had affected everyone else in the room, too, the same way as it had Athena. They all shared unspoken panic.

Finn slowly moved towards his mother and placed his hands on her shoulders to support her.
She suddenly burst into tears and began to wail vulnerably. It was the sound of a defenceless woman who had no escape.

'What am I going to do?' she sobbed, 'They know.' I stepped away from them, and Sophia came to stand by me.

'What's wrong with her?' I asked, confused. Sophia scratched her scalp, and her hand bobbed down her French braid. There was something she wasn't telling me, something that was on the edge of her tongue.
Finally, she caved.

'It's not you who has any of the *missing* powers, Kate.'
Her thick eyebrows scrunched, and she clamped her eyes closed, regrettably.

'It's her.'

CHAPTER 21

We sat outside in the beer garden, smoking furiously. Sophia continuously flicked her ash into the ashtray and swigged lemonade in large gulps.

'Do they know?' I asked, referring to the De Wyche's.

She exhaled, looking frustrated.

'I don't know what they know, but if they find out, my mother's a dead woman.'

'But how could they not know?'

'Because Akenna lied at her reveal,' she admitted, glancing her ice blue eyes at me. 'Maddock – your dad – he wasn't the rightful heir, neither was Jorah. It was always my mum.'

I listened in, remaining quiet, and watched her shift uncomfortably talking about it.

She glanced around us, making sure there were no prying eyes or ears.

'Why wasn't she just honest about it?' I queried. I

didn't understand it, she had sought after powers, why would she hide them?

'Could you live a life constantly peering over your shoulder?' she asked. 'Powers like that are more trouble than their worth. There's always somebody waiting in the wings; a power-hungry crook who, given half the chance, would slice your throat for them.'

I grimaced at the thought, and puffed on my cigarette again, disturbed by her comment.

'She knew what ran through her blood was more powerful than she expected, and she begged Akenna not to reveal the true nature of what she was able to do. She didn't want that responsibility.'

'Neither did my father,' I added.

'Because they didn't possess the savagery that was paramount to rule as the Mitral.'

I stared up to the sky to see the dying sun setting behind the trees and welcomed the cooler evening air. I knew it would be the last night where I would feel a sense of composure, because the time was drawing nearer for the event at Glentree Manor, and what could await me.

'What will they do? How will they know? As far as everyone else is concerned, Raven is convinced that I'm the one with those powers.'
Sophia blinked at me through a haze of smoke.

'If Raven's been watching you, which I suspect she probably has been, she will know it's not you. I have a gut feeling that Akenna has been forced to confess. He'll hang for his crime, if he hasn't already.'

'So then, we fight,' I argued. 'They can't take the powers from Athena.'

'Oh, but they can,' she scoffed. 'The curse …

remember?'

I blinked at her.

'Did I hear your mum say that was because of Finn?'

'It *was* because of Finn,' she certified. 'It was a curse or death.'

'What happened?'

She inhaled the smoke deep into her lungs, held it there for several seconds, and then released it.

'Imagine what he went through watching your parents being murdered. Imagine what that would do to anyone, never mind an eight-year-old kid. He was never the same again after that night. He wouldn't leave the house, wouldn't talk to anyone, he wouldn't eat or sleep – he was completely broken. Until Jasmine.'

'Jasmine?' I rived my head to face her as she stared ahead in a fixed gaze.

'When Finn was fifteen years old, he took a shining for this girl in secondary school. She was a normal girl in his class, but she made him forget everything. They were always together, always hanging out. Chamber kids aren't supposed to mingle with ordinary kids outside of school, it's forbidden, which is really stupid, since we spend most of our childhood being best friends with these people, but they can never find out about our craft.'

'And she did?' I asked, almost predicting the story.

'Everybody in his class did.'

My eyes widened, wondering what on earth he could have possibly done.

'I love my big brother, but he can be reckless,' she scoffed. 'There was this dickhead kid in his class who

used to always wind him up. Andrew Peters. I'll never forget his name. He'd had it in for Finn since they were kids, always bulling him, humiliating him, calling him a weirdo, just being your typical twat really.'
I knew this story was going to end badly, but regardless, I needed to hear it. I wanted to know everything there was to know about Finn Moon; the good, the bad, and the ugly.

'Andrew knew how to push Finn's buttons, and he knew the only way he'd be able to get a reaction out of him would be if he started to mess with Jasmine. So, he did.'

'What did he do?'

'Andrew started making fun of her. He'd get physical, push her around, mock her in front of others, push and shove her and completely alienate her from everyone. Finn warned him several times to leave her alone, but he continued to harass her. The final straw was Andrew groping her sexually in the middle of a class when the teacher's back was turned. That was when Finn saw red and totally lost it. He used his powers on him. He didn't even so much as move from his seat. Everyone said that Andrew was hoisted from his chair, flung across the room, and smashed through the third-floor window. He died instantly. He had no chance.'
My hand shot over my mouth as I gasped.

'The whole class witnessed it, but just couldn't explain it. However, they pointed the finger at Finn because he was closest to Jasmine. Of course, they all told the police what they had seen but there was no hard evidence to connect him with the actual crime, so they couldn't press any charges. The coroner recorded a verdict of death by misadventure. But there was a lot of finger pointing during Finn's final years at school. The De Wyche's caught wind of what had occurred, and they had no choice but to punish him for his foolish misdemeanour.'

'And they were going to kill him?'
She leant forward and stumped out her cigarette. 'Oh, yeah. They'd called the Chambers to witness and everything. But our great-grandfather, Apollo, pleaded and begged Jorah for an alternative punishment because of his age.'

'And so he placed a curse instead?'

'Not only a curse,' she said, shaking her head. 'He bargained his own life to save Finn's.'
I was stunned to silence.

'He forfeited his life so Finn could live his, and that's why he placed the curse. And now it can't be undone.'
I thought of how extreme it was, that his grandfather would sacrifice himself so that Finn wouldn't lose his. Finn would forever be in his debt. How could you carry that heavy burden around with you, knowing someone else's life ended because of your stupid actions?

'There's got to be a way?' I stressed, leaning forward to stub out my cigarette. 'Surely, somebody could reverse the curse, aside from Apollo?'
Sophia's chest inflated, and she stood up from the table. She was about to say something when her head did a double take looking out to the village high street.

'You have company,' she nodded.
When I followed her gaze, I was shocked to see Zoe and her Chamber waiting for me.

I stood up, confused.

'What is it?' I asked, stepping forward towards her. Zoe had that motherly dismay written all over her, with concern creeping into every corner of her face.

'We have to go the Fae Woods and initiate you immediately,' she said. 'It's time.'

CHAPTER 22

Everyone seemed to have a buzz about them as we reached the Fae Woods for the second time that day. I felt it all around me; the exhilaration between a group of friends who were excited about the possibilities this night could bring. It didn't sit right with me, how the group could drift between being panic-stricken and scared, to enthusiasm for the forthcoming ritual.

Perhaps they were relishing their last night together before the sacrifice? I found it to be an entirely different level of bizarreness that I'd involved myself in.

For a start, the Chamber appeared to be setting up a kind of occultist camp. I watched Danny construct an altar he wedged between two trees, using a folding wooden table. Darcie swooped aside of him and fluffed out a large black cloth and carefully neatened it out over the table. I squinted at it, to see a vivid gold pentacle stitched into the fabric. She then began to decorate it with candles and incense burners. They joked with each other as they carried out different tasks.

'What are they doing?' I asked Finn, utterly perplexed.

Savannah was dragging a rake across the leaves and clearing a large space, while Roman dropped a ton of firewood in the centre of a circle they were creating.

'It's for the initiation ceremony,' he explained, dipping his hands into his pockets. 'They're going to make you a fully-fledged Chamber Vent.'

'But I thought you couldn't be a Vent until after six months or something?'

'You can't,' he shrugged. 'But considering you were born into the Chamber as Antonia Wade; you already have a place by birth right. You only need to be initiated.'

I craned my neck to see his eyes pouring into the green terrain, scanning the coiling tree branches that draped sparingly from the thick tree limbs. He sighed, and I felt as though he was either delving into another memory, or he just felt uncomfortable because he was not officially part of a Chamber. It must have been frustrating to have so much power inside of him, without the ability to use it.

Zoe came stomping through the leaves towards us, clutching a bath towel. She probed both our faces with scrutiny and then offered it to me.

'It'll be dark soon; I need you to get undressed and wrap this around you. The boys are putting up the tent so you can get changed.'

'What?' I laughed dismissively, 'I'm not getting undressed again. What do you need me to get undressed for?'

'I'm not arguing with you, Kate. Clothes off.'
I tutted at her and stepped back, rejecting the towel.

'If you think for one minute that I'm getting naked again …'

'That's exactly what I think,' she snapped, glaring at me. 'Do you want to unlock your powers or not?'

'Yes but …'

'Then get undressed.'

She shoved the towel into my arms and left me glaring at her, visibly peeved. What was their obsession with getting naked all the time? Surely it wouldn't have made a blind bit of difference if I were clothed or not, merely to join their damned Chamber?

I glanced at Finn and caught the amusement that creased his cheeks. He flashed his eyebrows at me and chuckled.

'And as for you …' Zoe spat bitterly, snatching his attention. 'Go, take a walk. You don't need to be here for this.'

The woman was becoming overbearingly domineering. She took her High Priestess title to the next level, and often I found her curt words too brazen. Finn didn't entertain her with a response. He spun me around, told me I'd be fine and that he'd come back for me.

I liked that protective side to him, I felt safe, and I knew the way he looked at me when he uttered the words, that he meant every single one of them. I didn't want him to leave, but on the other hand, I didn't want him as part of an audience either. I just wanted it to be over and done with.

It was now growing dark. The sounds of the night were different. Rustling trees, the orchestra of grasshoppers buzzing, and owls hooting in the distance. It was a serene ambience, but that didn't shake my growing tension.

'Did you all have to do an initiation ceremony?' I anxiously asked Sav.

She tilted her head at me and smiled a reassuring smile.

'Stop worrying, and you'll be fine.'

'But did you?'

'No, we were family, born directly into the actual Chamber. We only do initiations if someone is joining us from another Chamber, but your case is unique, it's more complicated. The last time we did this was with Ellis.'

'And she got naked too?'

'Oh, yeah,' she laughed, 'We've seen it all, trust me.' A short while later, and it was time.

Sav had run me through everything that I needed to know before the initiation and had since changed into a black hooded cloak that had gold stitched into the arms and hemline.

She stepped out from the tent first, with her cloak sweeping along the dirt, and ushered me out. Luckily, the night was warm, but I still felt ridiculous.

She nodded at me, prepping me to be ready, and directed me down a short path towards the ceremonial clearing.

There now were candles everywhere, flickering in the light breeze. The altar dominated a circle that was made from stones and illuminated with candles and lanterns. Everyone else was barefooted, in the same robes as Savannah, and they stood outside of the circle, while Zoe remained inside it, in front of the altar.

As I got closer, I could smell jasmine and lavender incense coming from the table and could see some sort of glittering silver dagger, placed at the centre of it.

'Hoods up!' Zoe ordered. They all raised their hoods and bowed their heads.

'Ellis, Sister of the Morphing World, stand North,' Zoe commanded.

I watched Ellis's feet climb over the stones and into the circle, and she picked up a jar full of what appeared to be soil and held it aloft.

'Danny,' Zoe continued, 'High Priest of the Fading Moon, stand West.'

Danny stepped into the circle and lifted an owl engraved chalice.

'Roman, Brother of Protection, stand East.'
His jar contained a white feather that had been plucked from a swan, and he held it high above his head.

'Dominic, Friend of the Fae, stand South.'
Dom hesitated, but a moment later lifted a red candle up high.
Zoe ushered Darcie to stand in between Dom and Roman, while I stood amazed by what everybody was doing.

'Darcie, Keeper of the Black Mirror, stand South West,' she instructed, then signalled them to place the jars by their feet. I watched her turn to the altar and pick up the glittering dagger, the one that I'd spied before. Only this time, upon touching her hands, it changed colour. Blinding pinks and purple hues swam up and down the dagger. She stepped outside the ring, stabbed it into the soil and began to draw a massive circle with it around the group.

'I take this Athame and draw this circle in the name of Ovar. Only love shall this sacred circle come to bless.'

She crept silently back inside the circle, with her cloak swishing behind her and turned to Ellis, pointing the blade to her throat. She lingered for a while, and I glanced worriedly at Sav, who's gaze didn't falter from the group.

Zoe stepped back, and her eyes trailed their faces, as each hand suddenly jutted out holding a blade.

I jumped, but Sav placed a hand on my arm to calm me.

Ellis's dagger – a bright blue blade – was thrust towards the sky and she began to call out.

'Blessed guardians of the watchtowers of the North, I call to thee, ground my work and make it be.' Roman's green dagger mirrored her movements.

'Blessed guardians of the watchtowers of the east, air come to me, lift my words, do as I see.'

A yellow blur sprang from Dom's cloak, and it was his turn to puncture the air.

'Blessed guardians of the watchtowers of the south, spirits of fire, charge my words, burn our fear.'

As she side-stepped to Danny, they exchanged a crafty wink.

He cleared his throat and thrust the red blade above his head. 'Blessed guardians of the watchtowers of the West, let your water cleanse me now, and do as I vow.'

All heads raised towards Zoe and her stunning blade thrust skyward.

'Blessed spirits, the circle is cast. We are between worlds, beyond the bounds of time and space, where night and day, birth and death, joy and sorrow meet as one.'

'Now she's going to call upon her Goddess,' Savannah whispered, unable to take her eyes from the circle.

'Goddess?' I mumbled back curiously.

'She works with a Goddess who made herself known to her before she became the High Priestess. They live in the Elder World. Some of us will never get the chance to work with a Goddess. They often come to us during a turning point in our lives. They own their energy and vibration.'

'And Zoe's the only one?'

'From our Chamber, yes,' she whispered back. 'Although she had spent months leaving offerings for the Goddess, building a connection and attuning to her.'

Everyone remained creepily silent, and it was the first time I felt some ethereal, supernatural presence saturate our space. I couldn't help but cock my head behind me, always checking that there wasn't anything lurking and watching from the trees. Sav quickly nudged me to pay attention, and I turned back to watch the assembly.

'Gracious Goddess Maloon,' Zoe's voiced boomed towards the sky, 'I open my heart, my soul and my mind to you. I ask you to join me in this sacred space to bless my altar and my tools and to bless my circle and me with your love, protection and guidance. I align myself and my faith with you and to the supreme, Ovar. Welcome mother Goddess Maloon.'

'Maloon?' I asked Savannah.

'That's her Goddess, now shush!'

'Savannah,' Zoe bellowed, alerting her that it was time. 'Bring her into the circle.'

My heart started the react uncomfortably. I'd already been naked for half the Chamber. Now, I was going to be naked in front of them *all*. Nerves began to stir in my gut as my feet dithered walking on the cold earth. No-one raised their heads, but I could feel eyes lurking up underneath their hoods.

Zoe anchored her attention to me, but she appeared a far cry from the best friend I'd known all my life. She was stone-faced and unreadable and exuded dominance and control. She didn't smile or talk with her eyes but stared down the lens of her nose with caution.

'Who approaches the sacred space?' she bit towards Savannah.

'I bring to you the one who wishes to know the mysteries of this Chamber, and who wishes to honour Ovar and his Gods and Goddesses.'

'Which name will the seeker be known as in this sacred circle?'

My name? I was to have a name. Was I supposed to have picked one?

'The seeker will be known as Kate, Sister of the Aurora, the one who shines.'

I liked it immediately. It had a ring to it. For a split second, I saw Zoe's lips twitch suppressing a smile.

'Enter the circle,' she prompted, waiting for me to pass the threshold she'd carved into the soil. 'Drop to your knees.'

Savannah resumed her place within the circle, and I did as I was ordered, bowing before Zoe. A few months ago, had she asked me to do that, I would have burst out laughing and told her to piss off, but she was a High Priestess – people did what she asked, and this was necessary. She took the blade – or Athame as she called it - and pointed it towards my heart.

'By joining this Chamber, you become a part of a greater spiritual family. You are about to enter a vortex of power, a place beyond imagination, where birth and death, dark and light, joy and pain meet as one. You are about to step between worlds, beyond time, outside of the realm of your human life. Have you the courage for it?'

I lifted my gaze towards her and swallowed hard.

'I do.'

Suddenly she took the blade and swiped open my towel with one harsh tear. As it dropped to the ground, I felt the cold air react against my skin. My heart dropped to my stomach and began pulsing. *Oh, god, is everyone looking?* I tried to lift my line of sight to check their faces, but Zoe's hand grabbed my jaw and yanked my face back to meet hers.

'As a dedicant, you will learn and grow each day. You will seek knowledge and attain it. You will let god's and ancestors guide you. Are you willing and able to uphold our values and principles?'

'I am,' I mumbled breathlessly.

'I can't hear you,' she snapped, 'Are you able?'

'I am,' I repeated louder.

'And are you prepared seeker, to be born again, to begin in this day a brand-new journey, as part of your new spiritual family and as a child of Ovar?'

'I am.'

How long do I have to kneel?

The dampened soil caked my knees, and I was starting to get cold. My nipples were like bullets. Zoe inched closer towards me and thrust the blade a little too close to my chest.

'It is better that you should collapse into the blade than enter our circle with fear or deceit in your heart. How do you enter our circle?'

'With perfect love and perfect trust.'

She paused, it felt like she was staring deep into my soul, as though she were trying to establish my agenda. I must have passed the test as she stepped away from me, raised the dagger above her head then plunged it into the soil. I gulped, anticipating what her next move would be.

'Please get to your feet and repeat after me,' she instructed.

My legs wobbled as I rose to my feet, and I shuddered from the cold. I felt more exposed then than I did at the Melladonna. The energy was different.

'I, Kate, Sister of the Aurora, do of my own free will, most solemnly swear to protect, help and defend my sisters and brothers of the craft. I swear to keep secret, all that I must not reveal.'

I repeated her words and waited, praying it was nearly over, and they weren't going to ask me to drink blood or perform some weird sex act.

'The Chamber has deemed you worthy, Kate. You're welcome into the light and love of the God's and Goddesses, and I can now tell you, you are no longer a seeker, but a dedicant of this Chamber.'

A smile spread across my face that mirrored Zoe's, as she leaned forward to take a folded robe from Savannah's hands. She presented it to me, unfolding it and wrapped it around my shoulders. It warmed me instantly, and a rush of relief flogged me.

'This robe represents your role as a dedicant within the Chamber. It marks you before the Gods' as one who wishes to follow in their path.'
I tightened it around me and sighed in relief that it was all over.

'You can address the watchtowers and deities now,' she prompted, bending down to tug the blade out of the soil and hand it to me.

The black handle felt leather-like, but the colours that still surrounded the blade were spellbinding. I rolled my head up through the tree canopy's and pointed the knife towards them.

'Hail to the elements of fire, air, water and earth. Let it be known to all the watchtowers that I, Kate, Sister of the Aurora, am now a Vent of the Endocardium Chamber. Praise be!'

'Praise be!' the assembled cheered.
Zoe's face returned to her old expressive, kind and warm state, and she opened her arms out and dragged me to her, squeezing me tightly. 'Welcome home, Kate,' she cried. 'Back with your family, where you belong.'

CHAPTER 23

Zoe wasted no time in throwing me straight into my first ritual. She made promises of wine and food, laying out a feast on the alter to use as bait, so that everyone would join hands and assist me through the calling upon of Ovar.

Finn still hadn't returned. As he wasn't participating, I wondered if he'd gone home.

'OK, Kate, this is where it gets a little trickier,' Zoe announced, as I linked hands with Sav and Danny within the circle.

'Things are going to happen that might freak you out, and you might find it hard to follow us, but we promise you nothing untoward is going to happen and you don't have to be scared.'

'Didn't you say the same thing at the Melladonna?' I laughed, cocking an eyebrow at her.

'You're right,' she frowned, with a slight hint of guilt on her face, 'Ok, well we *aim* to keep you safe through this.'

'That's reassuring,' I scoffed, staring down at my feet. I kicked out at the dirt awkwardly and sighed. I wanted this ordeal to be finally over.

'So, when we're at a young age, we usually have a specific word that fastens itself to us,' Zoe continued. 'The word can be anything, but it's specifically attuned to you, to unlock your abilities. You'll know as soon as you hear the word.'

I wasn't following. Zoe's shoulders sagged.

'Basically, we can't use our powers without saying the designated word first.'

I blinked around their faces, still confused.

'Do I wave a wand before I yell *Alakazam*?' I mocked sarcastically.

Nobody laughed.

'You don't have to say it aloud, you think it in your mind,' Zoe barked, frustrated.

Dom broke the circle, unlinking his hands and took a few steps back from the circle.

'Why don't I give her an example?' he asked rhetorically.

His stocky frame shifted towards the logs that Danny had collected earlier. He stood before it and began to rub his hands together.

'Think of the word as a key. You have all these keys to unlock doors with; brass, silver, gold – but none of them work. Nothing will open that door. Those words are like the keys, and only one will unlock it.'

'OK?' I said, concentrating on him.

'So, I want to start a fire. Say I just pick a word at random.' He turned and waved his hands towards the logs. 'Nothing happens. I just *will* it to happen. But

…,' he paused and rubbed his hands together. 'If I conjure *my* word, *Ignite*, in my head …' Suddenly, his fingertips began to glow and spark. Within a split-second his fingers were aflame.

'Oh Jesus!' I panicked.

My first instinct was to try and find a bottle of water to throw over them, but he was not in any pain. In fact, the way his head turned and grinned at me – I'd be inclined to think he was showing off. Before I could grasp that he wasn't suffering in any way, his hands propelled flames into the logs, and in that instant, it became a fierce inferno.

My jaw was on the floor. There was nothing else I could do but watch it happen in total astonishment. I'd witnessed a man ignite a fire by using flames shooting from his hands. How was that even possible? I tried to remember how to breathe as the orange and yellow flames licked higher and hotter, the wood crackling and spitting out red embers all around.

Dom was clearly pleased with himself and shook his hands until the flames faded out. He wandered back into the circle, blowing at the smoke coming from the tips of his fingers, and then patted them off his thighs.

'You haven't seen anything yet,' Zoe chuckled, registering the awe on my face. 'Besides, this will work in your favour. You can stun someone's brain and create so much voluble chaos, that they won't be able to think coherently, let alone recall their given word.' They all ogled at the thought of it, all apart from Ellis, who had remained disconcertingly quiet throughout the whole event.

'When we do the incantation,' Zoe started. 'It's a

little different to what we did before. This time we're calling upon Ovar, and we can only speak to him in his tongue.'

'OK, then. Let's do it,' I said, now feeling more confident. I was aware that Sav had used her magic on me so that I was able to read the Ovarian language, but speaking it fluently was entirely different.

'We'll go as slow as we can for you,' Zoe said reassuringly. 'Just don't freak out. When our eyes turn white, it means we're under and we're connecting. Go with the flow and let it happen.'

Savannah squeezed my hand and smiled at me. 'The circle is safe. You need to ground yourself, so I want you to breathe in slowly, and hold it for several seconds before you release it.'

I followed her instruction, taking deep breaths in and out.

'Close your eyes,' Sav whispered. 'And imagine that your feet are blocks of concrete. Roots from the trees are emerging upwards from the soil and entwining your ankles and legs.'

Her voice was slow and hypnotic, and it started to soothe me.

'That's right, keep breathing deeply. Can you feel it? Can you feel the earth?'

I wiggled my toes under the damp soil that was cold on my feet. I began to feel strangely connected, as one with nature. I nodded my head.

'Imagine a bright white ball in front of you. Concentrate directly on that ball of energy. Imagine it is impenetrable, no one can puncture it. It's pulling you closer and closer to it.'

I imagined that ball of brilliant white light and

focused my mind on it. My body began to lightly sway, and the silence around me oozed, until I felt as though I was floating like a feather.

'Now repeat the words after me. Ovar, hara ous.'

'Ovar, hear us,' I flinched, confused why it was coming out in English.

'Aufcare ous. Cim zi ous hod lia ana conzassen.'

'Invoke us. Come to us with love and knowledge.' I stumbled on the word *Lia*. I'd heard that before. I knew it. It meant something to me.

'Hara unot pladrich.'

'Hear our plea,' I repeated.

'Hidez mami frecare mami lepuise.'

'Help me unlock my powers.' How was I doing it? How did I understand every single word she was saying? Was I speaking it in English or in Ovarkin now? I couldn't tell.

'Se cedas jic latek helar, scheger ana hidez audtri nal ildas namo vo sur godiv.'

'So that I can heal, protect and help others in the name of your divine.'

Silence rippled within our vicinity for several seconds, but then everybody began to join in and chant. It came in a low rumbling chorus of waves, pulsating around the circle. I could feel it in my chest, like a car engine chugging and rattling.

We repeated the words over and over, and I'd become lightheaded and nauseous. A vibration started to tingle through my hands and fingertips. My body began to get pins and needles. Something was happening.

The thick mass of darkness in my mind lit up like torch beams pinging on and off. Was I concocting this? Was this really happening?

'Aufcare ous,' I chanted, my breath short and quickening. 'Cim zi ous hod *lia* –'
My head snapped back instantly the moment my teeth bit on the word.

I felt an incredible wave of queasiness surge through my body. The coiled lights spun violently around the ball of energy, my legs gave way, but my body was hoisted as a mini tornado of wind ripped me up from the soil and pulled me into its spiraling chaos. Its ferocity was like ice against my skin. In a flash my body slammed onto a hardwood floor and all went still. The tornado ceased with a remaining wisp that curled into nothingness, and darkness engulfed me. I could hear my heart. I could feel my body, but I could not see into the black ink that surrounded me.

Then came a child's giggle from the depths of the darkness; a giggle, so pure and innocent, that it immediately dispelled any lingering fears I'd had. I felt at ease. A door creaked open in front of me and an orange light burnt through the seep. I slowly got to my feet, holding my breath so as not to make a sound, as the giggle was then accompanied by a man's voice, singing contentedly. The sound of plates and cutlery rattled in the background and I could hear the soft chitter-chatter of a female's voice.
I clasped my fingers around the edge of the door, and slowly opened it.
Someone quickly swept past me and I followed the direction of their shadow. I found myself in the kitchen of a very familiar home. It almost floored me how vividly I remembered the detail of the kitchen. It was the same layout as Zoe's, almost identical in fact,

but the only difference was the outdated furniture and colour scheme. It had teak looking kitchen units, a pine drop leaf table with high back spindled chairs. Cushioned vinyl covered the floors with colour coordinated Café related patterned wallpaper on the walls. The light seemed bright as a single fluorescent tube illuminated the area. But it did have a lovely, homely feel.

My eyes swept to a dining table where a mother and two children sat.

My heart collapsed the moment I laid eyes on her. She was stunning.

It was my mother.

It was so evident that this was her. I had her genes. I looked as though I'd literally been cloned from her. I took delicate steps closer to the table and stared at her face. I'd inherited her unique eyes; one blue, one green. I had her button nose and her freckles. She had an hour-glass figure, draped elegantly in a red silk nightgown. Her hands were perfectly manicured. Her face was a little rounder than mine, but she was still exquisite. I resonated with her, like I resonated with home. But this was a different kind of home, this was a heart that I missed from my life. A woman who melts away your troubles, wipes away your tears and promises you faithfully that everything is going to be OK.

Pens were scattered on the table, along with sheets of blank paper and a book that was almost identical to the Book of Shadows.

I immediately recognised the two little girls as me and Raven, dressed identically in pink pyjama's, our long blonde hair fell loose over our shoulders. I neared closer to them with my mouth agape, my breaths shallow and feigned. We were so adorable, it pained me to look. I was now a spectral visitor from the future, unbelievably watching my mother tell our younger selves to pay attention as my father dutifully washed dishes at the sink.

'Now, Antonia, it's your turn. Read that sentence to me and tell me what you think it means.'
Love and warmth radiated from my mother. She curled her own blonde hair around her ears and smiled affectionately at my younger self. Raven took a black pen to the paper and began scribbling and drawing, whilst the younger me nestled closer to my mother. I watched the child lean over the book and squint at it.

'Jic lia su,' She read in her young sounding, high-pitched voice.

'That's right,' my mother cheered, leaning in to kiss her forehead. 'And what do you think that means?'

'I know!' Raven shouted, lifting her head from her page.

'Ah-ah! Let Antonia answer, Raven.'

'I love you?' she guessed, glancing up at her our mother with huge bug eyes.

'Yes!' she clapped her hands to applaud her. She rose from the table, bending down to kiss the child on the top of her head, and then planting one on Raven's.

'And I do love you. I love you both very much.'
My father swept behind my mother and wrapped his arms around her waist, dipping his head into her neck. I felt a powerful prod of sickness hit my gut, thinking that he was the same vision from my nightmare. His face was full of expression and life now, but in my nightmare, those bulging bloodshot eyes would forever

haunt me.

'And I love your mother, very, very much,' my father said, bending his mouth round to kiss her throat, which welcomed a chorus of *'ewww's'* to pour out from the children.

My gaze drifted back onto the table, when I could see Raven's drawings. My younger self had drawn pictures of flower's that had been coloured in. Raven was colouring something dark; something sinister. My mother must have seen it too, because in that same instance, she pushed herself away from my father and ripped the drawing from Raven's hand.

'Raven,' she yelled, her face falling in dread. 'What have I told you about drawing *these* pictures?'

Raven sat rigid and confused by her mother's tone.

'Stop drawing these. Malecho, Raven! No!'

'I'm not bad,' she cried, curling her bottom lip upwards as her chin wobbled and tears threatened her eyes.

'She's just a kid, Allegra,' my dad huffed, moving past her towards Raven, who then burst into tears. He scooped her up into a hug and she clung onto him tightly with her hands wrapped around his neck.

'I'll take them upstairs,' he said, beckoning my younger self to accompany him.

I hadn't seen the full detail of what my sister had been drawing, but I knew it was bad enough to reduce my mother to tears and leave her visibly shaken. I slowly stalked her, wanting so much to comfort her and lay a hand on her shoulder, but I was a phantom presence in a memory – I couldn't physically touch her, could I?

Before my lingering hand could touch her, she ripped the drawing to shreds, marched over to a bin and disposed of it.

'Antonia,' my mother whispered, still with her back turned to me. I swept the room, confused. Everyone had left. 'You need to free us.'

My heart stopped. Blood rushed to my face. *Was she talking to me?*

Her body whipped round, and her eyes bore into mine with so much ferocity, that I staggered back. 'Jorah has contained our souls. Please find us.'

Her mouth was not moving, but her words found me. 'You haven't much time. Find Elias. He will know what to do.'

As she moved closer to me, terror paralysed me. I couldn't move. I wasn't prepared for this. I couldn't understand how she was talking to me in a memory.

'Your word is Lia –,'she said.

The door creaked behind me and snatched her attention. In that second, the ground caved beneath me and a black hole gaped open. It sucked me into it, and I began swimming through a fog, feeling the coldness against my skin again.

My pulse filled my ears. It was the only thing I could hear as I sank deeper and deeper, splaying my arms out to try and grab onto something – anything. The chill suddenly subsided, and I could feel my back was now pressing against something hard. A smell of damp soil filled my nostrils. My eyelids involuntary and rapidly flickered.

'Kate? Is she breathing?' Finn's panicked voice reverberated in my head.

My heart burst loudly as my eyes pinned open. I inhaled a huge lung full of air and could see five fretful faces hovering over me.

CHAPTER 24

'Give her some space!' Finn barked, growling at everyone who crowded over me. He cupped my face with his hands and found my eyes. His genuine concern for my wellbeing warmed me, and I couldn't help but react with half a smile.

That grin seemed to annoy him, and his stony face snapped away, as did his hands. He stood up from his crouch and huffed.

Zoe was at my side in an instant, and squatted by me, ushering a bottle of water in my hand. She rolled her eyes at Finn disapprovingly.

'Is there any need to be like that?' she snarled up at him. 'She connected, so stop panicking.'

Finn glared at her and crossed his arms. Was he a little overprotective? I didn't mind - I liked it. It showed he cared.

I flicked off the cap of the bottle and downed the cool water, gulping as it quenched my thirst and soothed my parched throat. Zoe's eyes swept back to me, and she placed a hand tentatively on my arm. I was lathered and felt clammy and irritable with everyone watching over me.

'Talk to me, what happened?' she prompted quizzically.

'Could I have a minute?' I asked apologetically. I needed room to breathe.

Finn and Zoe stayed close, while the others dispersed.

'I saw my parents,' I finally exhaled, bringing my knees up to my chest. 'And I saw Raven and me. We were kids, in what must have been our old home.'

'Was it like a real memory?' she asked.

'I don't know for sure what it was. Either I had time-travelled, or it was a flashback – or even just a dream, but it seemed to be a real enough. The kids were drawing and colouring, while my mother was teaching them the Ovarkin language. The next thing I knew, she was freaking out over a strange picture Raven had drawn. She sent them both upstairs to bed, leaving us alone. Then she turned to *me,* looked at *me* face-to-face, and asked *me* for help?'

Finn's head swung forward. He kicked the dirt with his feet and distanced himself from us.

'What do you know, Finn?' Zoe asked, dubious of his movements.

He nervously scratched his head, and double glanced Dom and Darcie.

He must have caught Dom's attention and waved him over. Dom trudged over to us and glanced expectantly at Finn.

'Do you remember those crazy pictures Raven used to draw, Dom?' asked Finn, rubbing his nose. Dom twisted his face in thought raking through his memory, then finally had a light bulb moment and nodded.

'You mean the weird eye thing?' Dom asked to which Finn nodded.

'Yes, she used to draw an eye,' Dom explained. 'The eye had two pupils inside of it, one larger than the other. She first started drawing them when she was around three years old, and nobody could understand how a kid of that age could even conjure up an image like that. It freaked everybody out, especially your parents.'

Dom kept tight-lipped and rolled on his heels awkwardly. Was it too much of a vague memory for him, or was he holding something back? Perhaps we'd have gotten more out of Darcie.

'It means something,' Zoe insisted, rising to her feet. 'Especially if you went directly back to that memory. And what did your mother say?'

'Did you get your word?' asked Dom, hovering behind Zoe.

'Lia. I think it's Lia.'

'Love?' Zoe's eyes flashed impressed. 'Of all the words.'

'She told me to free their souls. That Jorah has them incarcerated in some way.'

'He does,' Dom confirmed matter-of-factly. 'As we told you yesterday, he has them in some sort of container or instrument and it's locked away somewhere at Glentree.'

'She told me to find Elias,' I continued. 'That he would know what to do.'

'Elias?' Dom gasped. 'Elias Wade? Your grandfather?'

'My what?' I quizzed.

My mouth gaped open in disbelief. I had grandparents as well as parents that I never knew existed.

How many more shocks was I going to get?

I was surprised my brain hadn't exploded from the information overload the past few days.

'How am I supposed to find him? Is he even alive?' I asked.

'Oh, he's still alive,' Dom answered with a proud look on his face. 'Not that he involves himself with the Chambers or with other Vents now.'

'He moved to the middle of nowhere years ago,' Finn added, 'But, I probably know a way to seek him out.'

'Then we shouldn't waste any time, Finn. We only have until tomorrow night.'

*****

The morning came with a pounding, monstrous hangover that had me flinching into my pillow. I had no idea what time I'd gone to bed, how I got to the bed or what I did before bed, but I knew by the waves of nausea gurgling in my stomach, the swaying room, the dehydration and the coating on my tongue, that I'd had way too many drinks.

I inhaled the odour of the pillows, and it had a distinctive aroma of hair gel, body wash and Finn.

I sat up way too fast and felt the pressure build-up in my swollen brain, forcing me to sink back into my pillow.

I winced and pinched the space between my eyes and nose.

And then it hit me as I struggled to adjust to the morning light. I wasn't even in my bed. I was in *his*. I gasped loudly and patted down my body to check I was still clothed.

I was clothed, but they weren't *my* clothes.

I was wearing an oversized white t-shirt and a pair of shorts that I presumed belonged to him. The drunk fear floored me entirely.

Did we? How did I get end up here? Someone, please fill in the missing blanks - I've got several hours of my life unaccountable!

I couldn't penetrate the thick black fog that clouded the events from the night before.

I tilted my head slowly to my right, and Finn was there, zonked out, right beside me with his back turned. I mouthed the words, *holy shit,* and shrank in shame.

He was shirtless, and I had no idea if he was naked from the waist down or not. I mean, surely, I'd have been able to recall if we had sex or not?

I sighed a little too loudly, which caused him to stir – but only for a moment – and then he nestled back into his pillow again.

I took the opportunity to scope his bedroom and get an idea of what he was about. A bedroom says a lot about a person's character.

For a start, the room was small and cluttered. It's pale blue-white walls covered with Marvel posters from *Iron Man, The Avengers* and *Thor*. I pulled a face, probing a dusty old display cabinet full of collector action figures from timeless sci-fi films. I combed through the chest of draws that had socks and underwear spilling from them. A collection of boxed trainers left in untidy piles against the back wall next to an open wardrobe that had a jumble of clothes spilling from it. And as you'd see in any typical man's bedroom, in a corner he had a dusty TV with an obligatory X-box shoved beneath it.

It was like being inside a teenagers dark and dingy man cave. I stared down at him and sighed. His broad, muscular back was smooth and rose, up and down in rhythm to his slow breathing.

He had bed hair, a chaotic bouffant of thick ash-blonde thick with dried gel.
I forgave him for the state of his room and smiled down at him.

He stirred again, and rolled over onto his side, draping his sculpted tattooed arms over my stomach. He was a lazily ruffled, beguiling sight if I ever saw one. His eyes slowly opened, squinting to adapt to the morning light.

'Morning,' I mumbled shyly.

He groaned and rolled on to his back, exposing his gym-sculpted torso, that instantly pooled my mouth with saliva. There was only a light coating of blonde hair over his prominent chest, but every muscle was defined, right down to his pelvic bones.

'Morning,' he purred back in a gruff voice.

His eyes finally widened, and an ocean of their blueness arrested me.

'So,' I dragged my eyes away from him, sat up and fidgeted with my hands, 'I need a cigarette, a gallon of water, painkillers and a drip. In no particular order.'
A suffocated laugh came from his mouth buried into the pillow.

He lifted his head. 'I'm not surprised, you lightweight,' he teased hoarsely. 'I had to tackle the third bottle of wine from you, throw you over my shoulders and slog you home.'

The blood rushed to my head with dread.

'And on the way, you spewed all down my back.'

'Shit!' I squirmed humiliated. I shielded my face with my hands and wanted to crawl into a hole and die. 'No?'

His mouth curved upwards. 'Yep. It got lairy, really quick. The others will be suffering today too. That's for sure. '

I clasped my hands around my neck, struggling to swallow. My throat felt like sandpaper.

'In all seriousness, though, like I am actually about to die.'

I could feel that all familiar gut-churning sickness begin to jerk around my chest, and I bolted upright, throwing my hands over my mouth.

Immediately, Finn placed a warm hand on my back, and I heard him yawn out the word *echotis*, and within a glimmer of a second, a heat rushed up my spine, my nausea completely dissolved, my head cleared, my eyes renewed to their full sockets, and I felt like I had strength again. My head aimed at him in astonishment. Just like that, he'd cured my hangover.

'You're welcome,' he smirked broodingly. He stretched and propped himself up on his arm and focalised his attention on me.

'What?' I asked shrugging.

'If you're so thirsty, why don't you give your new-found powers a go.'

I frowned at him.

'You have psychokinesis,' he explained, 'There's a fridge full of bottled drinks down in the bar.'

We exchanged a flirtatious glance. This would be the test to see if my powers were unlocked. I had my unique word and now was time to put it to the test. I sat up straight, crossed my knees and closed my eyes.

'Wait,' Finn bleated, quickly adjusting his position so that he sat upright. 'Why don't you try it on something in my room first? I don't need an entire fridge full of broken glass downstairs.'

'Right,' I nodded, surveying the room to pick an item.

'There,' he said, pointing towards a black cap hooked on a peg on the back of an open wardrobe door. 'Now close your eyes and visualise yourself holding that cap. In your head, say your word.'

I nodded again and squeezed my eyes shut. I breathed in deeply and slowly exhaled. I pictured the black cap and willed it to unhook from off the peg. I held out my hand in anticipation and focused hard. I tried to imagine it gliding across the room, towards my hand.

I strained to concentrate on the word *Lia*, inside my head.

Nothing happened.

I slouched and opened my eyes to see it was still very much on the peg.

'You're not concentrating hard enough, Kate,' he complained.

'Well, this is second nature to you. I haven't done this before!' I argued back, becoming frustrated.

'So, learn. Focus your mind. You have an extra capability of the brain now. Think of it as though you have electronic impulses sending signals through your nerves to your muscles. Your hand is a magnet. You want that hat in your hand. Use some mental force and will it to happen.'

I huffed, agitated and arched my back, readying myself.

I can do this. I have the power within me. Move the damned hat.
This time, I kept my eyes open and fixated directly on the hat. I blocked out everything else surrounding it and used all my energy, beckoning it to move.
Move dammit, just move.
Lia! Lia!
The hat began to shake.
Concentrate.

I felt a pulsing from my fingertips and a physical sensation rush throughout my body. It was like a surge of electricity, sparking through my veins. I felt my teeth grind together rigidly, and my eyes were nearly popping out of their sockets. I controlled the muscles inside of me, using them like magnets to propel the object to me.

Suddenly, the hat snapped off the hook and zipped towards me at near lightning speed. I barely saw the blur of black as it whipped by my face with a gust of air and I heard an almighty clonk off Finn's head.

'Ouch!' he yelled, shooting his hands up to his forehead. The hat dropped into his lap, and I sat utterly dumbfounded.

'God!' I yelped. 'I'm so sorry!'
He sniffed, checking his hands for any signs of blood, but he was fine. He burst out laughing and grabbed me by my shoulders.

'You did it! It worked!'
Adrenaline surged through me.

'But it hit your head.'

'Trial and error,' he breezed, brushing it off. 'Now try again, this time with a bottle of water from the fridge downstairs.'

I exhaled again, bracing myself.

I repeated the same mental exercise as I had moments earlier, attuning my power.

I visualised the water bottle in the fridge, opening the door and summoning to myself.

'Lia,' my head whispered, sticking out my hand. I applied my mind to its focal point, and within a second, the hard plastic slapped into my hand with the sound of sloshing liquid.

'Holy shit!' I laughed in complete amazement. 'Oh, fuck, it works, it works. I have powers. They work!'

'Show off,' Finn chimed, nudging me.

'Show off? Maybe I'll use my audible inundation on you next. Annihilate your thoughts with unspeakable volumes of music, mainly shit music.'

'Is that right?' he flirted, cocking an eyebrow.

'Try me.'

He grabbed me and playfully rolled me on to my back, shifting his weight over me and pinned my hands behind my head.

I was so aware of the morning breath that I quickly tilted my head away from his face. I knew it would smell like something was decomposing in my mouth. I kept my head turned away, expelling my breath elsewhere.

'I can overpower you; do you want me to get physical? I can be violent.' I warned, as he tried and failed to get me to look at him.

'No way, you maniac,' he cackled. 'But I'll take a kiss.'

I shook my head, breathing away from him. 'You might want to take a rain check on that kiss. I need to get back to the cottage, shower, get changed and clean my teeth.'

'Yeah you do,' he laughed, before playfully prodding me. He rolled away from me and sighed. 'I'm joking. I don't give a shit if you have morning breath.'

'I do.'

'Then we can do other things?' He flashed me a devious smile indicating what he wanted was not just a kiss, but I had to resist him. I'd been so distracted by Finn that I'd failed to call to mind that it was probably *doomsday*. At some point that afternoon, I was going to be taken to Glentree Manor, where I'd have to face my deranged sister. My stomach began to churn with dread, and I pushed him off me.

'What did I do?' he asked, startled.

'Nothing. I'm just freaking out about later.'

'Nothing's going to happen. We're all going to teleport there together. Savannah will talk to Jorah, as will her parents. And if anyone can see something bad happening, it's Darcie. She's been keeping a close eye on their Chamber, through her glass mirror, all week.'

'And in the meantime, is someone going to try and find my grandfather?'

He blinked at me. 'Are they?' I repeated.

'Of course,' he nodded, but his tone wasn't genuine. 'But they might not need to. Sav will lie to Jorah. How could Jorah question the legitimacy of what she knows when she supposedly knows all.'

'Except for the other Chambers powers?'

He scoffed and glanced away. 'She knows. She's careful not to write it down.'

229

'My mother told me distinctly to find Elias. I think we should listen to what she said.'

'Look, leave it to us, we have a plan in place. We know what we're doing.'

'Finn,' I swung my legs off the bed and began to fret. 'You can't get involved in this.'

'It's going to be fine, freckles. Go back to the cottage and get yourself ready. I'll meet you there in an hour or so, OK?'

I narrowly missed a run-in with his parents as he snuck me downstairs and out of the back door. They'd only just surfaced, and I could hear them mooching about in the kitchen.

'Here are your clothes from last night,' he said, handing me a plastic bag. He kissed me on the cheek and lingered in the doorway. I frowned at the bag first, and then at him.

'Did we … you know?'
He flashed his brows at me, surprised that I'd asked.

'In your state? Not a chance. What do you take me for? Oh, by the way, you might want to stop and get some cream for that carpet burn on your arse cheek. That position was wild.'

I rolled my eyes at him and shoved him playfully as he broke about laughing, clearly finding himself hilarious.

'We spooned. That's all we did,' he reassured me, before leaning in to kiss my forehead.

He watched me leave, waiting until I was rounding the corner, where I gave him a little wave and blew him a kiss. It must have only been little after 8 a.m. Few people were out and about as that damned sun was growing in the sky again.

I felt hot. I grabbed the scruff of the jumper, the one that I'd borrowed from Finn, and began to waft it furiously to create some air that would cool me down. I wanted to get home quickly but had only got a few steps on the cobbles when I heard my name barked out from behind me.

I turned to see a torrent of fiery red hair powering towards me. She was wearing a white dress and sandals, and her face burnt with acid rage.

'Beck?'

What did she want with me so early in the morning? Why was she lingering around the pub? Why was she there?

She looked like shit. Usually, there wasn't a hair out of place with that girl. But that morning she appeared as rough as a bulldog licking piss off nettles. Her eyes were raw and blotchy from a blatant episode of tears. She hadn't a scrap of make-up on, and it appeared as though a brush hadn't been through her hair yet. She kept swinging her head from me to the pub and then back again. I realised then what beef she had with me.

'I thought I told you to stay away from him,' she snapped, gritting her teeth. She started to well up with a crazed stare on her face.

It was way too early to have a catfight in the middle of a quiet street, and I didn't have the energy for her meltdown. Instead, I backed away from her and sighed.

'Not now, Beck,' I moaned, flashing my attention back towards the pub.

'It's me he wants, not you!' she spat, snivelling. 'You're nothing to him, just another easy notch on his bedpost?'

'Right,' I scoffed, turning away from her and dismissing her with a hand wave. 'Whatever, Beck. I can't be bothered with your drama this morning. Stop stalking me.'

'He *will* be with me, Kate. Mark my words.'

'OK, great, whatever. I'm excited for you,' I huffed, turning down the main street. 'You know, you ought to seek some professional help for your disorder. It's bordering on harassment now.'

I heard her suffocate a scream behind me, and as her footsteps leapt and thumped behind me, she screeched out a word that rang in my ear and stunned me.

'Azorza!'

I suddenly became disorientated. The world swayed around me, uneven and rocked me sickeningly off-balance. I staggered on my heels, trying to shake off the confoundment that rattled my senses. It was like a whistling teakettle, and when I refocussed out of the hazy, blurred vision that had centred me only moments ago, I couldn't make sense of these new surroundings. Extreme panic set in as I stared down a cobbled street, one I'd never seen before.
Where am I?

There were shops and houses that I'd never seen before. As my senses sharpened, I couldn't recognise anything. Where was Jack?
The last I could recall was waving him off to work, making a fuss of our tabby cat who meowed for food around my feet, and then – this? I became scared. Did I have a severe brain abnormality that had driven me to a random place?

'Kate?' I heard the stern voice behind me call out. I turned to see a pretty redhead wearing a white dress and flipflops step towards me. She had huge vivid blue eyes and a smattering of freckles across her face. She studied me for several seconds, almost tiptoeing towards me cautiously.

'Yes?' I asked, sizing her up and down. 'How do you know my name?'
Her lips thinned alarmed.

'We need to get you to the hospital. You're really not OK.'

'What?' I snapped, raising my hands to clasp the sharp pain that began soaring through my head. I hissed out through my teeth as it tore into me. 'Who are you?'

'Jesus! How hard did you hit your head?' she laughed in a friendly, giggly tone. 'Remember, we had a collision just outside of this village. Your car got towed away.'

'What?'

I had no recollection of any of it. I couldn't think straight. My brain was blocked by some unknown force that hurt as I tried in vain to recall it. I wondered if I was suffering from a bout of vertigo as I couldn't stand still, and it felt like the earth was tilting on its axis.

'Dear me, you really shouldn't have refused the advice from the paramedics to go to A&E and be checked out.'
Paramedics? What paramedics? Who is this girl, and what is she talking about? Where the hell am I?

It felt weird. 'I need to call my fiancé.'

'Jack?' she asked, turning to hold my gaze. My head was still spinning. 'You already did, silly. That's the first thing you did.'

'We crashed … in our cars?'

'Yeah, well it was no more than a small bump, but your car is worse off than mine – and so was your head. Look, the hospital is less than a mile away, the garage said they'll have your car ready within a few hours, and I'm worried you have amnesia or concussion. Please let me at least drive you to the hospital to get you checked over, or I'll never be able to rest easy.'

I stared into her kindly blue eyes as she pleaded with me, still so flummoxed as to where I was and how I got there, but I knew in myself I wasn't OK. I probably did need to see a doctor. I nodded in agreement, and she offered out her arm. I interlocked my arm with hers, and she directed me up a cobbled street, towards a small car park.

'Where are we?'

She shrugged. 'God knows, some small village out in the sticks. I don't know about this area. My car's just over there.'

We approached a small red car, a Kia I think it was, and she unlocked it, walking me around to the passenger side. I carefully slid in and noticed an air freshener dangling from the review mirror and instantly inhaled its strong strawberry aroma. She slammed my car door shut, ran around and jumped into the driver's seat. I leaned my weary head back into the headrest. It was heavy, mentally fuddled and dazed.

'What's your name again?' I asked, wincing through my mangled senses.

She leaned forward and glanced into the rear-view mirror, completely changing her posture. She licked the pad of her thumb, cleaned off the smeared black eyeliner, adjusted her hair and then shot me a spiteful glare.

'Oh, I think you know my name.'
I frowned and looked at the rear-view mirror. I momentarily caught sight of a black shadow move quickly behind me.

'It's Beck, and I'm your worst nightmare, bitch,' she growled.

Before I had the chance to react, a hand lunged aggressively from behind my seat and pinned a cloth over my nose and mouth. I tried to wriggle my head free of the grip, but the hand fastened tightly over my face, securing it in place. All I could smell was a strong chemical that burned into my flared nostrils. I couldn't breathe, and inhaled air through my mouth with difficulty, the whole time kicking out with my feet and arms, with muffled screams seeping through the cloth muzzle. *What's happening? Who is doing this? Am I being kidnapped? Oh, god, someone fucking help me!*
And then, my body went into a spasm and collapsed. I lost the battle and consciousness and dropped into a black hole of nothingness, out cold.

CHAPTER 25

A piercing screech enflamed my ears and stunned my senses as I came around.

My eyes were open, but I couldn't focus my line of sight. My vision was blurred. Images jerked like a pixelating TV with a limited signal. My head lolled back against a cushioned headrest, rolling from side to side, but I couldn't feel the lower part of my body.

'Beck,' a voice barked in the distance. 'Come.'

A cascading of heels clinked loudly against a hard floor, and I could barely make out her red hair. I strained to remember what had happened and where I was. I couldn't move from the shoulder's down. My body felt as though it had been superglued to the chair, impossible to move an inch.

'You did well,' Raven's voice sharpened, and my memory quickly nudged me into reality.

The last thing I could remember was leaving Finn's place and getting stalled by Beck outside the pub. I couldn't remember the actual altercation before everything developed into total mental confusion. What had she done to me?

'I'll write you a cheque for half the amount now because you're forever in my debt, and you will do as I say as and when I demand it. Comprende?'

'Yes,' I heard Beck whisper in a strangely submissive tone.

Slowly, my focus aligned with my surroundings. My heart sank, now contained inside Raven's nest. Panicking, I tried to move, but paralysis halted me. Only my eyes and head could rotate as I tried to register the situation.

My chair was positioned at the end of a massive mahogany table, served by high-back antique-looking chairs with crushed red velvet fabric covering. My eyes scanned around the table and I could see that I was now a captive within the De Wyche's Chamber.

All the assembled around the table were dressed in funeral-black, wearing vampish clothes and hideously loud mystic jewellery. The table itself laid out for a banquet. It was something straight from the Victorian era. A statement chandelier with glimmering glass droplets hung directly above the table, illuminating the red runner that ran the length of the table. It highlighted the tall, silver candelabras, weirdly shaped chalices, and three steel cloche domes.

At first glance, the room looked as though it was one of several main ground floor rooms in what was effectively a grand Stately House. It had a soaring ceiling and an area so vast that voices echoed. Prestigious artwork adorned the shimmering gold walls; a grand piano sat next to a high-arched window that draped with matching gold velvet curtains. Dimmed wall lights framed the walls and there were huge wooden, double doors that sealed the room.

This place could only be Glentree Manor. From what information I'd gathered about the house, it certainly had all the hallmarks, including a creepy atmosphere. It also carried a smell of stagnancy and staleness.

I travelled the faces which surrounded the table. Each of them appeared hostile and unwelcoming. Raven sat at the opposite end of the table from me. She was in the process of tearing off a cheque from its book and offering it to Beck. Beck's entire demeanour had changed while in Raven's presence. She was avoiding eye-contact, recoiling into herself, chewing the inside of her cheek and shifting her feet involuntarily. She seemed jumpy, on edge and nervous.

'Use it wisely. I've helped to build a designer empire with this business. Don't make a mockery of my generosity. I want to see results, Beck.'

'Thank you,' Beck swallowed, lingering by her side.

Are they designers? I sneered at the thought of it. *Designers of what?*

Raven's head rolled down the table, and she jerked in surprise to see me sneering towards her. Her eyes hooded and glared with heated wrath.

'And look who's finally joined us,' she said coldly, raising her chin. 'Welcome back to reality, *Antonia.*'

'Um, Raven?' Beck winced, inching slowly away from her, clutching the cheque in front of her chest. Raven inhaled and narrowed her eyes to black slits, visibly irritated.

'You said that if I did this that you would, you know?'

'A cheque isn't good enough for you?' Raven bit, without turning her head.

'It's just that Finn and …'

'Finn!' she exploded viciously, slamming her fist down on the table. 'Is that all you care about? Finn fucking Moon. What is it with all of you idiots lusting after him? He's a nobody with no use of his powers. Your taste in men is exasperating!'

My own heart swelled at the sound of his name. I had so many questions. What did she want with Finn? Did he know I was gone? Would he come looking for me? How long until Darcie would see me through her black mirror? Would the Chamber come to my assistance?

She began massaging her temples and sighed heavily. 'You are single-handily obsessed with that boy, and I'm tired of hearing your petulant whine. It's exhausting.'

Beck lowered her head, sulking.

'I will discuss the dark binding with my mother, Tabitha, later. Do not infuriate me any more than you already have, Beck. Now go and make yourself presentable for tonight, you look a plight.'

Beck scuttled quickly out of the room, avoiding eye-contact with everyone, including me. So much for being the *hard girl*, eh! She'd handed me over for personal gain. And, what did dark binding entail? What were they going to do with him?

Her eyes drifted back to my face and narrowed to a squint. She registered me flinching and the inability to move, which tugged the corners of her mouth to a demonic grin.

'I had Seth paralyse you from the neck down. It's only a precaution until I'm confident that you will behave and cooperate with me.'

My eyes flicked to the blonde, gaunt-looking, square-jawed male aside of me. His washed-out, blue eyes lingered on me like reflecting pools of curiosity, but they squeezed shut and his head lowered to the table. I felt as though he were trying to tell me something with his demeanour, but his expression had disappeared before I had the chance to identify it.

'I presume you understand why you're here?' she asked with calm authority.

I couldn't comprehend that I once shared the same womb with it. She had my face, but she wore it differently. She enhanced her eyes with dark make-up and covered her freckles with a foundation that didn't match her natural skin tone. Her eyes were the shadows of her dark, toxic soul, and hollows of madness. Her cheeks weren't as plump as mine. Instead, they furrowed with scorn lines where she could not smile naturally. Malice had ravaged her face. She adopted a permanent sinister snarl that made her appear ugly.

'You think that I hold the missing abilities that you need to absorb before Jorah croaks it,' I bit, snapping like ice.
Her lips twitched and pressed into a thin line, and she straightened her back, lifting what seemed an exact match of the Endocardium Book of Shadows. She lingered on my reaction. *Has Beck stolen the book from our Chamber? She was such a snake. No-one would ever forgive her for this crime.*

'So, I see,' she mused, beginning to flick through its pages. 'I don't know where to start. A Chamber which breaks the Mitral law by visiting an alternative Melladonna, without the knowledge or permission of the Mitral or his council. A Chamber that plots against their bloodlines to compromise the sacrifice. A Chamber that has agreed to lie to the Mitral so that I won't make beneficiary?' She tutted down at the pages shaking her head. 'I'm disappointed, truly disappointed.'

'They're trying to protect *me*!' I barked, fearing the worst for my friends.

'Protect you?' she laughed heartlessly. 'Antonia, they were the ones that dragged you into this mess. They brought you to Oaks End. It could have all ended so peacefully. I was all set to come and absorb your powers in London and, if you survived it, I would have had Beck erase your memory, and you could have gone back to your quiet miserable life none the wiser.'
So that's what Beck did to me? She messed with my memory to kidnap me and deliver me to Glentree.

'And they're not protecting you. They're protecting themselves,' she insisted.

'That's not true,' I cried out. My feet began to tingle, and my toes were able to move. The minute my body was released, I'd make a run for it. I had to warn them.

'They're going to die for their crimes.'

'And what about *your* crimes?'

'My crimes?' Amusement curled her lips.

'Using your powers against another Chamber Vent. You're breaking the Chamber law.'
She stared right at me with raised eyebrows and parted lips, before slouching and running her hands through her hair.

'Oh, dear. You are a sad little creature, Antonia.'

'My name is Kate!' I roared angrily.

'Kate,' she scoffed, 'I don't care what you call yourself or how much of a legitimate Chamber member you think you are. Your exposure to our world is a mere four days, but I've lived in our world my entire life. I've earned my place in this family, in this bloodline. You think that you can just take the initiation and suddenly have a role within the Chamber? You're misguided. I am the only one who can be the next Mitral. Jorah has chosen me because he trusts me. He will entrust me to manage all the Chambers, to inherit his powers, his empire, his home and his fortune. He doesn't care about one pitiful little Chamber in Oaks End. He cares that I find those powers and absorb them.'

She exhaled and caught her breath.

'As for the Chambers law? We *are* the law. Rules don't apply to the De Wyche's. The rules were set in place to enslave the weaker Chambers into our submission.'

My legs began to twitch, and I could feel the paralysis begin to wear off. I stared around the table to see the De Wyche's' heads bowed, all except two of them; a gap-toothed pixie and a skinny bloke with horrific mohawk hair. They both sat up straight, fixated in awe on her every movement, hanging on her every word. Did the other siblings fear her? She had a voice that forced them to listen. Had she always been like that? They were direct descendants from Jorah and Tabitha. *She wasn't.*

How could they allow her to control the family in that way?

'Why weren't the abilities documented if the Chamber was so hellbent on keeping them in the bloodline?' I questioned, decidedly being cocky with her.

She scowled at me and folded her arms.

'Excuse me?'

'The fact that somebody went to great lengths to keep the beholder of those powers out of the Mitral Book screams volumes about the state of your Chamber. Someone doesn't trust them to fall into your hands.'

'Well, until we can get to the bottom of that, Akenna has been detained until further notice,' she bragged. 'If found guilty, he will hang in the morning, along with your so-called friends.'

My thoughts turned to the conversation I had with Sophia about Akenna. She already suspected that they'd turn on him. Was she right about them knowing it was Athena who had the powers too? I wanted to challenge her.

'And if he isn't? What are you going to do? Torture everyone until someone comes clean. How do you know the abilities are only in one person? They might be spread out through various people. That's a lot of Vents to consume against a ticking clock.'

The sensation was slowly starting to return up my legs, as far as my waist. I had to be smart about my movements.

'Jorah wasn't the rightful heir and consider what happened to him. A decrepit old man, dying years before his time because of his delusions of grandeur and greed. He was a fraud to the ancestors, and you will be too.'

She did not erupt like I thought she might. Instead, she sank back into her seat, her smoggy grey eyes

turned black as coal and filled with a crazed fury, so intense I thought her head might explode.
The veins pulsed in her neck as she ground her teeth and tensed her facial muscles.

'Nova.' She calmly turned to her sister, who wore waxen white contact lenses. She was a hideous goth that offended my sight. White as a glacier, she wore black eye shadow, black winged eyeliner and eyebrows like thin checkmarks. Plum lipstick matted her lips that had several piercings. Her haunting appearance was like something summoned from your worst nightmare; something you'd conjure up for a Halloween masquerade.

'Set up the screen. I think it's time my sister here learned a thing or two about our Chamber.'

'Is that necessary?' Seth interrupted from the side of me.

A low hiss escaped her mouth as she scorned him with a wrathful scowl. I felt the tension between them as he tutted and slumped back in his chair, shaking his head in disagreement.
Was he going against her? He seemed agitated, breathing heavily and restless.

Nova pulled out what appeared to be a small black remote-control unit and pressed a button, directing it towards the blank canvas wall to the right of us. A large screen began to descend from the ceiling. It was like those in-built home cinemas you'd find mainly in affluent celebrity homes.

'I have eyes and ears in the Endocardium Chamber,' Raven boasted, craning her neck to view the screen. 'I have a lot of people on my payroll. Policeman, doctors, nurses, council members, MPs, in fact, a lot of people in high places. Money can make folk do anything – including sniffing out a *rat*.'

'I thought Beck was your mole?'

'She is,' she agreed, 'But blood's thicker than Roman's dick.'

I blinked at her confused as her eyes grazed past me, and she snidely smiled as someone clonked into the room out of my line of sight.

'Did you bring it?' she asked someone behind me. Who was it? Who else had betrayed our Chamber?

'Yes,' she answered. Immediately the hairs on my back stood on end.

Ellis?

She glided past me and headed straight towards Raven. My blood ran cold at the knowledge of her betrayal. *How could she?*

'Sweet, adorable, gorgeous, Ellis. Who would have thought?' Raven gloated, laughing.

'Ellis?' I cried out, in disbelief.

Her tousled brown hair dangled effortlessly down her body in waves, and she stood tall with her hands behind her back, standing at Raven's side after handing her a small, crumpled piece of paper.

Ellis flicked her hair behind her shoulders and shot me a look of proud ignorance. She wasn't the same Ellis I'd recently grown to know. She somehow was stood alertly, her facial expressions were harder and more devious, and she appeared unphased by Raven's malice, easing into her company.

'How could you?' I cried breathlessly.

She shrugged a shoulder with a nonchalance that knocked me sick, before stalking the table to stop behind one of the male Vents. His inky black hair touched below his collar, and he had conflict festering beneath the surface of his hard face. She leaned over him, wrapping her arms around his neck and dipped her lips to his cheek and lightly kissed him. He pulled out his chair and yanked her down into his lap, taking her mouth with passion.

'What can I say?' she laughed poisonously, 'Oscar gets me.'

I winced away.

What about the poor Roman?

She was married to him!

She was having an affair with Oscar De Wyche the entire time. That would kill Roman and could crumble the Endocardium as a whole Chamber.

I suddenly linked what had unravelled in Zoe's house and Fae Woods to Ellis. My gut instinct was right. She *had* used her powers on me.

'My god! It was you. You used your powers on me.'

She smirked knowingly and nodded.

'Indeed, that was me. Revenge for meddling with my sister's boyfriend. She asked me to do that, and quite frankly, I think that it was my best illusion yet.'

I ground my teeth with deep-seated loathing and glared furiously at her.

Raven lifted the piece of paper and frowned down the table at me.

'This is Athena Moon's handwriting and, correct me if I'm wrong, but these are instructions on how to find Elias Wade.'

What?

I don't know anything about any instructions.

What is she talking about?

I looked away from her, squeezing my nails into the palm of my hands as the feeling came back. My pulse accelerated, and my body bristled, sensing an overpowering danger that I hadn't felt until then, even when paralysed.

'Why would you need to contact Elias Wade? Perhaps to reverse a curse?'

They'd sussed it.

There was no hope.

I cringed into the table, and suffered quietly, dreading the disposition of my friends.

'The only reason they'd need to reverse the curse would be so that the Moon's family could put up a fight,' she explained, unveiling what I already knew. 'And the only reason they'd put up a fight would be if I suspected that one of them was the person harbouring the abilities.'

I felt a wave of nausea overpower me and managed to lift an arm and press it over my stomach.

'Nova,' she barked, giving her a nod to play the images on the screen.

Immediately, a bloodied body image filled the screen, lying lifeless in a ditch with its head caved in. I was ill-prepared for such a sight.

'Let's start with our Isaac,' she began, entwining her hands in front of her. 'That body you see there was a thug who tried to rob him at knifepoint. Isaac can throw balls of electrically charged energy that will kill you. That thug's head exploded when Isaac had no choice but to defend himself. Next,' she ordered.

The image that followed was of another body, slumped against a tree with blood spilling out of its mouth.

'Cora also had a similar problem with a pervert who tried to grope her in the park. She can shoot deadly beams of kinetic energy at people, which also have devastating effects.'

She nodded towards Nova again, and the image flicked to two girls laying in adjoining hospital beds. Both showed horrific first-degree burns on their faces, their skin melted and peeling away from the bone.

'Ah, Jett,' she nodded proudly. 'These two bullying bitches tormented my sister for months in school. The name-calling, pushing and shoving, the online abuse – it isn't something we can tolerate. Jett can generate corrosive acid. I think those images speak for themselves. Not so pretty, now, are we girls?'

I grimaced away from the screen unable to view the images further and, as I turned my head towards Seth, it seemed he couldn't either. His head bowed, and he fumbled with a chalice in his hands.

'Oh, this one made even me feel a little nauseous,' she callously mocked. 'Some girl tried to have a fight with Nova in the carpark roof of a department store. Wasn't it over a broken parking ticket machine or something?'

Nova nodded smugly.

'Well, she certainly got her ticket off the face of this planet. Mind control. Love it. Any witnesses said they saw the girl appear to be in a trance-like state, walk towards a balcony, and calmly jump to her death from the top floor. Her body exploded upon impact. Horrific scene. Blood and guts everywhere. That one was rather brutal. It made the TV news who alleged that it was drug induced. Nice.'

'Stop,' I winced, unable to watch or hear anymore.

Raven exhaled and gave the nod to Nova to turn off the images.

'Do you see a pattern here, Antonia?'

'Kate!' I barked back.

She smirked at me.

'Between us, we can paralyse you. We can control your mind, steal your senses, leave you temporarily deaf and blind. We can project your worst fears into your mind, create illusions, and you won't know what's a mirage and what's reality. Oscar can hypnotise people and manipulate teleportation. Jett can control and manipulate the air and wind. And me? Well ...'

She paused, staring down the table at me. Suddenly, her voice was behind me and beckoned me back to the screen. My head snapped to find a clone of herself there.

'I can create multi-versions of myself at the same time,' she said eventually.

My mouth hit the table, darting from one Raven to the other. How was that possible? She'd cloned herself.

'Or, I can mimic anyone else,' she boasted, cocking her head the side, 'I can be the worried best friend calling you.' I felt faint. It was Zoe's voice she was using. 'Or the besotted boyfriend.'

And Finn's.

My body collapsed and heaved. How was she doing this? Finn and Zoe's voices were coming from her mouth.

'I can even project my voice into a place without being present.'

She cleared her throat and began to cackle, resuming her cold, formal tone. 'I could place you in the woods and have them searching for you for hours, following your cry for help. Except you'll be here, watching me be appointed next Mitral.'

'You're sick!' I yelled, finally released back into my mobile body. I lunged forward. 'You're delusional. A narcissistic, mentally unhinged, feral piece of shit.'

'And you're a nobody who should have been slaughtered along-side our parents.'
Her icy, vicious words sliced through my gut and knocked me sick. How could she say such a thing?

'There's no room for weakness in our Chambers. We have abilities only the rest of the Chambers could dream of. While the likes of Zoe are making lotions with dried herbs or they're chanting for luck and knowledge, we are the ones making the difference out there. We are cleansing our lands of the despots and criminals.'

'You *are* the fucking criminals!' I screamed. Everyone's head snapped towards me, shocked by my heated anger.

'No, we save taxpayers and governments a lot of money by killing off the criminals instead of having them locked up in our already overcrowded prisons. We're doing the world a service, and you should be a lot more grateful.'
I couldn't believe the words I was hearing.
Raven sickened me.
Ellis sickened me, as they all did. I couldn't trust anyone.

'I won't tell you another thing,' I sobbed quietly. 'You've been brainwashed. We are good people, and our parents were good people.'
She snarled at me and rolled her eyes, leaning over to pour wine into her chalice.

'No, our mother was a temptress whore and our father a parasite. He was a leech who sponged off this family for years, and he couldn't even do the one thing that many others would have killed to have the opportunity to do. He was so weak that he couldn't handle the responsibility of being the Mitral. That's such an embarrassment. Jorah was the strong one. He took me in and raised me like one of his own. He offered me solace when my anger and confusion were at an all-time high. I'm proud to call him my father and I will make him proud when I inherit his legacy.'

'If you do,' I spat.

'Oh, I will,' she laughed hoarsely before yanking the dome cloche up and revealing the contents beneath it. Hot bile jerked from my stomach and stung the back of my throat as I convulsed and heaved.

A severed head sat in a pool of pink blood, with its mouth agape, eyes gouged out, and blood smeared across its face. The head swam in potatoes and vegetables and had me delirious with nausea.

I whimpered, but the sound that burst from my mouth was what I could only describe as a strangled gurgle of terror.

'Raven, enough!' Seth raged, stamping his fist down on the table. 'Ellis, stop.'

Everyone suddenly broke out in a chorus of laughter, and as I opened my eyes, I saw the head replaced with a roast chicken. Raven stood with a carving knife over it and began to slice into it.

'Nice job, Ellis,' she snorted. 'Seth, since you don't want to play our illusion games and you're so bothered about my sister, why don't you take her to her room. Subdue her and make sure she doesn't escape.'

Seth's head lolled, and he huffed aggressively. I became wobbly on my knees as I stood.

'Antonia,' she smirked, slicing up the meat. 'Although that was an illusion, don't make me turn it into reality. I'd strongly advise you to behave yourself. I would hate to have to decapitate your mother's lovely little head.'

I winced away from her, turning my body repulsed.

'Now let's eat and prepare ourselves for tonight. It's going to be quite a show.'

CHAPTER 26

He navigated me along the plush red carpets down a never-ending corridor that was dimly lit with wall lights. I must have counted at least eight rooms as I shadowed him, all of which had the doors closed that triggered me to wonder what mysteries lurked behind them.

My eyes explored the ceilings where crystal chandeliers adorned, and expensive looking artwork embellished the walls. As I moved along the hallway, one piece arrested my attention.

I swallowed hard, recalling the story that Dom had told me about Raven and her weird drawings of an eye. Exactly as he'd described it, the painting detailed an eye with two distinctively round pupils inside of it. One pupil was painted grey, the other, a dark grass green. Was this the image that I too had witnessed her drawing as a child? An image that upset our parents so much?

I stopped and craned my neck at it, frowning

at the bizarreness of it. Seth paused aside of me and nodded towards it.

'Raven painted that,' he explained with a stone face. I remained silent, but I couldn't help but question why she'd draw one eye with two pupils inside. It didn't make any sense.

'What does it mean?' I asked curiously.
He flexed his cheeks and began to chew the inside of his mouth.

'She repeatedly sees a girl in her dreams with this eye deficiency. One is perfectly normal, but the other has two irises' in it. It freaks me out.'

I glanced at Seth, dubious of him. He didn't seem to be like the others. He didn't show any signs of malice or aggression. He wasn't being icy with me or even forceful. Instead, he seemed as though he was supressing some internal pain. I couldn't quite figure him out.

My attention skimmed passed him, down another corridor. I was intrigued to know how many rooms the house had, and how many possible *escape routes* there were. Perhaps, if I kept him talking long enough, I could stall him, clock an exit and make a run for it.

'So how many rooms does this place have, then?' I asked.

'Thirty-six,' he answered, itching the end of his nose. 'That's without counting the cellars and storerooms down below. This way,' he instructed, walking along another corridor.

'I heard Raven mention designers?' I said, assessing every crevasse of the doors we passed. Seth's head snapped back, and he began to angle his head in every direction before his eyes lowered to the ground again.

'Keep walking and don't raise attention to us,' he mumbled lowly. I hesitated with my steps, but he nudged me to keep moving forward. 'We're being followed, so just let me do all the talking and don't ask anything you shouldn't.'

What? What did he mean? Why was he telling me that?
I wanted to turn my head, but he nudged me again, as if to advise me against it.

'We are interior designers, all of us. The De Wyche's Designs. It's our family business and a world-wide successful one at that,' he said loudly with cool confidence. 'Great care has been taken to upgrade and modernise this house, but we have to retain the listed architectural features. It was built back in the 17th century… Jacobean…originally a lot larger than this.'

I kept my eyes forward, listening to his tone change. He sounded more like a Stately Home tour guide than an enemy who was about to detain me. We walked on, for what seemed like forever, and this was only the ground floor.

'How big is this place?'

'Big.' He glanced behind him again and I wondered who was following us.

'It was built to house aristocratic families. It has a lot of formal rooms, impressive architecture and huge landscape gardens. As far as I'm aware, it's always been the ancestral home of my bloodline.'

'Insightful,' I yawned sarcastically.

He turned to a room, and quickly pushed the old oak door open, ushering me into a vast space that snatched my breath away. The room was literally the size of Zoe's whole ground floor area, decorated in silver wallpaper, thick, grey carpets, an old marble dressing table, huge wardrobes and a four-poster bed sweeping with silk fabric.

He closed the door behind us, clicked it shut and immediately began to act shifty. I scrutinised him as he dipped down low to check under the bed. He got to his feet and opened the wardrobes, checking inside for any signs of intrusion.

'What are you doing?' I asked, completely puzzled by his actions.

He marched over towards the high-arched windows and peered out from behind its closed curtains, before snapping around to face me. His long finger pressed to his lip, and he slowly backed up against the wall, pointing that same finger up towards the ceiling. My eyes rolled cautiously, and I soon spied a security camera attached to the wall, blinking red, presumably monitoring our every move.

'The system doesn't have sound, but don't draw attention to it. I told them I'd sweep the room and restrain you to the bed. Jorah has asked Raven to take you to his quarters when they've finished dinner. He's called for all four Chamber Vents to convene here as soon as possible. The ceremony will take place, here, *tonight*.'

He strode over to me and pushed me aggressively back on the bed. From his pocket he removed paracord bracelets and then grabbed my arms. He attached the bracelets to my wrists and the bedpost and grimaced at me.

'I have to do this, I'm sorry. They can't suspect anything.'

'Suspect what?

'That I'm helping you,' he said, securing my other

wrist.

'Wait. I don't understand. You're one of *them*!'

'Only through blood. Do you honestly think I want your sister controlling the rest of my life as the new Mitral? Creating further madness and mayhem. I want peace as much as the other Chambers do, but she will never allow it. You don't know what she's capable of. You don't know what she plans to do. The ongoing fibrillation will continue, for possibly years.'

'Why are you telling me this?' I whispered, eyeing him cautiously. 'How do I know I can trust you?'

'The same way as I want to trust *you* not to rat me out.' He finished binding me and stood up at the base of the bed.

'I've been feeding your Chamber information for months.'

'Through whom?' I asked, gobsmacked.

'Savannah,' he huffed, burning his eyes down at me, waiting for the penny to drop.

'Wait!' My mouth hit the floor. 'You mean, you and Savannah are …?'
He smiled but dropped his expression quickly.

'Does anyone know about you two?'
He thinned his lips and shook his head.

'No. Not that I'm aware of. We've been meeting up in private for a while now. Keeping things on the hush. We've always been careful not to get caught with each other. If Raven knew, you could only imagine what she'd do.'
I waited, letting it digest. I'd never have guessed Savannah would be sleeping with one of the De Wyche brothers. Not in a million years.

'What's going to happen, Seth?'

He began to pace the room.

'It's an ambush. The Chambers are summoned here tonight, but they're using you as bait. They know Finn will come with his family if he thinks you're in any type of danger, and it's his family they want.'

'They know it's Athena?' I yelped, searching his face for answers.

He nodded, defeatedly.

'Akenna had no choice but to tell them. They all turned on him. He was backed into a corner. The way they behaved towards him makes me ashamed to be related to them.' He pulled out a stool from under the dresser and flopped down on it, facing away from the camera. 'Raven's going to force Athena up to the altar, and she's going to demand that you absorb Athena's powers and gift them to Raven.'

I collapsed with a sigh, dreading it.

'Jorah will allow them to use violence against you if you don't cooperate. There's no getting out of it, Kate. But what they don't know is, you can *pretend* to absorb those powers.'

'What do you mean, pretend?'

'If you absorb the powers and gift them to her, they won't take effect for several hours. They'll think it's legitimate. However, there's a specific word you can use to sabotage the citing, a sort of mind flare that disenables the absorption, if you will.'

I blinked at him, confused.

'Elias is the only one who knows what that word is.'

'My grandfather? Why's he the only one that knows the word?'

He shrugged one shoulder and chewed his bottom lip.

'I don't know. Akenna was the one that told me. Elias was also close to Apollo, so he knows how to reverse the curse too.'

'How do we get to him?' I asked in panic.
Seth sniffed and abruptly stood from the stool and began to pace again.

'I sent Akenna to go find him. They don't know he's gone, and we don't have much time. I'm trying my best to stall them, but if Akenna doesn't get back in time, I don't know what we're going to do.'
He sighed, whilst I lay on my back grimacing up at him, fearing the worst.

'Now listen,' he huffed. 'Akenna is the one who has to perform the sacrifice. They're forcing him to do it, he has no choice. It's not how it used to be where the beneficiary would take a blade and stab the Mitral through the heart. It's done differently now, with electricity and needles…a process that stops the heart in three stages.'

'Like a lethal injection?'

'Sort of. When it's completed, some of his blood is then drained into a chalice and is then poured into a capsule for Raven to drink. The capsule Akenna is going to give Raven is going to be a placebo. It's not going to be Jorah's blood. It's going to be mine.'
It became clear that he'd carefully thought all of this through, to the very last detail. But how long had he been planning this for?

'Raven's plan is this; once Jorah is dead, she's then going to ambush the Chambers and she's going to order my brothers, sisters and cousins to annihilate everyone. She wants everyone dead. She's going to take everyone's powers into herself.'

'Then we have to fight!' I insisted, outraged by her plan.

'And we will,' he assured, before starting off towards the door. 'Someone's coming.'

He moved closer to the base of the bed and frowned down at me.

'I have to pretend to paralyse you again. Can you do some acting for me now?'

I nodded up at him.

'Seth?'

He glanced down at me.

'What if he doesn't find Elias in time? Or he doesn't get back for the sacrifice?'

His gaze dropped regrettably to the floor.

'Then god help our souls.'

CHAPTER 27

The door suddenly burst open, and I lay rigid as Raven stomped through the room and over towards the bed. She stared down over me with a broad smirk, and then flashed a look of satisfaction towards Seth.

'We'll take her to father's room,' she commanded, 'but after she's seen him, I think you and I ought to have a little chat, don't you?'

Shit! What did she know? Had she sussed Seth? Had someone been listening outside of the room?

The way she spoke sounded so presuming and abrupt. I suddenly became worried for him.

Seth cleared his throat and exhaled loudly, before cutting me loose and yanking me from the bed.

'Not paralysed then?' she stated, eyeballing me up and down, before glaring towards Seth. He dropped his head and shoved me forward.

I was practically frog-marched down corridors that seemed to bring us into another wing of the house.

'Wait here!' she insisted, arriving at a room which had two large brown doors. Isaac stood off to one side, seemingly on guard. I figured it must have been their fathers' room.

Raven immediately disappeared through the doors with Seth and I was left outside, held again by the arm, under the scrutiny of Isaac. He wasn't pleasing on the eyes. Aside from his ridiculous purple mohawk and winged tattoos on either side of his face and down his neck, his ears were plugged with huge round black studs, in holes big enough to slide a finger through. He was gangly and bony, with acne skin and a constant unchanging look of smarminess affixed on his face. He donned a ripped grey t-shirt that exposed his tattooed chest which consisted of snakes and skulls, and he wore skinny leather jeans and shiny black Doc Martin boots. I roamed his body, grimacing.

Raven wasn't away long before she opened the door, reached out to me and pulled me inside. The stench of trapped sweaty moisture offended me the minute I stepped inside the room. It smelled like no one had opened a window in months, and god only knew what was festering in there. The room was unnervingly darkened. The arid air was so foul that I had to raise my t-shirt over my nose just to breathe comfortably.

We turned a dark corner, where dimmed wall lights illuminated a large space. I couldn't make out the details of the room or the colours of the walls, all I could make out was the King-size bed in the centre of the room, an old man hunched over with his back against the headboard, and a slender, middle-aged woman sitting on a chair beside him.

Raven yanked me closer towards the bed, and I noticed an oxygen concentrator machine was set up next to him. Wires and tubes were flowing out of it linked to his dishevelled looking body.

'Come closer,' he ordered in a voice that was guttural and rasping, like he'd spent years abusing it with cigarettes, drugs and alcohol.
A bedside lamp suddenly flicked on and I lurched back.

The man was barely a corpse. A constant exhale escaped his mouth, like he was clinging to life. He was skeletal, with cream coloured, silk pyjamas hanging from his bones. His face was sunken with sagging leather white skin flopping into his wrinkled neck. In his nose was a nasal cannula; a long plastic tube inserted into his nostrils, that wrapped around the ears to secure it in place. There was a constant hiss coming from the tube. I wanted to rip the tube from the oxygen-tank and drain his life force, but behind his beady eyes, I saw no life – just an endless depth of ink. His rotten, black teeth were snapped and broken, and his thin lips were dry and cracked.
I cringed as I ogled at him. *So, this is the monster who murdered my parents?*

'Antonia,' he whispered, raspy and breathless.

My eyes darted to the woman sitting aside of him. She was slightly hunched, in a modest pale pink shirt dress that fell to her ankles. Her ginger-tinted hair was loose, thin and long and draped past her shapeless thin figure with split, bushy ends. She had a lived-in face. Her shoulder blades were prominent and protruding, which made her appear willowy and brittle. I guessed that she was Tabitha, his wife.

Raven stood next to me, in a stance that showed that she was overly protective of the couple. His arthritic veiny hands were unnaturally twisted, and he struggled to lift his shaking finger and point it towards me.

'You live,' he gasped.

'Not for long,' Raven scoffed with a chuckle under her breath.

Tabitha leant forward and slapped Raven's hand so hard, I felt the sting radiate through my own. *Did I just feel her pain?*

'You will not speak of such horrors. Your sister lives, and she will continue to live,' she ordered, emotionally-charged and defensive. Her eyes examined me, as if she were in awe.

'Such beauty,' she sniffed, holding back tears.

'Your sister shall live,' Jorah echoed, managing to nod. 'I forbid you to harm her.'

What? He doesn't want to harm me. Wasn't he going to kill me when I was five years old, along with my parents?

I felt the bitterness radiate from Raven's skin and witnessed her fingers curl into a fist. He went to speak but resisted. Instead, he strained to search for his wife to talk on his behalf.

'Antonia,' she started, rising to her feet slowly. She was smaller than I was, and I felt if I blew hard enough, she'd fall over. It was unbelievable to me, that these people ruled all the Chambers. 'Jorah won't make it past the morning. He's too weak. We have to go ahead with the sacrifice tonight.'

I glanced at past her focused on him, debating whether to launch my attack right then.

'You can have a great life here at Glentree, Antonia,' she continued. 'You can live here; you can work for our business. I can make you a lot of money and I can offer you a very comfortable life. All I need you to do is cooperate tonight. Absorb the powers, and gift them to Raven.'

I wanted to argue. I wanted to tell them to go fuck themselves, but I couldn't. I had to be clever, compliant and act like the dutiful sister who was going to help the transition sail smoothly. After all, they were still in power and anything could change at any time, so I had to build their trust. I bit down on my temptations and nodded to them.

'The Chambers have been called here, Raven. Find Akenna and have him prepare the ceremonial room. Send your cousins to help.'

Find Akenna?

The blood drained from my face. He needed more time.

'Antonia,' said Jorah, breathing with difficulty. I found it hard to look at him. 'I'm sorry we didn't meet sooner.'

I swallowed my detest for him and forced a half-smile.

'Me too,' I finally uttered limply.

I'd have killed you a lot sooner, you peace of deteriorating shit.

His haggard face sagged away from us, and he stared blankly off into the distance.

'Leave us. Let him rest,' Tabitha fussed. 'Send for your siblings and cousins before the ceremony. He wants to say his final goodbyes.'

'Raven,' Jorah whispered a little louder. 'A word…please.'

Raven nodded, briefly showing some pain in her face. She ripped her eyes away from him and nodded at Seth. He grabbed my arm again and ushered me out of the room. I was happy to be released from there, inhaling and gulping clean air in the hall.

'I'll take her back to her room,' Seth said, reaching out to grab my arm again.

'Ah-ah!' Isaac barked. 'I'll do it. You have some explaining to do. Wait here for Raven.'

My insides dropped and we both exchanged a worried glance towards one another. They knew. They had to. Why else would she need to pull him for such an intense chat? Isaac grabbed me by the arm aggressively and yanked me away from Seth and pushed me forward down the corridor.

'Move!' he ordered. 'It's nearly go-time.'

CHAPTER 28

'The Chambers are arriving now,' Isaac gushed, peering out of the window through the curtains. He rubbed his hands together and snidely laughed while bound to the bed. He'd forced me to change into a red robe, which he said everyone would be wearing for the sacrificial ceremony.

'Can I see them?' I asked, yearning to see the outside world and catch a glimpse of the Chamber Vents. I longed to see Zoe or Finn, so I'd feel a lot safer knowing they had arrived.

He turned his head and shot me a warning glare.

'Did I say you could talk?' he challenged.

I wanted to slap that stupid mohawk right off his ugly head.

'I'm hardly going to escape, am I?' I rolled my eyes while thrusting my bound hands towards him. He ignored me and continued to stare out of the window, moving on to his tiptoes to get a better view. 'It's nearly showtime. I can't wait.'

'You can't wait?' I cocked my head up, astounded by what I was hearing. 'Jesus. If I weren't mistaken, I'd think you were almost happy that your father is about to die.'

His heels slammed against the floor, and he rotated on the spot, ripping the curtains closed again.

'Shut your fucking mouth,' he cautioned bitterly.

I refused to recoil away from him. He didn't threaten me.

'I'm not scared of you,' I bit. 'You're nothing but an upper-class, ignorant shit. You don't even care that your father's going to die. Look at you; you couldn't be happier.'

Suddenly, he lunged at me full of fury, raised the back of his hand and brought it down with such a force across my face that the power behind it knocked me sick.

My face blazed, and my cheek began to sting. No one had ever hit me in my life. I felt blood begin to trickle from my nose and bottom lip, and I could taste the copper-like liquid in my mouth. I winced through the pain and somehow managed to wipe my mouth against the sleeve of the robe.

'Does hitting women make you feel strong?' I mocked snidely. 'Because that was limp, you skinny little bastard. Those shit tattoos don't make you tough, you know.'

He gritted his teeth and rolled his knuckles into fists. I was beginning to get under his skin – deliberately.

'You know what, just you keep antagonising me. Keep on running your mouth. It'll taste all that sweeter tonight when I watch them slaughter you. I may have the honour do it myself.'

'You believe that, don't you?' I laughed. 'Jorah has forbidden it. He warned Raven that no harm should come to me.' His eyes narrowed into dark pebbles. 'I don't think he'll take too kindly to this, do you?' I told him, raising an eyebrow.

'You think I care what that decrepit old bastard says? To us, he's already dead and buried. The minute his heart stops beating, you're going to die, and I can't wait to sit back and watch it happen.'
I squinted at him, smiling smugly.
I liked antagonising him. I wanted him to wonder why I was smiling.

'Get that grin off your face before I slap it off you,' he yelled.
As he was about to charge at me again, the door burst open, and Nova filled the space.

'Isaac!' she barked. 'We need to change. It's nearly time.'
He sneered over me, flaring his nostrils. 'What about her?'

'There's a camera up there, and she's bound,' she tutted. 'Do the math.'
He continued to scowl at me as he inched away, cocking his head briefly up at the camera that was pointed directly at me. When they had left the room, I felt helpless and completely abandoned. Where was Seth? I needed to know what was happening.

As my head fell forward, I heard a scraping and creaking of something above me. I glanced up in the direction of the camera, to see it slowly panning around. The red light flickered intermittently and then suddenly, the entire thing came away from the wall and crashed to the floor. Broken pieces of glass and black plastic scattered the floor, immediately followed by a pixelated image forming at the door. I was startled but then delighted to see Sophia fully appear before me, dressed in the same type of red robe as I had on. She rushed over to me and pulled out some tissues from a box which lay on the bedside table.

'What did he do to your face?' she fussed, dabbing the wipes against my bottom lip.
I grimaced and hissed out as it stung.

'Sorry,' she cringed, dabbing it with a gentler touch. Sophia had Finn's eyes. They were perfectly symmetrical and were under thick sculpted brown eyebrows. Her eyes caressed my face as she tended to my nose and lip. She pulled herself up and sat next to me on the bed.

'I haven't much time. They're already seating everyone in the ceremonial room.'

'Is Finn here?' I asked, searching her face.
She nodded at me with a crinkled brow and a concerned look.

'He's going out of his mind with worry. When he heard that you were gone, he ran straight to his car and sped off in search for you. We had to go after him and stop him. We have to be cautious about this.'

'Ellis is in on it, Sophia.'
She clamped her eyes shut and exhaled vehemently.

'She disappeared during the night, well after your ritual. When Roman woke up this morning, all her stuff was gone. Darcie located her through the black mirror. We all thought they kidnapped her at first, but then he found a note saying that she'd left, and it explained all. He's a mess.'

'How did we not know?' I quizzed. 'My intuition let

me down badly.'

'She had us all fooled, Kate. She created an illusion around herself as all sweetness and light when she was anything but. She was a conniving, heartless traitor.'

'And Seth? You know he's been seeing Savannah?' I asked.

'She told us this morning after you were gone.' She sighed and glanced away from me. 'I don't know what she was thinking, but if I know Savannah, I know that she can read people. She told us everything. He was originally going to run away from Glentree and try to do a disappearing act, start somewhere anew. But then this happened last minute. He called her straight away.' Her head jutted towards the door, and she stood up. 'They're coming back!'

'We can trust him, right?' I persisted.

'Right now, Kate, I don't know who we can trust. Do what they say, let us take care of the rest.' She faded right in front of me, cloaking herself at the precise moment.

Nova and Isaac burst through the door again dressed in golden hooded robes. They both stared down at the broken camera and then threw an accusatory glare my way.

I shrugged innocently. 'It broke?'

I was untied, taken out the room and pulled along the corridor again, this time with more urgency. I felt fine until we arrived at the ceremonial room door, suddenly overcome with an aggressive sense of danger. It hit me like a ton of bricks. I couldn't move.

'What are you doing?' Nova croaked, attempting to yank me from my spot. Something was off: very off. I felt the gruelling sensation of oncoming doom and

271

like everything was inevitably going to end in bloodshed. Nausea winded me.

'I can't,' I fretted, shaking my head, trying to turn away.

'Stop struggling!' yelled Nova, glaring at me with her vicious white eyes. The girl's appearance terrified me. 'Don't make me hurt you,' she shrieked. 'I don't care if I drag you in half-dead, you *will* do this right now.'

Isaac stepped behind me and pushed me forcibly forward as Nova dug her huge fake black nails into my skin.

My legs uncontrollably shook as I got closer to a door. When they opened it, my heart plummeted to my feet. The room was as big as a theatre. The lights dimmed. All but candles illuminated the focal point in the centre of the room. There appeared to be an altar, that resembled a pathology gurney, taking centre stage. My eyes prized around two semi-encircles of pews situated at both ends of the altar. It reminded me of a colosseum, except the rows weren't stacked.

A sea of red-robed Chamber Vents sat in their allotted pews, hoods up and with their attention fixed on the altar. There was the aroma of burning incense, so rich it caught in my throat.

I was accompanied to the opposite bank of pews, where the De Wyche's Chamber Vents sat. They were all robed in gold, distinct from all the other Chambers garb. I assumed they had done this as a statement to show their superiority over the other Chambers. They positioned themselves closer to the altar than the other Chambers were. Nova pushed me towards the front pew and shoved me down next to Cora, wedging me in the middle. I stood out by a mile by wearing red robes. Their eyes were all over me, scrutinising and questioning. There was no sign of Seth. Where was he? He'd gone to talk with Raven. Had something terrible happened?

The low hum of men's voices started to chorus around the room, so deep and penetrating that the sound vibrated through my body. It was akin to monk's chanting *Om*, eerily but also demonically.

I searched their faces, manically trying to cypher some recognition and was horrified to see Beck and Gia Carmichael, sitting within the Myocardium Chamber group. I hated her. She had used her powers and kidnapped me. And there she sat with her newly found family, in the front row, ignorant to her chamber sat just a distance away in the pews. By now, other Chambers must have known she'd been a traitor, and surely, they'd have turned on her and Gia - or were they merely biding their time?

I slid my gaze over to the opposite pews, and my heart sank as I found Zoe's face. Her hazel eyes fixed into mine with so much emotion on her face that I felt instantly like my home was within arm's reach. She mouthed something at me before dipping her head and shielding her face. I couldn't work it out, but as I turned my head, I could see Nova visibly flaring her teeth in Zoe's direction.

I could see everybody else, the Bloom's – except for Ellis – Quinn, Athena and Sophia, but I couldn't see Finn. Where was he? My focus suddenly fell onto a small man dressed in a black floor-length robe, tied with a red sash, emerging from a door directly opposite to the one I'd entered. I couldn't see his face for his hood was hiding it, but behind him walked Raven, dressed in a white robe with a red sash. Tabitha followed them, pushing Jorah along in a wheelchair, while another hooded figure brought up the rear wheeling along a small electric machine.

My heart drummed as it neared the time.

The creepy humming continued as the mysterious hooded man led them to the altar, where Tabitha positioned Jorah next to the gurney. The other hooded man reached down under the altar cloth, seemingly connecting the machine to a plug socket. He turned on the device, nodded at Tabitha and moved a little way off.

Tabitha sat on a chair next to her husband, and Raven stood with her head bowed behind them. The small, hunched over, old man, stepped forward to the centre of the circle and pulled down his hood. His head had wisps of grey tufts in the centre, but the rest of it was bald.

'My congregation,' his voice bellowed around the room. The deep throttle resonated with everyone and silenced the humming. 'We gather this night, for the sacrifice of our Mitral, Jorah De Wyche of the Elder Blood.'

The room fell still.

'Where is Seth?' I whispered to Cora, still searching around to find him.

'Please don't talk to me,' she shushed, leaning her body away from me.

'Seal the doors!' the old man demanded. 'I, Akenna, the council of the De Wyche's, will conduct this sacrifice.'

My lips parted in shock.

274

That's Akenna?
What happened?

Something didn't add up. Seth sent Akenna to find my grandfather. If Akenna was back, conducting the sacrifice, that had to mean that the De Wyche's hadn't noticed he'd even left. Maybe Seth wasn't in trouble after all? So, where was he? Where was my grandfather? Was he found in time? Did he reverse the curse? My eyes shifted over everyone's faces with so many questions running one hundred miles per hour through my mind.

I fidgeted in my seat, searching out for Finn again. The less I saw of him, the more I worried.

'All rise,' ordered Akenna. The pews creaked as the congregation all rose.

Akenna's eyes shifted towards our group and waved a hand to usher someone over. Isaac, Oscar and a middle-aged man who I'd never seen in my life before strolled to the altar. They lifted Jorah from his chair and carefully laid him out on the table.
Tabitha let out a sob and patted her eyes with a tissue. The three then returned to their pews.

He appeared too weak and brittle to be a Mitral. He was fast approaching the end of his natural life, and it was hard to digest that he was only fifty-five years old. *The consequences of greed.*
The black-hooded cloaked man approached the altar again and wired Jorah up to the machine. I could see him carefully insert a needle into his arm. Once he finished, he again slipped away.

There were three lights on the machine illuminating a yellow light, a red light and a green light.

'Chambers of the Elder Blood, tonight we bid

farewell to our Mitral and announce a successor in his name.'

Akenna stepped aside of Jorah and placed a hand on his forehead.

'Jorah De Wyche, my friend, tonight we shall offer you to Ovar, and the Goddess Horb of the Elder World. We return you to your ancestors, to your grandfather, Lourdes, your grandmother, Cleo, and all the others who blessed us before you. Let them accompany you into the afterlife and live forever in our blood.'

He shifted slowly towards the altar, lit two red candles and waved his hand over a golden chalice.

'Tonight, you have assigned your daughter, Raven De Wyche, to inherit your blood and your abilities. Into this vessel, we will drain the blood from your heart, and she will consume it in your name.'

My stomach churned at the very thought of it.

'We thank you for leading the bloodline Chambers. We thank you for your guidance, love and knowledge.'

And, no doubt, for slaughtering so many innocent people.

Why was he giving thanks to this devil? I wanted them to kill him and be done with it, and the world would be cleansed of one less heinous animal.

'Tabitha De Wyche, please stand.'

She rose to her feet, dabbing her eyes with a tissue.

'Tabitha, you have served well alongside your husband. You too, have watched over the Chambers. You have adopted Raven into the Glentree temple as your own. Do you consent to the God's consuming your child? Do you accept her as the Mitral?'

'I do,' Tabitha nodded, turning to throw a sweet smile towards Raven.

'Praise the Mitral!' shouted Akenna.

'Prez Alho Alsam!' the congregation chanted.

Kate! Kate!

A voice filled my head with a smooth velvet rasp that mushed my insides instantly.

Finn?

Did I hear that, right?

Don't draw attention to yourself. I need you to listen to me carefully.

How was he doing that? Could anyone else hear him? I grazed the faces of the Vents, but I still couldn't locate him. How was he connecting with me?

'Do you agree to retire from all mortal affairs as High Priestess of the Elder Blood and hand your duties down to Raven De Wyche?' Akenna continued.

'I do.'

Akenna turned back to face the congregation. 'Athena Moon, please approach the altar.'

Kate! When you read the incantation, repeat these words in your mind after every sentence. Retro Acheego. Do you understand? Nod once if you understand.

I gulped, beginning to get anxious about what was to come next. I nodded.

Good.

Remember. Retro Acheego.

Only say these words in your head.

I glanced down at the palms of my hands, and they were glistening with sweat. If only I could see his face, I'd feel better.

I'm not going to let anything bad happen to you, Kate. I'm right here with you.

It was when I saw Athena rise from her pew that I saw those blue sapphires glistening towards me. Finn was sitting right behind her, his eyes pinned on me. My heart swelled, and I let out a nervous gasp.

Calm down. Breathe. You're OK.

I swallowed hard and nodded at him before tracking Athena's slow and nervy approach to the altar.

'Vents of the Chambers, this night Athena Moon will have her abilities stripped and absorbed from her.' The gathered all began to murmur and throw looks of concern at one another.

'Quiet!' Akenna roared, his voice echoing like thunder around the room. 'She has the unique powers that belonged to Lourdes De Wyche. We must keep these powers in the bloodline, through the Mitral. On behalf of Raven, her sister …,' he turned his body in my direction and extended out his hand, '… Antonia Wade will absorb these powers and gift them to her.' A chorus of gasps and whimpers rippled around the room. A rumble of voices quickly erupted. Did the other Vents not know I existed? Did they not know I was back?

'I thought Antonia Wade was dead?' a male voice called out from the crowd.

'Where has she been?' another cried out. 'Has she been kept here at Glentree all along?'

'Quiet!' Akenna raged again, silencing the room. 'I will address your questions later. Tonight, is not about Antonia Wade. Tonight, is about Jorah's blood sacrifice.' The heat from every pair of eyes in the room burnt my skin. I dipped my head and pulled the hood further down my forehead. I was never one for attention, and the idea that I had all four Chambers eyes on me, made me want to dig a hole and bury myself in it.

'Antonia,' Akenna spoke loudly, 'Please approach the altar.'

My hands began to shake. When I stood up, I couldn't get a grip, my knees buckled and had to clutch on to the pew.

I'm with you. Breathe, Finn whispered in my head.

I used him as my focal point when I arrived at the altar. I couldn't make out most of the faces, for it was too dark, but I knew his face. I knew his eyes – and that's all the comfort I needed at that moment.

'Athena, please stand in front of Antonia.'

Athena's eyes cried into mine, glossy with water, her face void of hope. I wanted to tell her how sorry I was. I wanted her to know that I didn't rat her in it. Did she know?

Akenna handed me a piece of paper and nodded at me.

'Read the following mantra. You will then absorb the powers and grant them to your sister.'

The sheet of paper shook uncontrollably in my hand. I was never a public speaker – the thought of a room painfully quiet - while ears homed in on my broken voice, made me feel violently sick.

I cleared my throat, stared down at the words that were out of focus on the page, and took a deep breath.

'By the powers of the mantra belonging to Goddess Hanan, keeper of abilities that stew in the orb of renewal, I bless thee.' *Retro Acheego.*

I lifted my head towards Akenna, who gave me a nod of encouragement.

'The assault of focused will comes with the ejection of the moon. I take thee powers, and I strip you bare, the rain of fire, the mind of flare.' *Retro Acheego.*

As I lifted my eyes from the page I saw a single tear roll down Athena's face. Did she think I was absorbing her powers? Was she already mourning the passing of them?

'The carnage of senses, I rip from thee, my mystic whip, shall set them free.' *Retro Acheego.*

'The ring of shadows, the acid rage, the savagery of minds, the intellects page. I take from thee; I take from thee.' *Retro Acheego.*

Raven's sigh of relief was loud. I turned in time to see her cock a victorious smile. I hated her.

'Very good. Now turn to your sister and repeat the next verse on the page.'

I rotated around and stared into the eyes of the devil. The ferocious look of evil glinted from one eye to the other as she curled one side of her lip up triumphantly.

I wanted her to suffer. I wanted to see the devastation plummet her to the ground when she learned we were sabotaging her power. I guess, in my flash of visualising her suffering, I must have smiled smugly at her, to which her eyes squinted accusingly, and she flicked her hand up to halt me.

'Wait!' she snapped. 'Why did you look at me like that?'

I frowned at her and shrugged innocently towards Akenna.

'Don't look at him; look at me,' she spat. 'Why did you smile like that?'

Easy Kate, Finn warned. *There's going to be a distraction very soon. Compose yourself.*

I shrugged, helplessly flicking my eyes from Tabitha to Akenna.

'Raven,' Akenna pressed in a warning tone. 'Can we proceed?'

She glared at me with heated suspicion, lingering as she studied my face.

'Go on,' she barked.

I chewed my bottom lip and cleared my throat again, staring down at the page.

'Upon rain of fire and acid bands, I will these powers into your hands. Trusted one, keep them safe, lift your head, and they will grant you faith.'

Retro Acheego. Bitch.

Her head tilted back, and she closed her eyes, inhaling deeply through her nostrils.

What an act, I thought. The powers don't take hold for hours, let alone in a few seconds.

'It is time. Will you all please stand,' Akenna ordered raising his hands.

The rumble of feet and the creaking of the pews vibrated as everyone rose to their feet. I flashed my eyes towards Finn, who nodded at me proudly wearing a supportive expression.

'Jorah De Wyche, are you ready to leave this earth plane and enter the realm of the Elder World?'

Jorah was barely breathing, and his eyes were now closed, his body already resembling a shrivelled corpse. His rasping gasps escaped from his mouth, but no words came out.

Akenna nodded at Tabitha, who sobbed loudly and kissed his forehead.

'Goodbye, my love.'

And good fucking riddance.

Raven followed suit and placed a kiss on his forehead, then stood back wholly devoid of any emotion.

'With great sadness and a heavy heart, we release you, Jorah. The first button will leave you unconscious, the second will stop your heart, and the third will pierce the valve that will drain the blood into this vessel. Raven's lips shall drink your blood and inherit all that you are.'

Akenna's finger hovered over the green button, and then he pressed it. The process was now underway. Tabitha let out a loud sob and sank her face into another tissue, the entire time Raven's face was cleverly disguising her real feeling of happiness.
I stared over his body, thinking what a travesty it was that he wasn't merely brutally stabbed like old traditions would have it - what a thoughtful way for such an animal to die.

'Raven,' Akenna whispered. 'You must recite your mantra.'
She stood over his body, straightened her back and smiled.

'Ovar, jic diservire su. Jic bebois ildas blans dav blans godiv.'
Ovar, I will drink the blood of the divine.

'Jo corla detrav mamio vena. Jo vercommer mami, wicom jic tare jo.'
It will run through my veins. It will consume me as I do it.

'Ovar, jic unam ildas nuv godiv. Ana hod ses honon. Jic vol diservire su mamio cokar, mamio neco, mamio menes ana mamio seanim.'
Ovar, I will be the new divine. And with this honour, I will serve you: my body, my heart, my mind and my soul.
The yellow light flicked, and I had to turn my head away. It was so dramatic, so unnecessary, and I couldn't wait for the distraction to come.

'Acczep mami Ovar, gesub mami ildas privile dov Alho Alsam.'

Accept me, Ovar, grant me the privilege of Mitral.

The double doors at the side of the room clashed open, causing everyone to stir and glance over.

This is it. This must be the distraction.

An old lady, with short black hair framing her face, came charging down the centre of the room towards the altar, aided by a walking stick.

'Wait! You must stop!' she shrieked, wildly waving her stick in the air. 'That is not Akenna! And Athena is not the one.'

My head snapped to Akenna whose entire face was ashen. Tabitha jumped from her seat and protectively blocked Jorah's body.

'Are you out of your mind, Mina? Your son is dying! Show some respect,' she snapped.

Mina? My god, that's Jorah's mother!

'This isn't legal because that's not Akenna!' she spat, 'It's a *glamour* of him.'

What?

'Restrain her!' screamed Raven, her face now bulging with fury. 'We have no time to lose. Now press the damned final button.'

Akenna's hand reached out to push the third and final button. He hesitated, then his fist slammed down on it – everything in the room then suddenly froze.

It was like the entire room had immediately freeze-framed. People halted in their stances. About to breathe, about to move, about to speak – now on pause.

I heard slow footsteps coming out of the darkness of the room towards me. A tiny, hunched figure came into view, concealed in a dark green hooded robe that made it hard to distinguish its features.

I saw another movement out the corner of my eye and could see Finn rise from his pew.

Finn.

'You have only *three* minutes,' the figure hoarsely called out.

My body sagged in relief as Finn approached me. I lunged at him, not taking in what the man had announced.

CHAPTER 29

Finn swept me up in a bear hug and squeezed me. Everything melted away; my anxiety, my fear, and everyone in the world around us. At that moment, he wrapped me up in his strong arms, and I felt his warmth. I felt safe. I had my human shield who always made me feel like everything was going to be OK. I didn't want him to let go, but he gently eased me down and wrapped his big hands around my face. The warmth thawed me, and I became limp as his lips found mine, and he kissed me hard.

'Are you OK?' he panted, pulling his mouth away from mine.

'Who is that?' I gasped, nodding toward the figure who'd halted in the middle of the aisle.

Before he could answer, the figure's arm raised towards the Endocardium Chamber, and suddenly Danny stood up and searched around him with a dazed look on his face.

'Danny,' Finn called out to him from the altar. 'Be quick. We don't have much time. Only three minutes.' Danny sped from the pews and hurried towards us.

Finn broke away from me and turned to view Jorah's motionless body.

'Help me lift him,' Finn ordered just as Danny arrived. He tucked his hands underneath Jorah's. I watched as Danny mirrored Finn's movement, then he pinned his eyes on me. I quickly pulled out the wires and tubes that were attached to Jorah.

'Thanks,' said Finn. 'You're coming with us.'
I surveyed the room. Raven was still wearing the devil-may-care grin on her frozen face, staring down at her inheritance, who was to be removed right from under her nose. It felt otherworldly to be one of the few people in this room who could move. Even the candle flames were locked in time.

'You must go now,' a voice boomed out from the green-robed figure.

'What about him? Are you leaving him here?' I panicked, pointing towards him.

'I'm sure Elias knows exactly what to do.'
My eyebrows furrowed. 'What? That's *my* grandfather?'

'We haven't got time, Kate, come on, let's go! Hang on to me,' Finn snapped. His voice was commanding. I wrapped my arms around his broad shoulders and held on to him from behind, 'Hold on tight,' he insisted. 'On three -'

Danny counted, 'One, two ...' On three they hoisted Jorah up from the gurney. 'Now close your eyes,' Danny ordered.

I closed mine tightly and immediately there was a slight slap of ice against my skin and a whooshing sound that blared in my ears. It all happened so fast. The air shifted. The warmth of the room turned to an early evening chill of the open air. When I opened my eyes, we were no longer in Glentree Manor. We were standing by a sizable lake that was surrounded by trees. Finn and Danny laid Jorah down on the grass and held their backs as they stood up.

'Dan, you must go back,' Finn warned. 'You need to get as many people out of there and as quickly as possible.'

'Where exactly are we?' I asked, gawking around.

'The house is a little way beyond those Willow trees,' Danny pointed. 'The three minutes is almost up, and I need to get my family.'
He dissolved into thin air, leaving dark wisps of particles.

'Kate, listen to me,' Finn said with urgency, clearly wanting my full attention. The worry behind those eyes startled me. I'd never seen him look so full of apprehension.

'That man you saw, the man who stopped time for us. That was Elias.'

My eyebrows furrowed. 'My grandfather, yes?'

He nodded. 'I have to get to him. He's waiting for me.'

'Why?'

'To reverse the curse,' he huffed.

'But Akenna was supposed to find him and tell him. I thought that's what he'd already done?'
My ears were alerted by thunder in the distance, followed by an echo of a high-pitched scream that rippled around us. We glanced at each other in alarm.

'Who was that?' I gasped, turning in the direction of the scream.

'That wasn't Akenna,' he interrupted, snapping my attention back to him. 'That was Raven glamouring into him. She can duplicate herself and glamour the duplicates into anyone she wants. She detained him this morning. Seth managed to release him, but he never made it past the grounds. He's detained inside the house again.'

A thud aside of us snapped our gaze to see Danny re-appear with Zoe, Savannah and Roman. When Zoe saw me, she stumbled, almost knocking me over as she swung her arms around me.

'Thank god!' she cried, hugging me tightly. 'Raven's gone crazy,' she cried with wild eyes. 'She's ordered her Myocardium Chamber to kill us all.'

Danny disappeared again, not stopping for a moment to catch his breath, getting our Vents away from the Manor.

I glanced at Finn, disturbed.

'Elias can reverse the curse, and I need to get to him now,' he explained. His hand entwined around mine and raised the bare skin to his lips. His hot mouth kissed my hand, and pain folded into his face.

'I can't sit and do nothing, Kate, and I won't watch them murder my defenceless family.'

Zoe clutched my free hand and stood tall by my side.

'I'll look after her, Finn. You must hurry.'

His eyes flicked to Zoe, and he swallowed, giving a sharp nod.

'I promise I'll come back for you.' He softly brushed my cheek with his knuckles and then turned, speeding off into the trees, leaving me alone with the few escapees from our Chamber.

'What's happening in there?' I panicked, turning back to Zoe. She shook her head with thinned lips and her face full of anguish.

'You and Jorah were there one minute, and I blinked, and you were gone. In the time it took everyone to register that, Raven screamed out, and ordered her Chamber to kill us all. People started running, and then Danny appeared and grabbed hold of me and, now I'm here.'

I glanced up at the swaying trees and felt another stab of danger puncture through me. If Akenna never made it past the gates, then what happened to Seth? Had he lied to us? Was he still involved in this?

Within another minute, Darcie and another few Chamber Vents appeared before us – though I didn't recognise all their faces.

'Danny,' cried Zoe, rushing up to him before he could again transfer back into the Manor. He had blood splatter across his face and grimaced away from her as she tried to inspect his injury.

'Don't worry, it's not my blood,' he whimpered, throwing off his robe.

He scraped his hands through his hair, quickly kissed her lips and whispered something to her out of my earshot.

'Don't go back,' she pleaded, clinging to his hand.

'Zoe, stop. My dad's still somewhere in there – please let go,' he urged.

He yanked his hand away from Zoe and turned, immediately fading from view again.

'What's happening?' I asked Zoe. Her face drained of colour.

Her hands covered her mouth, eyes bulging in fear. 'They're killing everyone except their own.'

Those who had made it to the lake were surrounding Jorah's body, peering down at him.

'What's going to happen to him?' I asked Darcie, who was comforting Savannah, as any mother would do.

'We're going to incinerate his body and scatter his ashes in the lake.'

'What about his blood?' I queried.

'His blood!' she said, glaring at me. 'His blood is soiled. It's of no use to anyone. Those powers have died with him.' Her concentration wavered, and she was distracted by the black mirror sticking out of her robe pocket.

Another Vent, a petit brunette, burst in front of Zoe and me, her body was shuddering so badly I thought she was going to have a seizure of some kind.

'What did you see, Luna?' asked Zoe, tugging her shoulder round to face us. 'Who is injured?'

Her chin wobbled as her lips curled downward and she burst out into deep sobs.

Zoe pulled her into her chest and cradled her, turning her head to me in fear.

'No!' screamed out Darcie, falling to her knees. She was staring into the black mirror, wailing uncontrollably. 'No! Please Ovar, no!'

Zoe pushed Luna away and scrambled towards Darcie, dropping to her side.

'What? What's happened?' The panic in Zoe's voice resonated through me. I was terrified.

Darcie couldn't speak through her guttural sobs.

'My baby!' she screamed out.

'No?' Zoe gasped, shaking her head. 'He's fine. Danny's fine. He was right here.'

'I'm going back in there,' snapped Roman, barging past the few of us who were safe.

Darcie was inconsolable. Had someone injured him? He wasn't back yet. Zoe paced back and forwards muttering to herself under her breath in a shocked, trance-like state, and I couldn't be a bystander and simply hear the carnage unfolding any longer.

'I'm coming with you,' I yelled, following Roman. He didn't argue. He turned and faced the group who were mostly women. 'Anybody else?' he asked with urgency.

'I'm coming too,' an older man called out.

'Thank you, Bastian,' Roman answered. 'Let's go … now.'

We made a run for it, emerging through the trees on to a long, gravelled central driveway. It was in the middle of a well-tended, landscaped garden, which led directly to the main front entrance of the house.

'Keep up!' he shouted, breaking into a sprint. I had no idea what I was doing. I had no idea how I would fight, or how bad it was in there, who was hurt or how this would end. But I knew of their powers. I knew who to avoid and who I could fight. And I was gunning straight for my sister.

CHAPTER 30

We ran as fast as we could, but I soon had to slow down, clutching at my ribs, as a stitch quickly ripped my sides.

'Wait!' I gasped, heaving over.

The older man was Bastian Moon. I hadn't met him before now, but he was Quinn's brother and Finn's uncle. He stopped alongside me, catching his breath.

'What are we dealing with inside?' he panted, mopping his brow of sweat with the back of his hand.

'Oscar can manipulate teleportation,' I exhaled heavily. 'If we can isolate him, there's a chance Danny can make it.' I glanced at Roman apologetically, but his expression was dangerous, fixed into an avenging gaze.

'And the others?' asked Bastian, sizing up the three-story mansion.

'Jett can generate corrosive acid. She can manipulate the air and wind. Cora and Isaac can throw kinetic waves of energy. Isaac can also manipulate reality, like Ellis, so trust your gut feeling, not only your eyes. Nova is as dangerous as Raven. She can use mind control, rob your senses and use fear amplification against you.'

'I don't give a fuck what powers they have,' growled Roman. 'My brother and my dad are in there, and I'll kill anyone who tries to hurt them.'

'We need to split up,' Bastian suggested. 'I'll go through that main central door. There are other entrances on either wing of the house. Kate, you take a left, Roman take a right. We do what we have to do to get the Vents safely out of there.'

We nodded at each other in agreement. Bastian ripped away from us and sprinted forward, making the first dash to the front of the house. Roman didn't waste any time and sped off in one direction, me in the other.

My heart thudded with fear, as my feet slapped the gravel, running around the side of the house, desperate to uncover an entrance. As I rounded the corner of the building, my chest burnt through exhaustion - that's when I heard the commotion. Violent screams bellowed from within the building, along with men's muffled shouting. A sizeable ground-floor window close to me suddenly smashed outwards with a blue sphere of energy which dispersed as it hit the air. I legged it further along the wing, my heart in my mouth.

I had no plan. I had no idea what damage I could do if any, but I knew that I couldn't just sit by and do nothing. Finally, a large door beckoned me towards it. I pressed down on its handle, and thankfully it opened.

I entered and found myself in a long passageway standing on black and white, chequered marble flooring. Pieces of fine art featured along the whole length of its vibrant red walls. Alabaster head busts of Roman Emperors sat atop large wooden plinths evenly spaced along its way. I wasn't sure which wing of the house I was in, but the echoes of violence from the nearby rooms were incessant.

At both ends of the passageway were wide staircases. I decided to take the closest and ran towards it. My footsteps were quiet as they pounded the plush, carpeted stairs, lunging to take two steps at once. As I made it to the first floor, the pitiful cries sounded even closer. I peered down the hallway that was illuminated by dimmed wall lights and could see that every door along that floor was closed.

A sudden blood-curdling scream from above had me riveted on the spot. I had little time to decide which way to go; up another flight of stairs from where the distressed scream came, or along the hallway to confront the chaos and violence.

The woman's screams above me were unearthly, pained and asphyxiating. I turned back on myself and decided to follow her anguish, taking the final flight of stairs. Her howling was almost deafening as I reached the first door.

Without hesitation, I opened it and slid nervously into a sizeable but sparsely furnished room. The room was L-shaped, and the hysterical whimpering came from an area out of in my line of sight. My heart was hammering. I tiptoed further into the room.
My body began to tremble as I lingered behind a second door, slowly easing my head around to see who was wailing and why?

The sight I witnessed instantly sickened me.

Tabitha was on her knees, kissing the feet of Seth, whose lifeless body was hanging from a noose fastened to a meat hook secured into one of the old beams. I slapped my hand over my mouth and retched, unable to rip my eyes away from his face.

Oh, my god. It's Seth! He's dead!

His face was blue, his bulging eyes looked towards the floor, and his arms hung limply by his side.

Who the fuck did this to him? His flesh and blood? Did this just happen?

My startled whimpers snapped Tabitha's head round and her raw blotchy eyes pierced into me. I jumped back, sure she was going to charge at me or use her powers against me, but instead, she snivelled, her face drenched with tears.

'She killed my boy,' she sobbed. 'Raven killed my boy ... why?'

It was heart-breaking. I couldn't believe that Raven would kill her brother, a sibling who was once allied to her. She *was* capable of anything. She must have known that he was assisting us before the start of the ceremony.

I inched away from her and then quickly scrambled back into the central area of the room. My mind was racing. I gawped around contemplating my next move as I had to move fast. It was then something strange stole my attention.

Sitting on a mantle above a fireplace were two glass orbs that were glowing. Inside them, a multi-coloured mist that continuously swirled in different colours. They glistened in various shades of pink, orange and gold. I was intrigued because they were oddly captivating and drawing me closer to them. A sudden commotion coming from the hallway snapped me back into reality.

I opened the door and cautiously peered down the hallway. I could see that a battle had broken out at the far end of it. I was close to the flight of stairs and dashed towards them.

I flew down both flights of stairs.

As I reached the bottom, my stomach heaved, and hot bile rose to my throat. I stopped in my tracks as I could see that an enormous chandelier had fallen from the ceiling and shattered across the marbled floor. A pair of legs stuck out from beneath it, and blood oozed from the faceless body. Black holes riddled the surrounding walls where energy balls had burnt through them, and the debris of blood-stained shattered glass was all around. I counted at least five bodies strewn lifeless on that cold floor. It appeared as though they'd try to flee from the main ceremonial area and got caught before they could make their escape from the wing.

I grimaced as their limbs lay at awkward angles, their abandoned shells with chest's that could never rise and fall again. For some, their eyes remained open and unseeing; for others, they were gone. Their souls had deserted their bodies, and I hoped they'd been welcomed into the afterlife, now safe from this cruel and vicious world. I heard a cry from further along the passageway.

'Please! No! No!'

I quickly hid behind one of the plinths fortunately situated close-by. It wasn't the best cover, but there was nowhere else to hide. I peered out from behind it and could see a young woman being dragged along the hall by her blonde hair. I didn't recognise the attacker who, with both hands gripping her long locks, certainly seemed to have super strength.

'Let me go!' she screamed. Her assailant stopped and smashed the victims head against the wall. She yelled out as she slumped down in a heap, covering her face with her hands and curling herself into the foetal position.

'Please don't kill me,' she sobbed, pleading with her hands. Her merciless attacker stepped to one side without saying a word and waved over to Cora, indicating that she must finish her dirty work.

'I never liked you, Orabelle,' Cora snarled. 'Now you're going to hang up there,' she said, pointing upwards and in my general direction. I quickly ducked out of view. 'Alongside your mother, father and your siblings when we finally get to them too.'
She backed up in preparation for the killer blow.
The girl whimpered, 'No, no, please, no!'
A flash of blue lightning shot from Cora's hand, hitting the girl directly in the face which exploded on impact and her skull cracked open against the wall. Crimson red began to ooze out, immediately staining her blonde hair.

My hands quivered as they covered my face as this wasn't just executions; this was a genocide of all opposing Chamber Vents. My heart burst open as I focused on one dead face in front of me. His brown hair swept across his face, his legs snapped and deformed, and blood gushed from his nose and mouth. I focussed on him and then had a sudden realisation.
Danny! No! Please, god, not Danny.

I bit into my fist, wanting to scream out. A heart that used to beat with love and laughter was now still, and a mind that used to chirp quick-witted responses to tease his loved ones was now blank. He'd been slain pitilessly in his attempt to save more of his own. Danny was gone.

'String them up!' Raven's voice echoed around the room, and she stepped into my line of sight, overseeing the aftermath of the chaos and murder ordered in her name.

'I want their bodies strung up above the stairs, and when the rest of them come, they can see the pain and suffering their loved ones experienced, before we close in and finish them all.'

A loud male voice suddenly roared.

'Come on, then you evil bastards!' as he raced into their immediate space. I instantly recognised him. It was Dom. Before I could determine what was happening, he'd caught both Isaac and Oscar off guard by his sudden appearance, and immediately engulfed them with fire.

'Stop!' Raven yelled, watching in horror as her brothers began to scream out in pain. They flapped their arms in the struggle to put out the flames which were rapidly consuming them from head to toe. I *wanted* to watch them burn, to watch them perish most agonisingly. It felt good.

Raven's hand thrust out, and a force seized Dom, raising his body from the ground.

Lia, I desperately called out in my mind. I tried so hard to visualise screaming voices inside Raven's head, but she didn't even flinch. I tried it again. *Lia. Lia. Oh, why isn't it working? What the fuck am I doing wrong?*

As Dom's body rose higher, his arms and legs flayed frenziedly to no effect. He continued to rise to the very top of the building, three floors up. Raven left him there to linger, while her cohorts desperately tried to pat down the fires that now fully enveloped their brother's. Their screams ceased as they both fell to the ground. Jett manipulated the debris that lay around them, creating a mini tornado of fragments, dirt and dust particles and finally extinguished them, but it was all in vain.

What a cold realisation it was to see no real emotion on their faces, just shock, as they stared down at their charred, smoking bodies. Those demonic bitches didn't dwell for long and turned away to continue dragging the other corpses towards the bottom of the stairs. Raven didn't flinch as she nonchalantly gestured with her hand a motion that would release Dom. He plummeted to the ground with so much force that his head instantly exploded as it contacted the solid marble floor.

I snapped my head away. I didn't want to see him like that. Both Dom and Danny were now gone. This 'nightmare of all nightmare's' would continue until Raven's cruel cull was complete.
Why couldn't I stop it? I had no time to weep for them. Nova and Cora began to climb the stairs, and I slipped back out of view.

Suddenly, a hand wrapped around my mouth, gagging me and a cloak got thrown over my head. With some urgency, I was pushed downwards into a crouching position. I turned and was relieved to see Sophia, crouching with me, her hand pressed firmly against my mouth. She slowly removed it and touched a finger to her lip, a warning for me to stay silent. We both watched on as the cruel Vents went about their demonic ethnic cleansing, oblivious that we were only a few feet away from them.

All had gone eerily still. Even the De Wyche's were now silent in their movements. Both Cora and Nova were attaching ropes from the balustrades and bannisters up the stairway.

'We need to walk but slowly,' Sophia whispered. Her voice was so hushed that I could hear her heartbeat as well as mine. 'We will find another route out of here. I suggest we make our way back up the stairs, then work our way through the house and find an exit. The bulk of the bodies lay strewn on this ground floor. We can't make a sound, Kate.' she warned again. I nodded at her. 'Don't look at the bodies.'

My chin trembled as images of the carnage had already scarred my mind for all eternity.
She reached for my hand and squeezed it tight, and we slowly got to our feet.

'Don't worry. Nobody can see us, the cloak makes us invisible to them, but they'll be able to hear us if we're not very careful,' she whispered, at which point Nova's evil white eyes flashed in our direction. We stopped. She inspected the corridor with suspicion but turned back to the task in hand.

We drew shallow breaths and began to move slowly past Nova towards the top of the first staircase. Every hair on my body stood on end as I tried desperately not to make a sound.

'I'm not mopping that up,' I heard Jett complain behind us. I clamped my eyes shut, now feeling nausea lapping over me in uncomfortable waves. Sophia squeezed my hand tighter, pinning her shoulders to mine. As we hesitantly rounded the corner at the top of the first stairway, I glanced back down and saw nooses slipped around the necks of the deceased. I quickly jerked my head away, focussing on the second stairway.

We'd made it to halfway up the second stairway when Sophia paused. It was then she let out a horrific, morbid wail. Her body dropped to her knees, and our cloak unveiled us. Sophia had defied her instructions, a mistake that would ultimately be her undoing.

'Dad!' she cried out.

It was then I saw that it was Quinn laying there – stretched over three steps on his back. He was dead. It was a gruesome sight. He had a black hole burnt completely through his lower chest, and blood spatter all over the rest of his body. Inner body parts spilt out from its opening. He must have died instantly.

'Dad! Oh, Dad!' she called out again in a cry filled with so much pain.

We were now fully exposed, and it felt like every pair of evil eyes were now fixed upon us.

Nova and Cora had run up the stairs and were standing in front of us. Raven, Jett and another two of her ilk were behind us. We were now trapped.

'Get up, Sophia!' I yelped, yanking on her arm. She wouldn't budge. Her body was floppy, and she struggled to breathe through her strangled sobbing. She just stared down at her dead father, immobilised in pain.

'Please, Sophia!' I pleaded desperately.

Raven hissed up the stairs glaring at me through a

sinister snarl.

'It's over, Kate.' she crowed. 'Restrain them!'

'Yes, with nooses,' declared Nova, chuckling with delight.

As I felt them close in on us from every angle, my head snapped back, and everything went sheet white. My ears began to squeal like a tea kettle. It was then I heard my mother's voice. *Antonia. Use your powers to release us.*

How? I panicked, frantically asking her in my head. *You saw us. Set us free.*

Where?

I wanted to scream out, feeling the heat of the fury nearing closer to me. I anticipated death; assured that they were going to strike at any second. My mother then planted an image of the glass orbs swirling with colour into my head.

That was them! My parents! Jesus, they are there, in that room! I strained hard to focus on the orbs. I didn't actively have to be in that room to release them. I had the power to move objects, not in my line of sight. I focused again and used my mind to push and nudge spheres from the shelf. I felt like my forehead was going to split as every brain cell was working in unison to force them off. Finally, they dropped from the shelf, and I heard them smash as they hit the floor.

Antonia. My father's voice filled my ears. *I grant you all my powers.*

My word is 'Aggie.' You must act now.

Steal their eyes, ears and tongues, strip them of their abilities. Use your energy to its full potential.

My eyes opened with a loud thud of my heart. Nova and Cora seized me and dragged me to the top of the stairs, and Raven held a knife against Sophia's throat. I was dizzy, my head spinning so fast.

'Let her go … it's me you want!' I demanded coldly.

'You?' Raven spat. 'Don't flatter yourself. What I want is my father's body. I can still salvage his blood. Tell me where he is, or I will slice her throat open.'

'Don't do it,' Sophia warned. 'You can kill me, but you'll never be *our* Mitral.'
Raven grabbed Sophia's French plait and sliced it off, then held the razor-sharp weapon next to her jugular vein.

'Where is he?' she bit, her eyes as black as ink.

'Let her go, and I'll tell you,' I demanded, as the others encircled us. Their faces were unreadable, and no invitational smirks indicated what they'd do to us.

I used all my force, shouting *Aggie* in my mind, and the knife immediately ripped from Raven's hand. At that moment Sophia spun around and punched Raven so hard it popped her nose. As thick red blood began to trickle from it, she was momentarily stunned.
Sophia only needed that second of distraction and began to viciously attack her, yanking her hair, scratching her face, biting and kicking like some sort of crazed animal fighting for its life.
I spun around as I saw a man lunge towards me, blue electricity was sizzling at his fingertips.
Aggie. Take his sight.
He suddenly jerked to a stop and panic filled his face.

'My eyes!' he cried out, now unfocused and blinded.
It worked! My father had granted me his gifts!
Aggie.

A woman dropped to the floor aside of him, screaming that she couldn't hear or see while patting the space before her, desperately feeling for her surroundings.

Aggie.

Nova's hands shot to her ears as I willed her head to explode with voices, and it was enough to disarm her and temporarily paralyse her thoughts. She recoiled away from us, crying out in agony.

'Stop it!' she screeched, hunching over and covering her ears.

I wouldn't stop. I'd never stop.

Cora sprung a wave of blue kinetic energy towards me that narrowly missed me.

Aggie. I forced out what energy I could, and a ball of golden light left my right-hand hurtling towards her. It hit her stomach at high speed, catapulting her down the corridor and smashing her into a wall.

Raven's mouth parted as she looked at me in disbelief. For the first time, I detected some doubt in her expression. It was then that I could feel a thick liquid had landed on the back of my arm and began dissolving the fabric of my top, seeping through to my skin. I could smell my hairs singeing and my flesh burning before I felt the blistering pain bite at my skin. Jett had spat at me, and she was revving herself up to spatter me with more acid. My head screamed out, *Aggie,* with such vengeance that it tossed her into the air, sent her smashing through the large arched glass window, and plunged her to her death.

It all happened so quickly. Raven screamed out. Her frenzied reaction was to pick up the knife from off the floor and instantly plunge it into Sophia's heart.

Her watery blue eyes held mine for a few seconds, pooling liquid white. Her mouth spurted blood, her chest burst crimson, and that beautiful face became frozen in despair. She dropped quickly to the floor, slumping over as she landed.

'No!' I bawled out. I lunged towards her, but Raven subdued me as I felt my body rising. The force then suspended me a few feet above the ground. She lifted Sophia's head, glared into her eyes and began a demonic chant.

I kicked out my legs and arms as Dom had done during his demise, trying to free myself, but it was to no avail. She began sucking at Sophia's face. It was as if she'd turned to vampirism. I struggled in the invisible grasp, watching her suck the remaining life force out of Sophia, and to my utter horror, the more she sucked, the more skeletal Sophia became. She was like a deflating balloon. Every time Raven inhaled her, Sophia's skin tightened and went gaunt, her cheeks now sunken and hollow. Her eyes began to bulge out of their sockets, and she became deflated to the point every bone was protruding from her lifeless body.

Raven's eyes rolled to the back of her head before blinking black. She threw Sophia's body to the ground and stood taller, moving her limbs as though more power was seeping through her veins.

'You know what? I don't need Jorah's power. I'll simply take everyone else's,' she snarled, rising to her feet. She stepped over Sophia's body and shifted her attention to me.

'I'll claim their business, properties and wealth too.' Her face changed from smug to a demonic expression. She positioned her entire body to face me, curled her hands into fists and moved to pounce. I saw her body lunging towards me and felt that familiar ice-cold wind pricking my skin as we teleported from the house into the abyss.

CHAPTER 31

My feet crunched into a layer of twigs and matted leaves. She'd purposely and tactically teleported me into unfamiliar territory; woodland that was presumably somewhere within the confines of the Glentree estate. The damp, stagnant earthy smell, caused by an earlier heavy rainstorm, flared my nostrils as a whiff hit me. Darkness was rapidly closing in and started to play havoc with my imagination. In the distance, lightning flashed viciously across the sky and was not far away.

I had not one ounce of religious belief, but in my head, I was praying for my friends who were assembled by the lake that they remained safe.

Raven didn't appear with me, and I became suspicious. I stood alone as the trees began swaying in the increasing breeze. There was more than one storm brewing. The trees cocooned me in their folds, giving me the occasional glimpse of the sky up above, but the bristling leaves soon hunched back together.

I was alerted by a noise behind me. My heart jumped

out the starting gate, and it soon went into a gallop. I inhaled deeply and exhaled as I turned apprehensively to be confronted by a pair of staring charcoal eyes and a face that wore a grim smile of satisfaction.

'Alone, at last!' Raven grinned. Her words were accompanied by a blinding flash of lightning and a booming thunderclap.

Talk about making an entrance!

My sister had arrived, and there was a cocky assurance about her. She clasped her hands behind her back and casually circled me.

As heavy rain started to fall, I monitored my surroundings just in case she had back-up lurking somewhere in the shadows.

'I thought you wanted Jorah,' I asked, trying desperately to sound unphased. 'Don't you want to salvage his blood? Isn't that what this whole thing was about?'

She cocked her head with a cold glint.

'And be ambushed by the few that remain of your Chamber?' she said, shaking her head. 'I mean, of course, it would have been nice to have those powers, but those powers will inevitably come around again in future generations under my new reign. I have my own laws. I can take every single Vents' powers, as and when I wish. I might even take a trip to the original Melladonna and see what she has to offer me.'

She stalked around me with calculated ease. I suddenly felt a shift within myself – instead of fear – I felt irritated.

I'd shared a womb with this demonic witch. We came from the same loins, we grew at the same rate, and our journey started the same way.

How did it come to this? How did I wake up in this damned alternative life, fearing my twin?

'I know that you intend to incinerate his body and throw his remains in the lake. Maybe they already have? But, be warned, because I will seek out every one of them for this crime. Yes, I wanted his blood; however, I *will* continue to grow stronger without it.' As she circled me in slow, scheming movements, another bright flash illuminated our surroundings, followed with what sounded like a sonic boom.

My mind was attempting to unravel the powers that my father had passed on to me. Raven had violence in her blood and would strike me when I least expected it, so I had to be alert. I'd decided enough with the fear as she fed off it. She enjoyed watching me squirm. I had to stand up and be courageous and not recoil anymore. I wasn't going to show weakness. I had power – more power than she did – and I had a right to use it.

'You know, once upon a time I had hope for us, Antonia,' she sighed, 'I often wondered what it would be like to join you in your alternative world, one that was oblivious to our existence and incredible abilities. I also wondered what kind of relationship we'd have. Would we be one of those sets of twins that wear matching outfits? Wear our hair the same? Would we share the same men – or women? Would we stay up all night giggling about the same things in our little *twin* bubble? And then I'd snap out of it and plead with Ovar never to darken my life with such a tragic existence as yours.

I saw your life through a lens and felt angry that they robbed you of your true potential. They stole the life

you could have and should have had, and instead –
you became so sickeningly sweet that it made me
convulse with nausea. I longed for you to be as savage
as me, but you're not. You're so weak and useless. It
embarrasses me.'

I glared at her, digging my fingernails into my palms. I
was now drenched, and rainwater was dripping from
my hair and off my nose.

'Your handlers failed you, Raven,' I snapped. 'They
brainwashed you, conditioned you over the years, to
dissociate you with any human feeling or have any
compassion towards others. I don't think you'd know
the meaning of love, even if it slapped you in the face.'

'Love!' she scoffed, craning her head upwards as
the thunder and lightning rolled on. She clamped her
eyes shut and smiled demonically. I watched her chest
inflate and deflate as she inhaled deeply. 'Oh, Antonia,'
she laughed. 'If only you knew what was coming, then
you'd know that love has no place in this world. Love
is categorically the most pointless and hopeless asset
anyone could have.'

'What are you talking about?' I spat, utterly vexed
by her delusion.

'The apocalypse,' she sniffed, darting her cold eyes
back to me. 'The final cataclysm is coming.'
I almost laughed.
She stopped circling me and began to roll her head
around the woods as if she were searching out
something or someone.

'We have until the year 2025 and then the world as
we know it will end. Our kind, and there's many of us
out there, will be the sole survivors, immune to the
devastation around us. It's written in our historical

archives, and humankind's death warrants are already signed.'

I side-stepped cautiously, without taking my eyes off her.

What was this '*The End Is Nigh*' drivel?

'What are you talking about?' I complained. I had to keep her talking while I could mentally draw up a plan of attack.

'I've seen it since I was a young girl, in vivid dreams that were as clear as day. I hear the agonising screams of the burning tortured souls. Seeing the skies in a constant haze of ash and orange, with black smoke rising from the barren wasteland that lays in ruins, strewn with mangled and decomposing corpses. If the fire didn't get them, then famine and contagion would soon wipe out the survivors.'

I strained to make out her expressions as the fierce lightning flashed. Her concentration now focussed on every word that rolled off her tongue, as though she were seeing it happening.

'Cities will be left in ruins, devoid of beating hearts, birds in the skies, no pollinators, no crops, just contaminated waters to quench their thirst. No fuel, no transport, not a single flower or seed will survive what's to come. But *we* will.'

She stepped forward from the darkness, and I could see a smirk wind up her face.

I stood my ground, refusing to shrink away from her.

'And how does that work? If the world is burning, how will your kind survive?' I asked mockingly.

'There's a special place on this earth reserved for us, one that you will never see, my dear sister. But first, I must remain vigilant and continue to cleanse humanity of both the weak and the hierarchy. To build an army of the strong, in readiness. I *will* be supreme.'

It was at that moment I realised just how delusional she was.

'You're right, Raven, there is a special place reserved for you, but reserved for the worst of your kind. The kind who know right from wrong but do wrong regardless. The kind who smile into the anguished faces of the innocent as you rob them of their last breath. That place is *Hell,* and that's where you're going.'

'Hell!' she snorted, inching ever closer towards me. 'And what do you class as Hell? A fictional place that repeatedly threatened us as children, to keep us honest and controlled?' Her hands dropped by her sides and twitched. 'An endless flaming pit where bad souls are dragged to meet the fiery, red-eyed demons with barbed tails and horns? What do you think awaits me there?'

'Eternal pain with any luck,' I snarled.

'Hell isn't an afterlife destination located deep in the depths of the earth, nor is it in another dimension, you idiot,' she barked, clenching her jaw. 'Hell is right here *on* earth. And if I can contribute to de-populating and ridding the world of oxygen-thieving parasites, then I will. Me, my Chamber and Glentree will be the real *Hell* on this earth.'

'What Chamber?' I snapped. 'You've killed half the Vents; most of your Chamber is dead. Who the fuck do you think will serve you? Those who are left will hunt you down and kill you. Jorah is dead, and there is no Mitral. It's over, Raven. You've lost the battle. You even killed your brother.'

'And I'd kill him again,' she hissed venomously. Her eyes bulged at me, her jaw rigid. 'Seth was a traitor. He plotted against his Chamber and for what? *Love?*' she hissed, scrunching her face in disgust. 'For Savannah Bloom, that wimpish book nerd?' Her face hardened. 'Our family hasn't survived millennia by being weak. You may say my values are diabolical, but they keep me alive. And if you think that was bloodshed, then you haven't seen anything yet, dearest Antonia, because nothing will prepare you or anyone else for the shitstorm that's to come.'

As I sensed her aggression was increasing, I thought of how to disarm her. Could I strip her powers? Overpower her thoughts? Could I blast her away with my new-found energy force?

'What makes you so sure you even have Glentree anymore?' I asked brashly. 'And who will clear away *that* crime scene? Perhaps others will arrive from further afield to rid the world of the De Wyche's?' She cackled cruelly and slowly, her body began to leave the ground and rise.

Show no fear.

You can defeat her.

Fight for your life, Kate.

Fight.

I flexed my hands readying myself as she rose higher, always watching me.

'I'll rebuild my Chamber. We are experts at clearing crime scenes. Remember Fae Woods? Oh, dear. I'm so sorry sister... how can you forget! I'll keep a select few, for mating purposes and invite others from abroad to join me. We will start new bloodlines. Out with the old, in with the new.'

She lingered, glancing into my soul, before sighing in thought.

'Sleep tight, sis.'

As she lunged towards me, I pulled back my arm, mentally fuelling as much energy as I could muster. I felt the same tingling sensation in my fingertips and waited for the feeling to run through my hand. Once I felt the power, I straightened my arm and released it. *Aggie*. I sent out a gold beam of light which shot towards her.

She dodged the beam and instantly fired a hail of energy pellets back at me. The incoming glistening blue balls missed me, but I lost my footing, falling into the sludge. I felt glued to the thick mud. I attempted to get up, but my legs were skating in what was rapidly becoming a quagmire underfoot, dumping me back down into it. The rainfall was now monsoon-like. The raging thunder and lightning ensued directly above.

She sniggered down at me. 'Don't think I'm going to make this easy for you.'

Her eyes bulged, and her smile faded as the irises of her eyes glowed a brilliant white.

Black shadowy shapes began to emerge from her body, first forming into rippling sheets of black velvet and then morphed into identical clones of Raven.

I could neither breathe nor swallow as I watched them, one by one, form a line in front of me.

It started with two, then three, then six.

These were not apparitions. They appeared to be solid beings.

I was outnumbered and outgunned, so I readied to be overwhelmed - six to one. I needed help and fast. I already knew I was about to fight a losing battle, but regardless I had to fight. I would not allow her to kill me so easily. I was *not* that weak.

I attempted to get to my feet again, the ground beneath me began to shake, but the thunder wasn't causing it. Raven hissed and muttered something inaudible under her breath. At the same time, each of her clones' eyes blinked from black to a blinding white. They lined up, side by side, all levitating mid-air beside Raven.

I compulsively swallowed as I searched their cruel faces. Fear began to creep up my spine, no matter how much I tried to ignore it.

The ground trembled again, but this time it was a stronger tremor. I stared down at the earth as my heart hammered uncomfortably. It was like a Jurassic Park moment when a T-Rex is nearing, and it's that gut-churning feeling of impending doom.

Take a chance, Kate. It may well be your last one. Run and find a hiding place.

Was it the apocalypse? Was this the beginning of the end? I wanted to stand and defend myself, but my body was now sinking deeper into the mire. Raven ignored the ongoing tremors which were now visibly shaking the trees. Her attack commenced. She slowly glided towards me with her clones in sync.

A tree branch snapped loudly nearby, distracting Raven enough to halt her and her clones from their advance. For one single moment, we locked eyes. Her head cocked to one side as if quizzing the shift of sounds around her.

Everything then went disconcertingly still and quiet. The rain stopped abruptly. Then, from nowhere, someone or something zoomed past me, slicing through the space between my enemies and me with so much velocity, that a strong gust of wind trailed it, whipping through the trees at an incredible speed. We were no longer alone.

CHAPTER 32

Raven was silent and unblinking. With a slight tilt of the head, she combed the trees assessing if or what impending danger was hiding in the darkness. She looked back and pinned her hollow eyes on me. Whatever had put her on hold, she deemed that there was no immediate threat.

Another branch snapped, and my mind sharpened. I had to arm myself and prepare to defend any eventuality mentally.

I could feel that all too familiar *hair rising on the back of my neck* feeling taking hold. I knew we had a visitor lurking, although I didn't know whether it was friend or foe. I felt the intense need to cover my back. I needed to get alongside a tree for security, no matter how fleeting that was to be.

How was I going to do battle with seven Raven's as they made their attack? I had no preparation or training for this. There had never been a violent bone in my body, but now it was my time to kill or *be* killed. I was armed with powers, but I still didn't know how to use them correctly, but I had to try. It was like handing a child a knife for the first time and expecting it not to harm itself.

I swallowed so hard that it hurt. My throat was sand dry from taking too many raspy, shallow breaths, and it now burned with thirst.

The clones swooped down, as Raven held back and victoriously smirked as she directed from a distance. As I struggled to stand, one of them rocketed towards me.

I winced away and threw my forearm up as her face came closer and I clamped my eyes shut.

No, no, no, no! What's wrong with you? Fight!

The air was ripped from my lungs as another cold blast whipped past me.

I opened my eyes to see the clone swatted like a bug by the mysterious form, her body slamming into a tree trunk and dropping like a hot rock to the ground. The sound of something heavy landing in front of me came as a shock. The form immediately revealed itself. It was Finn.

My heart accelerated the second I laid eyes on him. *Had he got to Elias in time? Did he manage to reverse the curse?*

I wanted to scream out to him, sink to the ground and thank god for sending him to my aid. Relief swamped me, but he didn't look at me. Instead, he studied Raven's reaction to his reveal.

Raven's face dropped into a startled sulk. Her lips parted, and an angry growl hissed from her mouth. She flicked out her hands with a silent order, and then another two clones launched themselves at him.

I grabbed the opportunity to take flight and ran over

to a nearby tree. I steadied myself against it and watched as Finn's hand thrust out and grabbed the first clone by the throat. With a quick jerk of his forearm, he snapped its neck. It stilled, and he dropped it into the mud. He caught the second one with his other hand, locking around its neck, and arched back his arm in a stance that looked as though he was about to throw a spear. Raising his leg and bending his knee, he used his one arm to aim and the other to hurtle the clone through the air at lightning speed where it smashed directly into a thick tree trunk.

These clones were no match once in Finn's clutches, faint to his strength. They didn't wince or react to pain. They spilt no blood. They were more like automatons, recreated to kill or be destroyed. Raven's scorn flared through her nostrils, and she growled again.

'This won't end well for you, Raven!' Finn shouted, rolling back his shoulders.

She bared her teeth and narrowed her stare on him, seething with rage.

'I'm going to kill you,' she cautioned.

'You're talking shit,' he mocked, now with his rigid stance and legs spread wider than his shoulders. With one effortless movement, he ripped the cloak from his back, and I watched in awe as he rose from the ground, gliding much higher than Raven.

The remaining two clones swarmed him, but he overpowered them in a moment, forcing his hands around both their heads. I knew what was coming; their two skulls were smashed together and cracked open like eggs. The luminescent gooey substance that came away from their heads held no resemblance to human brain matter.

'Those missing powers you're so hell-bent on taking for yourself - remind me again of what they are?' His body now hovered opposite Raven. 'Regeneration, life-draining, aura-choking,' he began to count on his fingers. 'Um, let me see, holograms, pain infliction, age-shifting, power extraction, indestructibility? That's right, isn't it?'

If a single look could kill, Finn would have perished under Raven's scrutiny in that second. Her eyes were black holes, and her pupils were so constricted that I could only make out the target of her focus by following the movement of her head. It angled towards me.

'Oh, and what about memory reading, retrocognition or shape-shifting?' he continued. He grinned wickedly at her and chuckled to himself, folding his arms. 'They weren't on your list, were they? Let me guess you'd like to inherit those, too?' He lifted a single finger and pointed it skywards and began to move it around in a circular motion. The leaves below him began to rise from the ground and form a small tornado. Raven's head lowered at the same time as mine, and I could read her confusion by the tightening veins in her neck. Finn began to repeatedly tut, taunting her. The leaves fell back to the earth in a heap.

'Those powers you crave so much, you think it was my mother who had them?' He began to snigger as he slowly lowered to the ground. 'I'm disappointed you didn't work it out sooner. Lourdes De Wyche had a lot of abilities, forty-four in fact. An incredibly powerful man who put the fear of god within everyone he encountered. His daughter inherited most of his powers.'

Where was he going with this? Even I was startled with his strange behaviour and his newly found accustom to bloody violence.

'My grandmother is Mina De Wyche. Ah, good old granny, Mina.'

My memory flashed to the older woman with the walking stick, disrupting the ceremony. That was Jorah's mother and Finn's grandmother. My head spun, trying to process it all.

'She inherited a lot of Lourdes' powers and, in turn, so did my mother. But my mother was clever. She didn't agree with the evil code of the De Wyche's. She didn't appreciate their rules and regulations and the total control they had over the Chambers. So, she married into a family who were just as, if not a little bit more powerful, than the De Wyche's.'

'Apollo Moon was not more powerful that Lourdes De Wyche,' she spat, ravaged by wrath.

'Oh, wasn't he?' Finn queried, with an all-knowing smile. 'Apollo Moon was a very discreet man who sheltered the true extent of his powers. He held forty-nine powers. Powers that remained in the Moon's bloodline for centuries. Powers that bleed into every generation, including mine. Powers that escaped thieving hands and murderous eyes, and you – you vindictive, cruel delinquent - you think you're entitled to them? Do you think you can merely demand them? That pisses me right off.'

I felt a direct shift in the atmosphere around us and my stomach churned as the smell of viciousness seeped through every tree.

'I'm prepared to fight for it,' she quipped. 'Your family placed a curse on you so you could never use the powers, so, what does that tell you about the confidence they have with those abilities in your hands?'

For the first time, I saw his cheeks clench and discomfort lift his mask upon the impact of her statement. Had she sliced a lesion in his armour? Did that accusation ring some home truths?

'Back down, Raven,' he hissed, 'It's over. You're fighting a losing battle.'

'Then I'll die trying,' she growled. Her eyes emitted beams of white light, and a steady flow of black shadows again seeped from her body, quickly materialising as her clones. 'Did I forget to mention?' she smirked. 'They're immune to mental attacks. They have no brain.'

Immune to mental threats? So, only energy or physical force could stop them?

You've got to be kidding me.

With a wave, she urged them forward, and they began to move in on both me and Finn.

CHAPTER 33

Finn recommenced his battle. More skulls cracked open, bones shattered, and limbs were twisted and broken. I watched Raven's clones repeatedly destroyed, and I was now becoming desensitised to their grotesque and gruesome ends. They didn't scream or show any feeling of pain like human beings would. It was shell shock at first, watching the gore, brutality and bloodshed, my stomach heaving as Finn's hands eliminated each clone.

Finn was almost single-handedly slaying most of them, but every time he killed one, another would replace it. I needed to help Finn destroy them as the onslaught was becoming relentless. We had to get to Raven and end it.

I prayed for more back up. I prayed for the other Vents to help us.

Balls of energy became my only real weapon against them. They had been tried and tested, and I knew how to use them. I started repeatedly firing indiscriminately at them, initially with great success. They were dropping like flies, but still coming at us. The more exhausted I became by talentless use of my energy, the less effect they seemed to be having on them.

Finn was in danger of becoming swamped by them, and I decided to lock eyes with my sister. I saw the crazed look of murder within those blackened sockets. I took a deep breath and exhaled, preparing myself to tackle her. What good would I ever be in a Chamber if I merely cowered away? Perhaps I couldn't use mental abilities on her army, but I could use them on her. I homed in on her face and gritted my teeth. If I could attack her mind with so much noise, it could distract her and buy us more time.

She began to glide towards me, and I knew if she reached me, she would probably go in for the kill. I steadied myself as she loomed closer.

Aggie!

I waited. It didn't work. Maybe I wasn't concentrating as hard as I should have been? *Strip her power. Aggie!* Her pace accelerated.

Aggie, dammit, Aggie!

Why wasn't it working? What was I doing wrong? *Aggie!*

Suddenly, the most intense, head-bursting noise ravaged my head and forced me back down into the mud. I screamed out, blinded by the agony of it. It sounded like a room full of people all talking thunderously at once, entering my every brain cell. I couldn't see. I couldn't think. All I could do was claw at the mud and try to escape. The pain was excruciating.

I realised my sister had used deflection. She was deflecting my power back to me. A sharp pain bit into my cheek and my head fell into the cold earth. As the insufferable noise began to fade, a high-pitched screeching immediately replaced it. I became disorientated. My eyes unfocused, and with blurred vision, I tried to push myself up on to my elbows. My stomach tightened, and I retched. I felt a thick warm liquid oozing from my face and, as I reactively touched it, the syrupy texture transferred to my fingers.

I could smell the blood. One of my cheeks was numb and tingling. I blinked several times and slowly, my focus readjusted to see the dark crimson liquid dripping on to my top. She'd slashed open my face, and it left a gaping wound.

It's not supposed to end like this. She's going to kill you. Try harder.

My body felt weak, and I had little strength left. I'd failed myself. I'd failed the Chambers.

Finn was our last remaining hope, and I could still see he was still battling them, although the number of his attackers was clearly on the wane. My distraction was taking effect.

I tried to stand, but I was slammed back to the ground and forced on to my back. Raven stood directly over me clutching the offending razor-sharp dagger in her hand. My pulse throbbed in my ears as I saw the deadly intent in her eyes.

I refused to allow her the gratification of killing me where I lay, and I threw a forearm up to protect my chest as she raised the dagger behind her head and went for the fatal plunge. As she thrust the blade down, I raised my feet into my chest and kicked out with all the force I could muster, clipping the weapon from her hand. She instantly began to scream with rage and commenced a frenzied attack, clawing and scratching at my face, then hammering her fists repeatedly into my upper body. I desperately pedal-kicked at her in defiant defence. It was now hand-to-hand warfare.

I managed to kick her in the face with enough force behind it to momentarily stun her and buy myself enough time to roll out from beneath her and struggle to my feet.
I glanced at Finn as he picked off the last clone. He glanced towards me, panting heavily.

'Finn, it's me,' Raven cried from behind me. Her trembling voice resonated throughout our space and instantly had my back up. Confused, I spun around and was astounded to see she'd glamoured into me. Every single detail was identical to mine, my muddied hair, the blood-soaked gash on my cheek, the dirt and grime and my ripped clothes.
I panicked.

'No, she's lying,' I shouted, moving away from her. 'Finn, she's glamoured into me.'
He stood with hunched shoulders and frantically assessed us both.

'Babe, please,' she pleaded. 'Ask me anything – anything only you and I would know – you'll know I'm the real Antonia.'

'My names, Kate, you fucking cretin!' I snapped, hopeful Finn would recognise the anger in my tone as a dead give-away, but he didn't react.

'Finn,' I cried. 'This is ridiculous. Please listen to me!'
Before I could say anymore, his hand flexed, and a force lifted me from the ground. I felt my stomach rise

and fall like a rollercoaster drop. I was thrust through the air and landed against the base of a tree.
The agony that crippled my back upon impact made me scream out. Tree branches snapped and twisted, and then wrapped themselves tightly around my body until they ultimately restrained me. I caught my breath when I saw he'd unbelievably done the same thing to Raven. She was bound in the same way to a tree opposite me.
Finn paced the distance between us, giving nothing away. I studied him, and there was no indication that he felt anything but hatred towards both of us.
Raven decided to perform and burst into tears.

'Finn, please,' she dramatically begged as I watched on, my brain in overload. She sobbed dramatically and continued. 'What about us? Me and you.'
He flinched down at her and sighed.

'If I'm not Kate, then how do I know about the time you nearly burnt your mouth on a hot coffee that first morning at the café. Or when we took a drive out for breakfast and sat gazing across the lake. Or the way - the way you looked at me at the Melladonna?'
How did she know all of that? Was she spying on me that entire time? I sat there and trembled, wanting to speak up and defend myself, but I uttered not one word. Did Finn believe Raven's crap? Would he free her and kill me?

'Finnius!' A woman's voice echoed around us and snagged everyone to attention. It sounded like Athena. 'Finnius, help me!' she screamed out.
His ears pricked, and he dodged quickly away from Raven, staring nervously into the distance. I heard a

distortion in the voice that reminded me of the day Raven used voice mimicry of my ex-boyfriend.

'Finn,' I jerked my head towards him as he side-glanced me. 'Please don't listen to it. She's using voice mimicry. It's not real.'

She glared at me with twitching lips.

Finn's eyes clamped shut, but it wasn't in a way that he was stressed or emotional. He swayed unsteadily on his feet and staggered.

'Finn?' I panicked. Something was wrong. His breathing was off. 'Finn … what's wrong? What's happening?' He stared down at his hands as they shook furiously, and he tried to turn to me but lost his balance and dropped to his knees.

I watched in horror as his hands began to change. The usually thick balls of strength were shrivelling in size, becoming little more than mottled brown flesh with protruding blue veins.

'What's happening to him?' I shrieked, terrified. 'What are you doing to him?'

Raven shrugged. 'It's not me,' she said, staring at him in bewilderment. 'I haven't done anything.'

I frowned down at his arms and felt sick watching in dread as they dissolved in the same way his hands did. His muscles convulsed as they too shrank, and the skin began to sag from the bone.

My Finn. I couldn't understand it, nor prevent it, or stop it.

'I need to help him,' I cried, using all my might to try and prize off my restraints, but it was no use. 'I need to get out of this. Please, Finn! Hold on!'

'Oh, my,' Raven began to chuckle, before her laugh developed into an evil loud cackle as she morphed back into herself. 'This is brilliant,' she celebrated. 'The curse still stands. They didn't reverse it.'

What? How not? He went to meet Elias. Did it fail? Why would Finn come if he were putting himself at risk? Was this a self-sacrifice?

'He's ageing by fifty-years,' Raven laughed heartlessly. 'And now he's going to die, and I'm going to finish you and every single last one of your Chamber Vents.'

As Finn withered on the floor, deteriorating before my eyes, the branches that fastened me began to loosen. I snapped my way free and flung myself towards him, dropping to my knees.

'Finn!' I bawled out, reaching to touch him, but as my hand contacted his body, it went right through him, at which point his body crumbled away to ash. I froze, unable to speak. 'Finn?' My voice quivered.

I heard a slight gasp from behind me and craned my neck to see Raven's head trembling as her eyes drooped and hankered on me in pain. Blood began to trickle from her mouth as her face bulged red. Before I could scamper backwards to truly register what was happening, my eyes locked-on a blood-soaked blade that was thrust deep into her chest.

'Kate,' Finn's gentle voice came from behind me, and I felt him slink up beside me. He wasn't a pile of ash anymore. He looked every bit the youthful and gorgeous man with who I'd fallen head over heels in love with.

I moved away from him, startled and confused. Was it really him? Was he a hologram? Or a ghost?

Her entire body shuddered as she remained constricted against the tree trunk, and blood began to splutter from her mouth. Her drowsy unseeing eyes clung to me, almost pleading at me to help as her life began to ebb away.

I held eye contact, swallowing hard with no words to offer her in her final moments. Her teeth were stained red. She gurgled and attempted to speak but could only cough and splutter on the now free-flowing blood.

Someone concealed behind her pulled out the blade, and her head flopped forward. Her body relaxed in an awkward motion, and I watched her face harden, and her pupils dilate.

She was gone. Raven was gone. My sister, my twin, gone.

I reached out behind me and grabbed Finn's hand, and my heart swelled as I realised, he was very much alive.

'Who's there?' I asked, squeezing his hand tighter.

We both braced ourselves as a figure materialised aside of her body. My knees buckled, and my stomach exploded as the figure stepped out and closed the space between us. I let out a strangled gasp, and I heard the fright catch in Finn's throat too.

The figure slowly cocked its head at us, and peeled back its hood, to reveal a face that would scar and haunt my nightmares forever.

I'd seen those eyes before. The same eyes Raven depicted in her drawings and sketches as a child. Pictures my parents would confiscate and tear up because they were so inexplicable. The same eyes that never left Raven's memory. The same eyes she painted and hung as art around her home. The eyes that had two irises.

I couldn't breathe. Not because the entity existed

outside of Raven's paintings, and not because it had two pupils within one eye, but because this being had *my* face.

She was me. She was Raven. She was *us*.
She had my freckles, the same shaped eyes as me. Her left eye was a sapphire blue, and the left eye was the strangest feature: a double iris, one green, one brown.

Her hair was longer than mine, blonde with bright pink streaks through it. Her build was identical to mine, but the way she moved was careful, slow and deliberate.
She didn't speak, and that's what made her even more mystifying.
How? She wasn't a stray clone that had extended out of Raven. She wasn't a glamour. So, where did she come from? Who was she?

We locked eyes, and I trembled, too awe-stuck to move an inch, but the way she inspected me stirred a strange feeling inside of me.
Out of nowhere, I felt an overwhelming sense of sadness, like a part of my soul, had died.
And then – just like that - she completely vanished.
Finn quickly rose to his feet on high alert, like a cat who'd lost its pray.

He panted heavily and began searching the area for her. He turned, with a vacant stare and found my face.
'Who the fuck was that?'

CHAPTER 34

Finn appeared startled as he observed my eyes roll to the back of my head. It felt like I was being sucked down a deep, black hole, losing consciousness. My head began to spin as cold air suddenly gushed past me. Was I falling? I felt like I was falling. Moments later, the spiralling stopped, and as I dizzily steadied myself, I found myself standing outside a room. I had no idea where I was.

The door was ajar, beckoning me from the darkness and into the light. A voice tore me away from the door before I could push it open.

'Antonia,' a female voice whispered in a soothing tone. I turned around to face the darkness, to be greeted by a sparkling white light that surrounded my parents. They smiled tenderly at me, holding hands, radiating promise and youth. 'You freed us,' she said softly. 'Thank you.'

She stood smaller than my father, with blonde shoulder-length hair that almost covered her chiselled, charming face.

Her expressive blue eyes glistened at me. There was something extraordinary about her, perhaps it was her mesmerising beauty, or maybe it was simply her tenderness and loving heart. Nonetheless, I ached to know her.

'Every day is a new chance to make things right,' she stated. 'Make it right.'
I stepped closer, almost blinded from the intense light that glowed around them.

'Make what right? Raven is dead. The Chambers are dead?'

'Antonia,' my father answered, his big round brown eyes watching me delicately. 'We will find Raven's soul as we are now allowed to pass into the Elder World. There's still lots of time to save her.'
He stood tall at my mother's side, wrapping a protective hand around her shoulder. His eyes twinkled with untold stories and jokes, and his long beard moved with the curling of his smile.

'Don't worry about the past; focus on the future. The future of the Chambers lies in your hands.'

'My hands?' I gasped, 'How?'
The door behind me began to creek open, and I glanced back in its direction.

'Antonia …,' my mother's voice was fading, I quickly spun around to find the light that surrounded them was fast diminishing. 'We must show you; you must see the truth.'

'See what truth - Mum?'

'She's going to return, please make it right.'

'Who's going to return?' I squawked, watching as they dissolved to a silhouette. 'Mum? Dad?'
They were gone, returning me to the darkness.

I stood there, utterly perplexed, my mind completely boggled. What's behind the door? What did

they mean by she's going to return? Did they mean
Raven? And what do I have to make right?
I hesitantly pushed on the door. As it slowly opened,
repeated cries coming from of a new-born baby
temporarily halted my advance.

With the door now wide open, I quickly composed
myself and crept sluggishly forward. I entered a
hospital side room that was busy with activity. It had
cream coloured emulsion walls, one large inner
window that looked out to a corridor, and two grass
green chairs positioned either side of a hospital bed.
The room typically smelled of hand sanitiser and
chemicals. It was a strong odour at first, and I found
myself covering my nose. I stepped closer to a woman
patient who was in bed, nursing a new-born and
instantly recognised her. It was my mother again, but
she was a slightly younger version of the one who had
just visited me. Two nurses busied themselves around
her and the baby. A vital signs monitor was set up
aside the bed and beeped loudly and steadily.
My mother appeared every bit exhausted, alleviated
and mesmerised as she cooed down at the small infant
wrapped in a blanket, curling its tiny fingers around my
mother's pinkie finger.

As the baby's cries fell away to a whimper, she
ogled it with so much love in her heart and content in
her eyes, that you'd forgive her matted, sweat-soaked
hair that dangled over her face. She'd experienced a
hard birth.

The nurses left the room, and my father then
entered. God, did he look so very young and
handsome, wearing a youthful broad smile and proudly
holding a baby in each arm.

I paused suddenly, adding it up as it suddenly hit me. *If he's carrying two babies, and my mother has one in her arms, that would mean … omg … my mother had given birth to three of us! I'm one of three triplets?*

I stepped closer, feeling dizzy and confused by what I was witnessing. That tiny little human, with its little bruised head, swollen red eyelids, closed eyes, pruned feet and hands was one of us?

My mother's smile waned, and suddenly she became flustered and scared.

'Maddock,' she cried, alarmed as the monitor beeped irregularly. 'Maddock, something's wrong here.'

As the monitor's alarm began to sound, the nurses rushed back in and crowded around the bed, blocking my view.

'Do something!' my mother cried out desperately. 'Please!'

I watched as the baby was whisked away from my mother's arms and then as if someone had switched channels on the TV, I bizarrely found myself in a different room.

It was in the hospital waiting room. I scanned it, bewildered, as I had been fast-forwarded there. My parents were now sitting at the end of a row of seats, sobbing and sniffling while each nursing a vended coffee cup, their blotchy red eyes staring into space.

A doctor approached them with his head bowed, and as he mumbled quietly to them, my mother suddenly screamed out in anguish.

My heart swelled as my parents became inconsolable, hugging each other in apparent grief. What had happened to their baby and where were the other two?

As I stood contemplating what I'd seen, I was again instantaneously transported to another moment in time. I was now in a different hospital room, not unlike the one I'd first visited. Through the dim light, I could see that a baby was occupying a basket which was on the top of an unmade and empty bed. A man accompanied the doctor, the same one that had broken the news of the baby's death to my parents. He moved quietly towards the baby and peered over it.

'The child survives,' the doctor whispered, smiling over the sleeping baby. My eyes widened expectantly, and I circled the two men to inspect the infant myself. Its little body started to wriggle and kick from beneath a pink blanket.

'I hope you're doing the right thing, Elias?' the doctor asked.

Elias! I froze, my head ducked and jerked to get a closer look at him. My grandfather? Was he behind this deception?

My body began to shudder, and I could see my breath before my face as the temperature plummeted and froze the scene. I closed my eyes briefly, and when I reopened them, I had been forced further ahead in time. It was becoming very surreal.

I found myself standing outside a busy airport drop off zone. Snowflakes fell lightly past my face. I shivered and wrapped my coat tighter around my body to shield me from the wintry weather. I was standing close to my grandfather, who was dressed in a smart light-brown, woollen overcoat, and topped by a matching trilby hat. He held a baby carrier in which I could see a baby who was protected from the outside elements by a thick blanket.

My eyes danced around the immediate area. The illuminated sign above the building entrance read 'North Terminal' and I immediately knew I was at Gatwick. I'd travelled from this airport on numerous occasions, but it appeared different to when I last visited.

A thin covering of fresh white snow had layered the roads, taxies and other outdated vehicles. The intermittent roar of aircraft taking off from the terminal filled the cold night air.

Who was he waiting to meet? Where was he going? More importantly, why would he do this to his daughter? Why would he take one of her babies?

As my attention turned back to the baby, I jolted back in awe, as it opened its eyes.

The right eye was a sparkling blue, and the left was a startling sight if I ever saw one; it housed one brown pupil and one green. A rarity that was so magnificent, anyone could see that the child was unique.

Heels clipped behind me, and I turned to see a couple approach my grandfather. They were both suited and booted, middle-aged professionals who reeked of money.

The man was dressed similarly to my grandfather, in a long brown Crombie coat. The woman emitted a motherly aura. Her blonde hair was well-groomed, half-hidden under a scarlet beret hat. She wore an oversized white quilted jacket, a knee-length black skirt, black tights and strappy heels. The way her blue eyes lit up when she saw the baby reminded me of the loving stare my mother had recently given her child. She pressed her white leather-gloved hand against her chest and began to cry.

'Oh, my goodness,' she gushed, bending down for a closer inspection. 'She's breath-taking.'

I instantly detected her American accent.

Her husband firmly shook my grandfathers' hand and nodded at him.

'You're a good man, Elias,' he declared in a similar accent to that of his wife.

My grandfather grimaced and sighed. 'My daughter's heart is broken because of a great lie. I'm not a good man.'

'You're doing the right thing,' he assured my grandfather. 'We will keep her safe, as will our Chamber.'

Chamber? They were part of an American Chamber. Is that where they were taking her? I cast my mind back to when Finn told me of more International bloodlines.

'She's everything I expected and more,' the pretty blonde sniffed. She gestured for Elias to hand the baby over, but he hesitated.

'Elias,' the man whispered. 'You know the fate of your bloodline is inevitable. You know there's a chance they won't survive fibrillation when it happens. We must do this. Our Heart beats strong and united in America.'

Elias nodded defeatedly. He raised two fingers to his lips, kissed them and then used the same two fingers to plant the kiss on the baby's forehead.

'She is so special,' he said, his voice stumbling over the words. He handed the baby carrier over to the woman. 'When the time comes, she will return to us?'

'Of course,' the woman assured, grasping the handle of the carrier.

'You must never hide her true identity,' my grandfather warned. 'Tell her who she is and where she came from, but she will not be able to disclose it until the time comes.'

'Elias,' The woman locked eyes with him. 'Elias, thank you so much,' she said with an honest and gentle smile.

Elias peered down at the child, lingering on her face. It was as though he were sewing her into his memory for eternity.

'What's her name?' the woman asked.

Elias smiled lovingly at the child and flicked his eyes back up at the couple.

'Evanora,' he declared. 'Her name's, Evanora.'

*****

The fragrance of the damp forest had stolen me back to reality. I'd returned to Finn, who was squatting beside me, holding a fixed stare of anxiety.

'Are you OK? I was worried when you passed out! What happened to you?' he asked with urgency.

I was still in total disbelief as to what I'd witnessed back there in my flashback.

'I watched it all unfold, Finn. I went back in time. I saw our very beginnings. Me, Raven and Evanora.'

'Who is Evanora?' he quizzed.

'She's another one of us … we're triplets,' I stuttered. 'You just saw her appear here; it was Evanora that killed Raven! This is only the beginning, Finn. She's coming back. It's only the beginning.'

ABOUT THE AUTHOR

Rachael Harris was born, raised and still resides in Newcastle Upon Tyne, where she lives with her boyfriend and her baby daughter, Isla. She graduated from Northumbria University with a First-Class Honours in Journalism and a Master's degree in creative writing. Bloodline: The Awakening is her first novel, and she is now hard at work on Bloodline: Sanctum, the second book in the series.

You can find out more about her on www.raharrisauthor.wordpress.com or follow her on Instagram at https://www.instagram.com/r_a_harris_author/

Printed in Great Britain
by Amazon